GW00643206

Zoe Hearty and the Space Invaders

TE Norris

Copyright © TE Norris 2022

All rights reserved. This book or parts thereof may not be reproduced in any form, stored in any retrieval system, or transmitted in any form by any means–electronic, mechanical, photocopy, recording, or otherwise–without prior written permission of the publisher. For permission requests please contact:

This is a work of fiction. Names, places, characters and incidents are either the product of the author's imagination or are used fictitiously, and any resemblance to any actual persons, living or dead, organizations, locales or events is entirely coincidental.

Contents

Dedication

For Linda.
Love

The world breaks everyone, and afterward, some are strong at the broken places.
Ernest Hemingway

"And before we judge of them too harshly we must remember what ruthless and utter destruction our own species has wrought, not only upon animals, such as the vanished bison and the dodo, but upon its inferior races."
HG Wells

A Prologue

My name is Zoe Hearty, and I am a killer, but I am not a monster. Certainly not the monster they want me to be.

I made it easy for them to put me away. After Leary died, I had trouble thinking straight. Yet I did what had to be done, and I would do it all again. You might have done the same.

I am, in fact — and this is so cringy and embarrassing — your saviour. I hear you scoffing. I get it. I do.

I look around this cage of mine, the white walls, the metal fittings, the lone window barred and sealed. Hollow sounds of despair echo through the corridors. You put me here for a reason. You call me trash. Filthy Zoe. Crazy Zoe. I might do the same if I was in your place. But I know what I know. And that tears me up. I am your saviour, and I must make you believe me. Otherwise, we are doomed. Your fate, all our fates, mine too, depend on it.

I am not crazy. I wish I was. It would be so much easier. But I have never been saner in all my pathetic life. Logic, or logic as I saw it at the time, drove every decision as it drives this story. Believe me.

So, all I ask is that you let me tell my story. Let me attempt to persuade you. I get you may be incredulous, but keep this in mind: there is proof I have kept secret up till now. I'll share it with you, when you come to see me. Get me my day in court so I can tell my side, so we can fight this thing together.

Guthry, that pallid, disgusting creep, has given me access to this recorder. The "Doc" no longer considers me a suicide risk, so that is something I suppose. Considers it therapeutic, he said. And it's not like anyone anywhere is ever going to believe me.

1

His words, natch. But I am confident, Mr. Reid, you will see that I did what I had to, what anyone in my position would have done. I found a logical path and followed it through the turmoil of those desperate events.

Anyway, he is probably up there in his office perving off to the feed from the blinking light above the door. "Surveillance 24/7," said the committing judge. So welcome, Big Brother Guthry. Put your junk back in your trousers, creep, and wipe the spit off your upper lip.

Listen: they have promised me you will get a chance to evaluate my story, though God knows I do not trust them on that. The thing is: I am telling the truth and I think you will hear that too.

Did you do it? I hear you ask. I never denied it. Why would I? I was in no frame of mind to resist. The police gathered the evidence and it all pointed in the right direction. Me. And then they threw me in here without a trial to shut me up.

You will have to decide if what I did makes me a monster or not. But let me tell you this, long before they died, I grieved for what had been stolen from me. They were gone. Long gone. I do not and never will regret what I did. It was only fitting in the end.

So let me tell you a story of the death of a family and the cruelty inflicted on my poor babes. My poor dead sparrows.

Another Prologue

A telephone rings. A loud shrill sound that Reid both loves and hates.

This time it's his desktop phone. He glances at the digital number of the caller and smiles to himself.

The bait has worked and the fish has bit. He presses the button for the speakerphone.

"Brown, Reid, and Partners. Reid here. How may I help?"

"Guthry, from the Institute. Returning your call."

"Mr. Guthry! I hope you are having a wonderful day."

Not that I give a shit, you fascist prick.

As they exchange the necessary opening pleasantries, a knot of tense excitement grows in Reid's stomach. So close now. So close.

"Your primary interest, I understand, is one of our guests." Guthry finally comes to the point. "One of our more colourful and infamous guests."

"Indeed. Zoe Hearty. Thanks for returning my call so promptly." *Not that you had much choice, you shit. We do have you over a barrel.* "I take it you have had time to examine our final demands."

"I wish to point out that I consider this course of action foolish in the extreme, Mr. Reid."

"My firm's desire is solely to ensure that justice is done."

"Very noble, I am sure, but I am worried that you have no idea who you are dealing with."

"Zoe Hearty never had a proper trial. She was committed to your institute on the whim of a judge and his court order. My firm merely seeks the truth."

A cross between an exasperated sigh and mocking laughter sounds from the other end of the phone. "The only truth that concerns me, Mr. Reid, is medical. Your Ms. Hearty is a very ill woman, a narcissist with a severe personality disorder. She is also very clever and extremely manipulative."

"As I said, my firm´s interest is simply in upholding the law. There are a lot of questions surrounding this case—questions we feel have never adequately been answered. That is why we require her testimony."

"I appreciate that, Mr. Reid. But let me emphasise how strongly I feel that yours is a wrong and wilful course of action. The recording she made was purely for medical reasons. Therapy, if you will. It was never meant to leave these premises. Its wider availability can only inflame matters. Think of the families of the victims. Think of those she murdered. "

"And I am afraid you no longer have a choice in this matter. As solicitors for Ms. Hearty, we are entitled to everything. We will have that recording, one way or another. "

"I repeat, sir. Your client is a dangerous person. A fantasist. A woman of great charm, but a fantasist. She blames aliens, for heaven´s sake. Aliens. In this day and age. This path you are engaged in can only lead to grief…"

Reid clears his throat hard, stopping Guthry in full flow.

"Mr. Guthry." An emphasis on the first syllable. "I believe you know my reputation and the reputation of my law firm,. We tend to get what we want, and we certainly intend to get what is due to us: thus, I see little point in debating this issue further. We will look into the case of Ms. Hearty. We will shine a light on the alleged police corruption and investigate the nagging legal issues. Should we find nothing out of place, then so be it, but it is our contention that everybody, Ms. Hearty included, deserves a fair shake. We are not convinced she has gotten that to date."

"You and your company are making a terrible mistake." Reid can almost hear teeth-gnashing on the other end of the line, and it is music to his ears.

"The recording, Mr. Guthry? Zoe's story. When can you get it to me?"

A long silence filled with the sound of damp breathing on the other end of the phone.

"I will have it in the post by tomorrow morning. Registered, of course. Thereafter, I appeal to your sense of fair play and discretion."

"Make sure that it is. There have been enough delays in this matter. Now, will there be anything else? "

"No, nothing," Guthry's voice is deflated. "Nothing. But I do pray we do not all live to regret this."

And with that, there is a click and the line goes dead.

Chapter 1

We met when we were both high in a dive on the Northside. I was off my face and he was no better. But man alive, was he hot. I mean seriously smoking! His ass in those faded jeans. Buttocks of steel I tell you, and those liquid green-brown eyes. I fell hot and hard. He took me by the hand, and he smiled, his lop-sided, little boy smile. And that was that, apart from the shagging. He took me home, ripped off my clothes, while I tore at his and it was great. Do I need to say more? Hot, steamy sex, as a girlfriend of mine used to say, and lots of it, day and night and night and day. And tenderness in between. But, if I am honest, even then there were signs. Little hints that he was not as sugar candy, as gentle and centered, as he wanted me to believe. Nothing obvious: a hint of a frown, a throw-away remark. Sarcasm. But I was in love, so nothing could pierce the warm cocoon he wrapped around me.

I was studying to be an accountant. He was a few years older than me and in advertising. Already successful, despite being doped and stoned to the gills for most of his days and nights. Got his creative juices flowing, or so he said. Part of the charm back then, and I wasn't all that much better. It was what made him so alluring, I guess. I hated what I was doing, hated it with a passion. I saw him as a way out, an escape.

A weakness, I now see: running away. Something I was a bit of an expert on back then. Ducking shit. Avoiding responsibility. It all goes back to my parents: their protectiveness, their demands. Be a good girl. Smile. Sit just so. Study. Be well behaved. Accountancy would be a good fit, dear, don't you think, Zoe?

And all the time I was screaming inside. Let me out. Let me go. If I want to be a starving artist or a lion tamer, let me. It is my life. Mine. I

6

will live it as I see fit.

But I never had the guts to tell them.

Jimmy, though, was different. A pull yourself up by the bootlaces kind of guy from the other side of town. He came from a truly fucked up family, had educated himself, was driven, and made money. He had his shit about him and knew what he was doing.

I fell hard, and he took me under his wing. I was in love, but I was a fool. I was hardly the first.

#

The honeymoon period lasted a good long time. Great sex, great parties, great friends. Alcohol, drugs, trips on dhows in the Indian Ocean. Sex on beaches in India, in wild German forests, in the dark against walls in hotels, and in amusement parks. A wild ride. Too wild, I now realize. As though we were hurtling on a runaway engine into the future, unaware of the danger we were in. Heedless, irresponsible. We were not fully adults, and yet not children. A man-child and a woman-child in full-grown bodies.

Then I got pregnant. That was Sarah. It took a little time, some agonizing, but we did keep her, though he was a little more than reluctant to begin with. Jimmy proposed in a posh French restaurant. Flowers and rings and people clapping in the background, like a scene copied exactly from a Rom-com. Corny, I suppose, but it was sweet in its own way. I had rose petals in my eyes and a bun in the oven. I gave up studying, at his insistence, and started reading all the pregnancy books, bought all the toys, and decorated the room.

And one day, late in my third trimester, I was gripped by pain. A stabbing knife in my lower back drove me to my knees. Breathing deep and hard, sweat pouring down my face, and fear like a dark chill in my spine.

I cannot lose you, I prayed. Not now. Not so close. This child within me was already my everything. I got to my feet, hobbled to the phone, and called emergency. I don't remember how, but I made it to the hospital. I awoke in a hospital bed, an Indian nurse with almond eyes leaning over me.

"You'll be alright, now, love." Her smile was a summer's day and I believed her. I would be fine.

In the end, it had nothing to do with the pregnancy. I had developed a peptic ulcer.

"Too much chili, I guess," I remember saying, smiling at the tall, pinch-faced doctor.

I remember the look in his eyes, the naked skepticism.

Yes, I did still have an occasional drink. Not many. Just a few. When I was feeling down, lonely. Sitting in front of the TV, feeling like a beached whale. Chocolate, ice cream, pickles, and a glass of bubbly.

Jimmy was not exactly hands-on in those days. He was gone from morning until night and sometimes even on the weekends. And when he was home, I caught him glancing at me from beneath his eyebrows. There was something chilling in that look, like he was trying to work out what had happened to him and where he was. Who I was. He was casually drunk most of the time, but he was successful. A major account had landed in his lap and his campaign was a runaway success. His clients, his firm, were treating him like a Roman emperor. We, or should I say he, had money. He was rolling in it. From the outside, we looked like the ideal couple.

Successful professional family with a child on the way.

On the surface that was true, but there were other deeper truths. We did not talk much, and if I am honest, I was a little resentful. He had his life, while I was stuck at home. My parents did come to the wedding, faces tight and unhappy. We were already not on very good terms but they were completely peeved after I announced I was giving up my studies to be a "Hausfrau".

It wasn't all bad though. We still laughed a lot when he was home, we cooked together. We held each other and I still felt loved and embraced.

The alienation came later.

Chapter 2

Unequivocal love

She was born upside down and had to be pulled out of me.

I screamed, and screamed, little more than a wisp of strength left, after five hard days and nights. Her face was squished and blood-smeared. Her head was elongated and shaped like a cone. I remember sharing Jimmy's look of horror as we looked at our daughter.

The midwife smiled kindly. "None of that, now. She is a grand, healthy lass. She'll be fine. Happens a lot when they finally choose to show up."

Jimmy leaned down and kissed me then, whispering in my ear. "Remember the movie Coneheads? Dan Aykroyd. I think we have just given life to an alien."

A sputtering laugh escaped my lips; tired as I was. That was the thing, his irreverence always made me smile or laugh.

When Sarah was brought back to us, cleaned and swaddled, I fell in love. Actually, I don't think that's true. I think I was already madly in love. I just got to meet the object of my affection outside myself for the first time.

And in that intense wave of emotion, what shocked me, was Jimmy. I saw tears in his eyes. His lips trembled. I imagined I was seeing him melt, like candle wax, sweating and changing. The new Jimmy, when the wax hardened, was a dad first and foremost.

A soul reborn, if you will. The man-child abandoned.

Or mostly. The dad took the child's place, but Jimmy had too many demons for a transformation to be totally successful. The darkness had not vanished, it had just been driven deeper.

#

Jimmy was an only child. His father was a quiet man, who worked as a janitor cum handyman for the council. A quiet, temperate man who loved fixing cars and racing them. Soft-spoken. A chain-smoker. He died much too young. I only met him a handful of times. The mother was a roaring, abusive dragon filled with the belief that she was better than everybody else. She also suffered from what she termed an inherited drinking problem. She imbued her only child with a terrible need for her approval, an aching void that could never be filled. They lived in a two-up, two-down: a place her grandiose soul could not abide. Jimmy would never talk about it, but I always knew that she had warped him: the gentleness he inherited from his dad twisted into dense knots of need and insecurity.

They were churchgoers, so he became a godless heathen before he too became a true believer, and that had consequences of its own, as I will explain later. The last time I met her was before Sean was born. Christmas. An epic holiday row over the Christmas dinner, followed by eternal estrangement.

Jimmy never spoke of her again.

I did learn something from her of Jimmy's childhood. In school, he was clever. I imagine cleverer than his parents had ever been, good at everything, even sports, but his passion was writing. It was one of those rare inspirational teachers who set him on his path. Gave him that writing bug that would stay with him forever. But more than anything, Jimmy needed approval and success. The world of the admen, madmen was his compromise. A temporary cash cow until he wrote his magnus opus. And he was good in business, looked fine in a suit, could hold a room during presentations or over cocktails. My tall, handsome, broken man.

Then came the crash. The deep recession.

It's funny, Jimmy never took to Sean like he did to Sarah. She was Daddy's girl and his love was fully reciprocated. That left me and Sean to balance them out. Sean was Mama's boy. All very cliched, I know, but it worked. Mostly. They were good kids, well-loved. He never allowed the edges in our relationship to affect the family as a whole.

And when Jimmy was home, he was Dad: one-hundred-and-twenty percent all on and unsparing.

That was until the crash. Until I copped on to the affairs. Until the drinking got out of hand. Until he joined that cursed society.

#

Jimmy was getting older, becoming a dinosaur in his world. Losing friends and influence. His lifestyle once embraced was now barely tolerated; arriving pickled at work accompanied by long drunken lunches, from which he sometimes never returned.

He had earned his bosses a fortune, but his star was fading. The writing was on the wall in big, scrawled letters, but Jimmy was too wrapped up in himself to notice. The final straw: He admitted kissing (and for all I know fucking) a college intern at his last Christmas party. And then came the deluge, the downturn.

He was let go. A generous severance package, an engraved watch, and best fucking wishes for the future, but he was finished, and he knew it. His name dirt. He called me to tell me, and then he disappeared for three days, crawling back home in the early hours, red-nosed, smelling of stale alcohol and staler pussy.

He stood in the doorway of the ensuite bedroom of our McMansion tears rolling down his crumpled face.

"I love you. The kids. We can start again." He looked at me in that semi-darkness, and behind the tears were both shame and a deeper well of broken coldness that never thawed. Shards of his mother's self-hate buried in his soul.

"I love you too, babe."

And I did. For all his flaws, he was still a reasonable husband, and a decent dad. Was I aiming too low, you say? Too tolerant of his infidelities, too naive for believing he could ever be changed. Ignoring not just warning signs, but great Times Square billboards and sirens blaring, "You got yourself a dud."

You may be right, probably are, but I loved him. You know, 'The heart wants what it wants' etc...

"Come here." I held out my right hand to him and waved him to me.

He stumbled into bed, flopped like a sack of potatoes and I wrapped my arms around him.

"Time for a change. Time for a change."

His words were sighed rather than spoken. Moments later, he was snoring gently in my arms.

I felt hope that night, I swear. Hope for a new future. Hope that we could still be a family. Hope that we really could pull it all back together.

Looking back now, I want to cry at the richness of my then life as I take in these white, antiseptic walls around me, the metal commode, the blinking light above the door, the prosthetic eyes of Doctor Creep. My heart is bleak and empty and deep with anger.

Believe me. *Trust* me. Otherwise, we are all doomed.

#

I woke the next morning, late, to the sound of noise and laughter downstairs. I slid out of bed, pulled on my robe, and went to the bathroom. All the time I could feel a smile on my face and a tug of warmth in my heart.

I remembered his words. "Time for a change."

One thing about Jimmy: When he made up his mind, his mind was made up for good. No beating about the bush, my boy. No siree, Bob. The past, all done and dusted. "Been there, got the fucking t-shirt and the hangover to go with it, now let's make a new one," as he liked to say.

They were all in the kitchen. The kids were in the breakfast nook while the sound of Jimmy's "Weekend" Spotify flow blasted from the Harmon Kardon Bluetooth speaker on the kitchen island. An Aura something or other with glowing lights that looked futuristic; a prop in a spaceship on some 60's TV show. It had, of course, cost a pretty penny. Only the best for our Jimmy. He was in tracksuit bottoms, a Balenciaga T-shirt, swaying and jiving barefoot to the sound of some hip-hopper I did not recognise. Eggs sizzled in the frying pan, as the smell of bacon wafted from the oven.

He was still a little gray around the gills. Hard at our age to recover overnight from one of his extreme binges, though, he never did seem to suffer enough, given what he poisoned himself with. He turned when he heard me enter, a beatific smile on his face.

"Breakfast, Love. Pull up a pew. I'll get you a coffee."

I remember, smiling, nodding. Being happy. He gave the kids their eggs and bacon, then brought a plate and a steaming cup of coffee for me. He squeezed in beside me on the bench and put his arms around my shoulder kissing me on the cheek.

"See," he sighed into my ear. "We can get past this. We just need to keep a check on costs. Plan things. We can turn this around. I might even get a chance to write."

He smiled at me, seeking approval.

"I thought maybe we should think of selling up. Move away to the country. Find a house with a huge garden. Trees, grass, open sky. A safer place for all of us. Away from this crap."

"Dad!" Sarah scolded.

"Oops. Sorry, Babe. I mean stinky, horrible, smelly stuff."

Sarah giggled at him.

He reached out for my hand. Through the window, I could see the lone oak in our back garden; its leaves wearing a gentle fringe of green as the first leaves started to bloom. Clouds scudded past overhead in a bracing breeze as the branches danced. The sky was a wonderful interplay of blue and white, light and gray.

Spring. New beginnings.

I nodded, sipping at that warm, hearty coffee.

I nodded, feeling buds of hope blooming within me too.

"We should talk about that. Talk hard about that." I leaned, pressing against him.

Sean blew a raspberry when I kissed Jimmy and then Jimmy was up from the bench, chasing Sean and then Sarah around the house, stomping and growling like a big-ass bear until they all collapsed into a fit of squirming giggles on the plush carpet in the TV room.

Believe me when I tell you, we had good times too. Goofy times. Times that I wished had never ended.

Chapter 3

It was Autumn before we had everything organized.

Our new life waited in the town of Temple, in the Nire Valley. In the middle of nowhere, the nearest large town was a good twenty-minute drive away, through winding roads and misty hills full of heather and vibrant yellow furze. Enormous old oak and glorious rolling hills of pine and spruce. There was even a stretch of road that looked like the Dark Hedges on GOT; a spooky stretch on a dull day with trees towering above, but glorious when sunlight cast beams through the leaves.

The town, more a village really, had everything we would need, but the best thing about it was the beautiful river snaking gently over rocks.

Our house was a new build, that had been a holiday rental. A four-bed with a deck to the rear leading down to the river with our own wooden jetty.

We were standing there, arm in arm, looking down over the river, the sun on our backs, when I saw a red deer on the opposite bank of the river. It raised its head at us, its eyes liquid. Then it disappeared, and we were both sold.

The money we got from selling our other house left us in a fairly decent position, financially. Jimmy would have time and space to write.

The plan was for me to go back to studying. I would finish my degree in accounting. Finding online courses was easy. When I rang my parents to tell them, they thawed a little and wished me well.

They meant it, I think, though they never did bother to make the drive to see us and their grandkids in their new lives. Too self-involved in their Boomer retirement to take the time for us.

Jimmy also applied to sub as an English teacher in the local school.

He recounted his interview with the slim, young principal.

'Build up a little trust. A few retirements in the offing. See how we get along, eh! We pride ourselves on being a family, here. And I am sure you will fit right in.' "Leaning forward, eyes deep with compassion and sombre with gravitas," Jimmy paused and snarled. "Rod up his arse, that one. Obnoxious, officious prick," Jimmy said. "Five foot nothing, would blow away in a stiff fucking breeze."

"Jimmy!"

"Hold on to your knickers, Love. I was well-behaved and totally chill. Cross my heart. A proper boy scout with a shit-eating smile."

"So you do have the job?"

"A few hours a week guaranteed to begin with, and then we will see. Beer money, if nothing else."

"Jimmy!"

"Joking, pet. Just a joke."

Jimmy had quit. Given it all up. Sworn off the demon rum and all its associated evil spirits. Good for him, for us as a family, but it did not help with the bitterness. Jimmy had been big in his world and found brown-nosing a principal younger than him demeaning. I could see it written in his eyes. The failure like a scar in his iris—one that never healed, only grew day by day. A place of deadness in those warm eyes.

If the book did not work out? If he could achieve nothing further in his life? The emptiness. The pointless waste of the rest of his life.

I could feel the despair boiling over into anger. With me, the kids, everything. Not often and nothing violent yet, but it was there. A cancer of the spirit.

I know this now, of course, and only vaguely sensed it back then: the bitter emptiness filling the spaces in his broken, empty soul.

#

The kids loved the house.

We pulled into the drive on a beautiful day in a heatwave of an Indian summer, with the sun liquid gold on the trees. The foxgloves and furze swayed ever so slightly on the hill across the river and above the

15

house. Jimmy had barely stopped and set the handbrake before they were away; running squealing, arms cartwheeling to the deck out the back and down to the jetty.

The house was furnished and fitted. Jimmy had spent the week before on his own here and had returned with a beaming smile on his face.

"I love the place. It is a dream," he whispered to me as I lay in his arms after sex in bed. His arms wrapped warmly around me, the beating of his heart loud in my left ear.

"We can be happy there. We can."

He kissed me on the top of my head. I cry myself to sleep now, remembering the hope, the warmth and the swollen joy in my breast that night.

#

There was a large three-seat kayak, a brilliant shade of green, tied to the jetty.

Sean's eyes lit and the smile on his face reached his ears.

He looked at me, more in hope than expectation, and I nodded. I had stuff to move from the car, anyway, and to have the three of them out from under me would be a relief. And what better way could there be for them to come home?

"Yes. Go. Get gone. Be off with you all."

Jimmy laughed, I think in relief, and ran to the shed for the lifejackets and paddles while Sean jumped into my arms and Sarah grabbed my legs.

"Be careful with them out there, Jimmy."

He winked and said, "Safe as houses, love. Why don't you check out what I did with your house, Hausfrau?"

I stuck my tongue out at him, but I marched back up the hill to the deck with a jaunty stride. That was hope, you see, putting the spring in my steps.

I was carrying a cardboard box marked 'kitchen' from the car when I glanced out the sliding doors at the back of the house.

Jimmy was on his knees, all three of them in blue and yellow life jackets, his arms on their shoulders, talking as they listened with serious intent.

A lecture on how to respect the water and their safety instructions. Jimmy was deadly serious when it came to safety.

On his knees, his arms holding their small shoulders. Looking back, I believe that is one of the last purely happy memories I can dredge up from the depths of my brain.

If I had only known, if I had had the power, I would have stopped time then and there.

But we never do know how good life is till it goes up in the smoke of time and entropy.

Chapter 4

Surprising me, but more so himself, Jimmy was an effective teacher. Beloved even. He had enough gravitas to keep the kids engaged, and his passion was real. Principal *Small Dick* o Mahoney (Jimmy's words) doled out more hours from the "always tight" budget, and the contract was renewed at the end of Jimmy's trial period.

And that was a terrible shame. Jimmy could take no satisfaction in a thing which he was genuinely good at: a profession that might have given him and his life meaning.

In the end, the job was not glamorous enough for him. I was not enough. Not even his children were enough. His obsession lay elsewhere. It was his book. The writing. The thing he had always wanted for himself: a published work but more than that—recognition, respect, reviews. He never said it in so many words, but I know he pictured himself on TV, or writing articles for the broadsheets, making appearances on the radio, his voice taken seriously.

His work loved and respected and selling well.

A way back to the fifteen minutes of fame he had enjoyed in his twenties and early thirties; before he was put out to pasture. This time as someone serious. A person of consequence, not just a sleazy marketing man whoring himself out for the corporate shilling.

#

It was the rejections that did it.

That tipped him into the deeper darkness.

He was in his study working I presume when I heard him whoop. Almost a yelp.

Joy or pain?

I wasn't entirely sure. I was cooking in the kitchen, hands wet and a sharp knife in hand. Jesus, I almost cut myself.

Heart in my mouth, I threw the knife into the sink and dried my hands on my clothes.

Another scream. More jubilant but also somehow pained.

I ran to him, for it was unlike Jimmy to be so loud, if he wasn't chasing after the children or, if I was lucky back then, me.

The door to the study was closed, as always.

When Daddy is working the door shall remain closed. Rule number one and written in capitals in the constitution of our household. I knocked. Jimmy grunted.

"What?"

"You okay, Jim?"

"It's alright, Love. Come in. Come in."

I pushed open the door, still nervous.

He stood up from his chair and desk as I answered, straightening slowly, as if shaking off a stiff back.

"It is finally done," he said.

I remember the big, bright smile I felt bloom on my face.

"It is?"

"It fucking is! Fucking A, it is."

He grabbed me in a huge bear hug, squeezing the air from my lungs. He was laughing. I was too, as tears welled in his eyes. He let go, took me by the hand and showed me the screen.

"The End." Today's date.

"I did it. I fucking did it. And it's good. I know it is."

And I was delighted for him. I was. But one small, perhaps mean, little voice in my head was also saying to itself. "Thank Christ that is all over."

I know that sounds petty, but three years living with a struggling artist will do that to you. Try it, if you want to see what I mean. The dark moods looming over days he could not write. The long, interminable evenings with the scowling man who was my husband, sitting on the sofa together, but not really together as we pretended to watch whatever was on the box. That pale shadow of a man who locked himself into that dark and miserable room, day after day. Phoning in sick to work too often. Ignoring the kids. Ignoring me. Moping around like a sick house cat.

I mean, three fucking years.

Yeah! Yeah! I know some books have taken three times that and more, I started the Name of the Wind when it came out and loved it and have been waiting ever since, but trust me: if your better half is an insecure, middle-aged struggling writer with mood swings, then you are bloody happy when the thing is done. Ecstatic. Over the freaking moon happy.

So I shared in his jubilation and with good reason. We informed the kids, went out for a meal, had a bottle of bubbly we could ill afford. Drove home, slightly merry and definitely over the limit, but what of it? This was a once in a lifetime moment. The genius that was Jimmy was committed to paper. The world could go blow itself. His moment was at hand, or so he said.

And he was happy. With me. With work. Whistling on his way to the local school, mind you, like he was the star of dancing in the Rain. Skipping down the bucolic lanes rimmed with gorse and heather. Helping the kids with their schooling. Helping me too, with various other things, she said to herself, smiling.

#

What was the original name of the bloody thing again?

Bleeding Alleys of my December Mind was the first attempt at a title. Not at all pretentious, was my feedback.

Then came *The Prince of Mallow Script Lane.*

That made me a little nervous. Neither title sounded magnum oposesque, if such a word exists, and I am fairly sure it doesn't.

For Jimmy, euphoria gave way to frustration, fairly soon. This was work. And work he was ill-suited for.

The editing, the drafting, the redrafting. The endless moans and groans.

Mr. Scowling Man became Mister Long-face Scowling Man. And I mean 24/7, 365 days of the year.

Mister Long-face Scowling Man sounds like a song, huh. Well, if it was a song, it would be a dirge, the background music to my life for the next two years.

And then, when it was all ready, and we were older and grayer, he started sending the tome to agents. Email, online submission forms, even old-fashioned postage: stamps and envelope licking included.

Nothing.

Emptiness.

A blank screen, a postbox filled with nothing but bills. No accolades. Only torn hopes and evaporated dreams, day after day.

Rejection again.

Like when he was young.

Like it was his mother again.

"Not good enough, James. Simply not good enough. A waste of space and fresh air, just like that useless lumpish creature you call a father. And you never will be anything, mark my words. Never. You are just like him. Not an ounce of spunk in the two of you. Barely a brain cell between you both."

Holding her almost empty, but soon to be refilled, glass over him, while he drops the report card on the brown carpet of their tiny "dining room".

While tears bloom in his eyes.

I wish I could have reached out to him then. To have held him tight and warmed his soul before the ice in his heart blossomed in the cracks she created. I would have whispered in his ear that it was not his fault. I would have made him look up at her: to see the almost lascivious way she licked her lips and that gleam like a hint of silver in the corners of her eyes.

Enjoying the moment, as she crushed him. Allowing all her myriad inner demons to pounce on this poor little fellow who is about to pee his pants with sadness, and does so as she slaps him hard on his right cheek.

"Go clean yourself, child. You are no son of mine. A foundling if I ever saw one. You disgust me!"

It sickens me.

If he could only have written that story.

If only he could have touched that pain, he would have had

21

something real. Something he could have been proud of. That might have sold. That would, at least, have given him back something of himself and his self-worth. He never did.

Chapter 5

Jimmy turns to look at me, a cheeky grin on his face.

He winks.

"Sean, could you move your bleeding face out of the only part of the back windscreen I can see out of. And stay still, for all our sakes."

"Wasting your breath," I say. "He´s coked up on sugar and fat. Try and tame a drunken monkey, why don't ya."

Today was a Good Day.

A very good day.

An agent.

No contract yet.

But an invitation. A genuine invitation. To the big smoke. And that must mean something, says my writing man.

"I mean, these are serious people. If I am being invited, it must be something good. They want me."

He smiles at me again, a brittle sort of smile.

Truth be told, I am not so sure. I have a sneaking feeling that this too might go nowhere fast. Don't get me wrong. It´s not that I don't care. I do. I really do. It is just that I need this to work out, too. For him. For us. To keep this family sane.

Anyhow, for that moment, it suffices to have a human amongst us again.

Old Scowling Face has become A Bundle Of Cuddly Warmth And Joy.

The beers help.

Him.

And that whiskey.

Only one, mind. Hardly counts.

Which, of course, explains why he is driving, although, I had but a single glass of red.

And yeah, he has been on the sauce again for a year or two, and so have I. Sobriety failed. I have had the occasional drunken tantrum to put up with. As, honestly, has he.

Nothing more. Not yet.

We drove to Mr. Bumbles. Local organically sourced produce and a five-star (ish) local celeb chef. A big old house, a grand dining room with all kinds of pastiche references to the past. Oil paintings of lords and ladies of yore gamboling in green fields, or riding to the hunt in their masses. The cheap romanticizing of the rich bitches and gentle lads of the past.

We spent way too much money for tiny portions of food the kids barely touched.

But that's Jimmy.

Reliving the good old days, don't ya see?

When he could ask the "Garcon" what the best wine was and order it without swallowing a turd. When it was all on the house (or at least on the company).

When he was young and in form, I guess. When he was still hot shit.

What a shame: He could always have been my hot shit.

#

The light rose behind us.

I might struggle now to describe this for how can I truly remember, but please do believe me. This is all true.

The light is complex.

Like light from a ridged bottle in the evening. Not a glare, more a constant distortion.

Behind us.

Above us.

Way above us. And yet all around us.

But streets that were soot dark but for the gentle glow of our rolling headlights are now not. It is like being in a city bathed in streetlights fashioned by ash, not sodium.

Imagine a dead fire burning. A buried corpse rising and putting on makeup and the sick gleam on its face.

Nothing human. Nothing earthly.

This is the light that is behind us.

That is chasing us.

That is hunting us.

I turn in my seat.

"Jimmy!" My voice comes in strangled squeaks.

I am scared, for the kids, for Jimmy. For myself. I feel cold.

Like my bare feet had been placed on concrete in winter. A cold that began almost benignly but became a burn that invaded my legs and ate its way into my lungs.

My breath fogs the windscreen,

"Jimmy!" I yell.

He starts, jerks the wheel toward me. "What the fuck!" Deep breaths. "What the fuck is the matter with you, Zoe?"

"Look. Outside. That light!."

"Jesus, woman. You almost gave me a heart attack. We could have crashed."

His lips are pink and damp with spit. His eyes appear almost fanatical in the ashy light. Dark holes that beg to be left alone.

"There is something wrong with that light. It´s really, really not okay." I keep my voice low and turn in my seat, checking on the kids who had been reduced to a sudden panicked silence.

Jimmy glances into the rear-view mirror. Turns away. Looks back. A long, hard look.

"It is like something is following us. Above us. I can't see what, but it seems to be getting closer." His voice is a low, harsh whisper.

"Dad, what´s happening?" The fear in Sean´s voice is a terrible jolt. Jimmy straightens and raises a shoulder.

"I think I´m sober again, Zoe." He cracks half a smile. Typical. Strong when in a sticky spot. It is the daily grind of life he can't handle.

"Let´s see how fast this thing can go, shall we? All together now.

Zoom!"

"What do we say, Sean?"

"Zoom"

"Sarah?"

"Zoom."

"Zoom it is, ladies and gentle frogs."

"Jimmy. The kids."

"I know. Fast, but still safe. Okay? Cross my heart and hope to fly."
He starts tapping my thigh, a gesture of reassurance. It doesn't work; I
want both hands on the wheel.

"Great. Flipping fantastic." I don't mean a word of it. My stomach
is in my mouth and my hands are shaking.

"Do you feel that?" I asked.

"What?" Jimmy is leaning forward, the car accelerating, eyes fixed
on the road.

"That cold."

Jimmy shakes his head, irritated.

"I feel it," Sarah said in a quiet voice.

"Me too."

Those words are fit to break my heart. I turn in the seat, and reach
back to hold their hands. Icy. Frozen. Blue lipped. Small frames
shivering, like we are lost in a winter gale.

"Get us away from this, Jimmy. Please."

"Doing my best, love. Doing my very damned best."

Is that excitement in his voice? An adrenalin rush? As if he is
starring in his very own heroic car chase?

And with a popping sound, the light is gone.

The blessed dark of night returns.

Like a weight of granite rock has lifted from above me.

Sean smiles. Sarah giggles. Then I do too.

Jimmy eases up on the accelerator.

"Well, that was something, wasn't it?"

"Something bloody weird."

"I suppose."

"You suppose?"

"There will be an explanation. Air-force helicopters or some such."

"You said it yourself. It was following us. Coming after us."

"Deep breaths, Zoe. Calmez vous. We probably just overreacted."

He reaches out to me, and rubs my neck.

"It was nothing. Really nothing. We overreacted. What were we thinking? I mean, what else could it have been?"

I know he is trying to calm us. Sarah and Sean are both sobbing quietly. Sniffling. In relief, I imagine.

And his voice is soothing. It runs like a river over me. A river rolling over stones.

And that is calming in its own way.

But, and it's a big fucking but, his hands on my neck are freezing, like the hands of a dead man. Cold and damp flesh stroking me.

Why did he lie?

About the cold. He must have felt it, too.

I move my neck away from his hand and it drops away. I turn in the seat, towards him.

I swear, on his face is the strangest look I have ever seen. His eyes are still dark pools, but his lips are curled in something that looks like a half-smile.

As if he had just experienced something wonderful. Joyous.

I shiver. A shiver that runs through me like a wave.

"Take us home, Jimmy. Take us home, please."

My voice sounds hollow, robbed of substance.

"Zoom?" Jimmy bellows loudly.

"Zoom," from Sarah and Sean together. A little laughter now amongst the tears.

"Zoom, zoom, zoom, zoom."

If you can't beat 'em, zoom with 'em: So we zoomed-zoomed our long winding road back home.

#

"Nobody else has reported anything."

"Say what?"

"Here. See for yourself."

27

We are sitting on our couch, staring at the empty TV screen. The kids are finally down. They wanted to sleep in our room, and share our double bed: Me on the bed beside them, Jimmy sitting opposite on a settee. In the semi-dark, like we were huddling in a bunker, waiting for disaster to strike at any moment.

No wonder, I suppose. They did have a fright and I don't think they have ever seen their parents afraid before. Not like that. Only natural that the poor dears would be terrified too. They are both asleep now, gently breathing, faces warm and relaxed: Sheepy and Raggy-the-Bear tightly clutched against them. Tokens of protection against the great dark world.

I am nursing a glass of red, Jimmy a malt whiskey.

He pushes his phone toward me.

"See for yourself."

Twitter. The website of the local paper. The feed of the local Facebook page.

"Nada."

"But it can't have only been us?"

"You wouldn't think so, but then again, that stretch of road is quiet. Especially at night. And hardly anyone lives that far up the mountain." He laughs. "There are a few farms and about a billion sheep. The rude, wild living fellas."

"And they are not on Twitter?"

"Apparently not."

He glances at the fire opposite, staring into the roiling red flames. I snuggle deeper into the sofa.

I want to reach out to him, to hold him, but there is a gap between us. Only inches, but it feels like a chasm.

I wish I could remember why. I wish we could return to the ease we once had, but the very air between us is strained, has been for a long time now and neither of us seems to have the words to stretch across the gap and reach out for the other.

"I don't know. Do you think we just imagined it? A hallucination. I mean, what was it even? Light and cold? Nothing more."

Jimmy nods, still staring at the fire.

"Say something, dummy." I tap his arm playfully, and he turns and stares at me. The anger on his face is a dash of cold water.

"What the fuck did you do that for?"

"Whoa, Jimmy. Love? What's gotten your goat?"

He stares at me with those eyes that seem darker than they used to be, filled with emotion I can no longer comprehend. There was a time when I could read him like a book. Now that book is written in a cypher and I have lost the key.

He shakes his head as if coming out of a trance, or forcing himself out of a trance.

"I just think it seemed real." His words are slow. Long pauses between the words. "Realer than I have felt in a long time. Something..."

"Yeah?"

"I dinna ken," he says smiling at his woeful Scottish accent. "It might be something for a new book. A grain of a new idea."

I force a smile and groan inside. I had hoped this too was over: this writing lark. Had hoped he might see sense and focus on the teaching. Grow up. Grow beyond. Do what he was good at rather than that which drove him mad.

"I have, I don't know, something...a feeling. Call it sixth sense. I am on to something here. A germ of an idea, but it is exciting."

"I guess that is good. Only..."

"Only what?"

"Nothing. Nothing. You still have the meeting, right? About the book? You haven't forgotten?"

And with that, the tension drains out of him, like a boil lanced. The darkness, gone in a moment. His eyes vibrant again. He smiles, a happy smile reminiscent of the one he had left the house with."

"God, I had almost forgotten that. Strange, huh? And that was all I could think about a few hours ago."

"The *Big Meeting*."

"Right. This is the one. Publication at last. Fame and fortune await. Onward and upward."

He holds his almost empty whiskey Glass out to me and I clink mine against his. The tinkling sound is hollow. The silence drowned out by the crackling of the hearth fire and the loud beating of my uneasy heart.

29

Chapter 6

The Day is come. The Big Day. Hallelujah. The day is come.

The day of *The Meeting*.

That meeting.

And Jimmy is as skittish as a newborn foal. He has been growing his beard out: looks good, if I do say so myself. No Nancy-boy goatee for My Jimmy. No sirree. This is the real deal: it would put your average lumberjack to shame. A deep-rug, king of a beard, if you see what I mean. Wild and luxurious. Makes me tingle inside and, lately, so does he. The pessimism is gone. In its place is a new Jimmy. The good one. The one who appears like the sun in winter on the good days and whose memory I miss when he retreats from us.

So, please, please, God be good to me and give him good news.

Please.

We need this now more than ever.

For not everything is sunshine.

Jimmy has been missing a lot of school, locked up in his room. Research, he tells me. The white light gave him a concept, one that excites him, consumes him.

But still, he is warm with me and helpful around the house.

Better than it has been for a very long time. Except, there have been hints that his contract at the school might not be renewed. Gossip conveyed to me in hushed tones in the shop by the other mothers. My "friends".

We know how beloved he is, they say. We know the children listen to him. Sympathy is written large on their faces. Oozing sympathy like

30

slime, as if doing me a favor. Sure: it would be a shame if she didn't know, poor dear. And her with the two little ones at home.

So Jimmy is fucking up big time and could lose our only guaranteed source of income, because of an obsession with a white fucking light. And does this worry me with our savings dwindling? When you move into a house, they don't always tell you that there is rot in the ceiling or that the plumbing is on its last knees.

Bill after bill dropping onto the floor near the letterbox like clanging hammers.

I know we should have gotten the house checked out first. That's what my folks used to say. Buy in haste and regret in leisure.

Well, that's not us. We are a bit too impulsive for that kind of thing. My education has petered out too—that's on me, not on Jimmy. I will get back to it. I will. I promise.

We are not penniless. Not yet, at least. But Jimmy needs a big advance, or he needs to keep his job.

I need him like this and better. Need him to be in a good place.

But, boy, does he clean up good.

Dressed up for the long drive and the 12:30 meeting in the offices of the "Big Lads".

Black jeans, gray seersucker jacket, bluish-gray shirt, brown loafers, long legs, quick smile, chiseled chin, broad shoulders, liquid eyes, and that beard.

Well, you get the picture.

Still ain't half bad, my man.

Sometimes I don't understand what has come between us.

After breakfast, he kisses the kids goodbye. He grabs his keys from the sideboard near the front door and reaches back to me. He wraps his arm around me, all gentle-like, and leans down to kiss me. His hand cups my face.

There is love there. Warmth. Things we have been guilty of not always sharing.

Love and a last true kiss.

#

Grabbing his arm, I walk him to the car.

He checks his pockets—wallet, keys, a printout of his invitation, printout of the thick tome on A4 paper wrapped up neatly with cloth ties.

Ready.

He unlocks the car, opens the door, and turns to me.

I am there on the porch, arms wrapped around myself against the early morning cold. A spring day, threatening to be mild. Clouds flit across the sky, some sun-kissed, others gray and low and bearing a threat of rain. Sparrows flit in and out of the cherry tree; blooming white as a bride in the center of our garden. A blackbird is hopping along the moss-tinged grass, berating me and the world.

Jimmy smiles at me and that smile is the smile of the man I fell for. It is the smile of the man I loved. The man I lost. The man who lost himself. The man I need back.

He scrunches down to get into the car- the curse of a tall man in a bog-standard sedan. I see him put his stuff on the passenger seat, pat the car on the top of the dashboard, and then key the ignition.

With one last smile, he turns the wheel and is gone.

#

We got no message from him that afternoon.

I waited till four and then rang.

No answer.

Voice mail.

Shit.

I told myself, maybe that is good news. He might still be in his meeting. Or out for lunch, discussing contracts and what not.

Don't be a panicky old biddy. We can wait.

The kids were back from school. Doing their homework.

"Where is Daddy?" Sean asked at about six. Daddy drawn way out, as only a boy can.

Daaaaaaady.

I did my best to ignore their impatience. I did my best to ignore mine.

I confess. I could have been more worried, but I had a feeling about what this meant. It wasn't a car accident or a mugging. It was the bitterest pill: Rejection. Again. That stake that sinks deep into his otherwise inviolable heart. In a way, I hoped it would be an accident. A mugging. Something minor. Something unforeseen. Not the inevitable. In my heart, I knew what it was: him lashing out at their temerity. You plan to reject me. Who do you think you are?

I can see the progression. He strides confidently into a building—could be an old redbrick with stately lines or a modernist temple of glass and steel—introduces himself for his 12:30 with Herr Yada-Yada. On the way up in the elevator, he is all sunshine and charm. Then he has to wait. Fidgeting. Nervous sweat slipping down his back. A half an hour later, he is ushered into the room of Yada-Yada. Swanky rooms, full of books, with a distinguished desk of cherry wood.

Mr. Yada is polite, dismissive, basically disinterested.

"We thought we had an opening for a project such as this, but I am sorry to say, Old chap (in my mind, Yada is a tall, thin bespectacled Brit with the posh accent of one of his social status two generations ago), that vacancy has been filled. Sorry for the inconvenience and all that. One must go with what one loves, not what one merely likes. I am sure you understand. But chin up, Old man, I am sure there is a loving home for your work somewhere."

And Jimmy being Jimmy, does what Jimmy does best.

He rises from his chair, leans over the desk, and in a loud voice tells Mr. Yada what to do with his company, his unctuous words, and his whole family. And his friends. And his fucking dog.

Which more or less guarantees that Jimmy will never be published anywhere but Amazon.

And then he knocks something from the desk, strides out, and disappears into the city of a million dreams.

A million miles from home.

We don't see him again for a week.

#

Frayed at the edges.

Fending off questions from the kids.

Worrying about the bills and my husband who hasn't been teaching school all week.

Small-dick O Mahoney is asking valid questions.

Questions I can't answer.

"Is he ill?"

Don't know.

"When will he be back?"

Haven't a clue.

Sorry *small Dick*. You know as much as I do.

Not what I say, of course.

"Flat on his back with a recurrence of the lower back pain that has been troubling him all year."

"Of course he has been to the doctor, and I am sure the anti-inflammatories will kick in soon."

You cannot know. The creeping fear. The embarrassment. The doubt. We are poor and getting poorer, and the man I tied my lifeline to is nowhere to be seen. And I know. I should have done more. I should have finished college. But truth be told, I love being with the kids and God knows they need me. I will finish the course. I swear it.

I have to, for all our sakes.

I have just never found studying easy or fun.

A pain.

Just have to do it. Get through it. Be the adult I never quite feel I am.

I love the kids; I will do anything for them.

So, this is just one more thing.

#

He arrived back on a Thursday.

The look on his face told me everything.

The look *of* his face told me more: Pale and blotchy skin, circles like bulls-eyes targeting his eyes, hair a rat's nest of grease.

I saw him though the kitchen window. He felt my eyes upon him and glanced up. His look made me step back, shocked at what I read there.

Anger. Frustration. Hatred even. Not of me necessarily: of the whole poxed-up world that refused to give him the breaks he felt he needed. No, the breaks he deserved.

If others could have fame and recognition, why couldn't he?

No remorse. No recognition of my pain and anger. No knowledge of the pain he had caused his children.

Not even embarrassment.

I dried my hands and walked through the hallway.

I was pulling open the door when the bell rang.

I stood there facing him, arms crossed, torn about whether to let him in or not.

"So?" he said.

"So!"

"Did I ever tell you the story about that film star Richard Harris?"

"You did, Jimmy and more than once."

Jimmy ignores me.

"He left for a weekend to watch Munster play a club game in England up near Manchester. Was supposed to just be gone for the weekend but he ended up on a tear and was gone for two weeks. Came back late at night to his wife, lost for something to say."

"I remember."

"And you remember what he said?"

I nod.

"So, why didn't you pay the fucking ransom?"

He raises his eyes to mine, expectantly, a smile curling his lips.

"Not funny anymore, Jimmy."

"No. I suppose not."

"Is there any point in me asking where you have been?"

"If I knew, myself, I'd tell you, Zoe."

"You dickhead."

"They turned the book down. I just lost my head. Lost it all."

"You sober now?"

"Since yesterday. I drove, you see. Slept in the car last night. Feel like shit warmed up, if that helps you any."

"Not a word from you. A whole week. The kids worried sick."

"But not you? You weren´t?"

"On the piss and sniffing after skirt. I know you, Jimmy. I knew you'd be back like the bad fucking penny you really are."

He reaches out to me, as if to caress my face again. I slap his hand away. Anger flares in his eyes.

"Do it, Jimmy. Do it, you, shit. Hit me like you want to."

He lowers his face and kicks the ground with his now scruffy loafers.

"I understand you are angry, Zoe."

"You selfish shit. Angry doesn't cover it. Whatever you feel about me, what you did to the kids? I mean one call. One fucking call. Is that too much to ask? Is it?"

"I lost my phone. It was just gone. That first night."

"And you couldn't think to borrow one. You must have stayed somewhere. Did none of your sluts have any technology? Don't fucking lie to me, Jimmy. You couldn't be bothered. That is the A and O of it. Out of sight, out of fucking mind."

"I screwed up, babe. I know. But they kicked me down. Tore my work apart. Made me feel tiny." A sniffle now. "I just lost it. With them. And then I felt so ashamed. I couldn't. I just couldn't. Return here. To see the look in your eyes. The pity. I couldn't. I am so, so sorry."

"You don't deserve us. Me. The kids."

He looked up at me then, his eyes red and bleary, snot running down his face, but there was no longer any contrition in the face. The anger was back. He was looking up at me from below on the lower steps of the porch. Looking up, in his own mind, into the face of his mother.

"Let me in, Zoe." Venom in that voice now.

"I don't know that you belong here any longer, Jimmy. With us. In this house."

"Don't be so fucking melodramatic woman. I messed up. I said sorry. This is my house. Those are my kids. I will not be told no."

Steel in his voice, and a degree of panic.

He lunges for me. Up two steps and grabs me by the upper arm. Hard. A vice-like grip.

"I belong here, Zoe. With you and the kids. I will be good, I promise. We'll get back to normal. I will make amends. To you. To them. Do not fight me on this. Do not. Okay?"

All the time squeezing. Fingers digging into the fleshy area above my elbow. His hands are so large, they completely enclose my forearm. His fingers with his too-long nails dig deep into my skin, and I know he does not need to do this. An extra pinch of pain. A mark for me to remember.

This is no accident of misplaced strength. I wince in pain and he squeezes tighter.

"Do we understand each other, Zoe? We'll get back to normal. I'll go to school tomorrow and clear the air with Small Dick, and then it'll be all good again. Back to normal, see. You and me and the kids. What do you say, love?" The last five words carefully punctuated.

He squeezes just a tad harder. I know he can squeeze much harder. I know he knows that I know. He is letting me feel his strength. In his own warped way, probably thinks he is demonstrating restraint.

In all those years together we had experienced a plethora of emotions. I had. We had. Caused by him. By us. Joy. Ecstasy. Frustration. Anger. Never fear. Never. Until that day on that doorstep.

He looked into my eyes, and I saw it again. That sheen. The sheen in his eyes like scummy oil on water I had seen the night the Light followed us.

If I said no, if I defied him, I thought, he might squeeze and squeeze and squeeze till I have nothing left. Until my arm breaks, until, perhaps, my will breaks.

A voice inside me, my mother's, saying, think of the children. This is the small sacrifice. Think of those children.

So, I lowered my eyes and turned sideways to let him pass.

He kissed me on the cheek as he entered the house, his stink like a dark jungle miasma. He patted me on the head saying: "It'll be all good, Zoe. All good. Trust me on this. You'll see."

I rubbed my arm as he passed down the hallway. Rubbed the pain away. On the outside. The wound on the inside was likely never to heal.

Chapter 7

I dreamt.

I was in our bedroom.

It was after midnight. The witching hours.

Deep within them.

And I am lying asleep on my bed. I hear a noise. It sounds like something breaking. I start. Sit up gasping for air.

What the hell just happened?

Another noise like the stairs creaking as someone tip-toes down.

Noises that are not just the house cold-settling at night.

Sweat on my face. My armpits. Greasing my bum.

My heart racing, thumping.

What is that?

I swivel out of the duvet and stand. No sign of Jimmy. The blinds are down, but a faint light seeps through the gap below. A gray light. Like ash and death.

I walk out the room towards the stairs.

Another sound below. Somebody cursing. A stubbed toe? Jimmy?

Please God, let it be Jimmy. I feel almost naked. T-shirt. Shorts. Should I phone the cops? Alert somebody. Jimmy isn't in bed. It has to be him below.

Has to be? But what if it isn't?

I start down the stairs in slow motion, part of me screaming, "Don't be the blond in that crappy slasher movie. Ring the police, would you? Don't be a fool of a Took.

It′s no good. How can I say this: I am compelled. I have no choice.

I reach the last step in pitch darkness. Muscle memory assures me I am at the bottom. A faint hissing sound from the dining room. Straight down the hallway. First door on the right. Eyes adjusting to the darkness, faint light glows from beneath the door. My heart is pounding now. My palms are damp with sweat.

Turn around. Go back. Nothing for you to see here, nothing at all. I told you: stop being a fool of a Took.

Too late. My feet move. I do not control them. Someone whimpers. It takes me a moment to realize it is me.

One foot after another down that long, dark hallway.

One foot after another simple steps stretch into eternities.

I reach the door. Pale, ashy light that illuminates nothing seeps through the cracks around the door. My hand reaches out. I feel the cold metal of the ornate handle on my palm. I hesitate. I mean, I would rather turn back up the stairs, but the compulsion does not allow for hesitation.

Boom.

My heart.

My feet cold.

Bathed in that ashy light.

Freezing.

Like in the car.

A cold that sweeps through me.

My hand on the handle hurts: a bright cold hurt as if dipped in ice and held too long.

I press it down and push the door open, an inner voice still screaming to stop, not to do this. Do not. Do not. Fool, fool, fool!

The door swings open.

The light in the room is ash and cinders. Light, but no earthly light, and Jimmy stands at the window staring out. His hands are spread across the window as if in supplication.

Yearning and longing.

I feel it from here.

His need to go out.

I see it his posture, his body, his need.

It is almost sexual.

39

The light comes from outside like light from a car parked in our driveway shining through the open, curtained window. A greasy, ashy light.

He hears me. I see his body stiffen, as if disturbed. Disappointed.

He turns and faces me. His face is nothing like I ever want to see again.

That is not Jimmy. I cannot describe him, for words fail me. His head swivels on his body and his tongue darts out—thin, red, long and quivering—from beneath lips that no longer exist.

His face.

It is Jimmy. It is. It is Jimmy the monster.

I wake screaming in the dark, cold in my bed, and Jimmy is not there. I wrap myself in the duvet, heart thudding.

I lie paralyzed, shivering under the covers till the morning chorus sings, and the world I know has returned.

When I finally get up as the alarm rings, Jimmy is cooking breakfast, and the kids are flitting around the bathroom.

Everything seems normal, except the nightlight is gone. On the floor are flakes of lethal glass I sweep up quickly.

It was a dream. I pray that it was nothing else.

Chapter 8

Obsession.

No other word for it.

Jimmy said he would be good, and he is. Attentive. Back at work, all regular and keen-eyed. Coaching the kids' football twice a week with occasional games on Saturdays, parent-teacher meetings, volunteering for the meals on wheels. The whole shebang. Almost as if he likes it: small-town life. The ordinary. All the expectations of being extraordinary wrung from him like a dried-out sponge.

On the outside, looking in, it must seem to all those bustling busybodies in this little town of ours that everything was going well. Such a nice couple. Grand kids. Settling in well after that rocky period.

I know better. I see the anger flare within him every so often, like the flames on a gas BBQ. Damped quickly and controlled, but latent and potent. And then there is that slight droop of his mouth, like the beginning of a clown's sad mask, a sign of age and despair rather than resignation. The rash of dermatitis he has developed on the back of his hand, and the way he compulsively scratches it in the evenings at home after the kids are in bed. That is, in the rare times we are together, when he is not on his computer.

Sometimes I understand Jimmy only too well. We left our lives behind for this rural idyll, hoping for… I don't know what exactly. A change. An improvement. In our surroundings, but also in our selves. A screwy idea, I see that now. All we have for it is more space and time. Our surroundings are certainly healthier. Not sure about us, though. And, yeah, we do have more time.

Time to look in the mirror. Time to dislike the changes that we see.

He walks with the kids to school except when it is raining and leaves me behind in this empty house. The hollow space.

This ennui tugs on me. I guess I miss having the kids running around my feet, but at least the online course does eat up some time. Exams, presentations, reports. A tough schedule not helped by the fact that I am out of practice with this learning lark. I struggle through. Keep on keeping on. I fear I will need to have something to fall back on, in case things go pear-shaped.

Sometimes the morning will have flown by and the kids and Jimmy are back for lunch and I have nothing ready for them.

The kids complain mightily, but Jimmy waves them off. "Shoo, begone, demon children. Foundlings, I swear. For no real children of mine would treat their Mama so. Your mother is busy with her studies. Isn't that right, love? Sit you down, and I'll conjure up sandwiches for us all."

"That's right, Dad. Can't possibly be ours, these little rug rats. Much too evil for words."

And the kids smile or scowl at our banter, but they are still good kids. And when we sit in the kitchen nook with the sandwiches and glasses of milk or a jug of Jimmy's signature raspberry, apple, and orange juice smoothie, all seems right with this world.

And we chat and laugh, and they brush their teeth and set off back to school.

Like I say, sweet as hell. But still off-balance. Off-kilter.

You can't see it without looking closely, but it is there.

In his eyes.

That haunted faraway look.

And in the evenings, even when he is with me, I feel him yearning. Like a tug in his heart where I used to own real estate. I can feel him trying not to glance at his watch to get away, first opportunity he can, to lock himself in the dungeon in the basement. He calls it his study. There, he spends his evenings and, mostly, sleeps. His computer is there, his gym equipment and the single, spare bed we bought "just in case".

Except *just in case* has become the rule, not the exception.

At first, I thought it was another woman. What else? An affair, though where he would have gotten the time, I didn't know.

But it wasn't that. I wish it had been.

The reality was so much worse.

#

The other end of the light. I see it through the cracks beneath his door. Not that strange ashy light but the blue light of a computer screen.

His obsession is in there.

Something to do with that night in the car. With my dream. But also with Jimmy and the pain in the backside he so often is. Maybe he is working on something. If so, he hasn't mentioned anything, and why all the secrecy?

At night, I sometimes stand outside his room.

There is silence within but for the faint click of his old Apple keyboard, so maybe it is work? Him writing again.

This is not new. The hours spent behind a closed door click-clacking away. But why is he so secretive about it? He never did let me read the old manuscript when he was finished, but at least he talked about it. Told me his frustrations and plans.

Now he is stumm. As silent as a winter's field.

Did I ever tell you?

I read the manuscript, well began it, when he was gone. Snuck into the room. At first, I could not find it anywhere. He had hidden it. I know Jimmy, though, and I found it hidden in the wall behind his bedside table. Some poems, a few naked pictures of me from back in the day, an old Nokia he was secretly hoarding for some strange reason. No charger.

An old Nokia, for feck's sake.

They may be indestructible, but without a charger, they are as useless as any other brick. Weird. And his manuscript. I read it, or at least skimmed the first fifty pages. It was fine.

A review I dare not give Jimmy, for fear of his wounded pride.

I mean, it wasn't bad, just not good, or at least, not good enough for his dreams. Something to read if nothing else was at hand. You might buy it at the airport. It'll be a little dusty from hanging around on its shelf. But what the hell, you might say. I need something for the downtimes between sex and sangria. Why not? So you read the thing. Might even enjoy it. But is it memorable? Not really. Easy to forget. The work of a journeyman, not a master.

Poor Jimmy.

Should have stuck with the advertising.

So, what the hell is he doing in there, night after night?

#

And then he sort of tells me.

"Hey babe, we have nothing planned for tomorrow? Right?"

I am washing carrots in the kitchen on Saturday morning. Jimmy is taking Sean to the match later down at the club.

Sean is a knot of nerves. His first time in goal. I feel for him. The first place they look when the shit hits the fan is the goalie, but Jimmy is reassuring.

"The reflexes and the balls skills of a Cluxton, so he has. That right, Sean?" Sean glances up, pale-faced, the strain evident in his face.

"He'll be fine," Jimmy says.

"What about tomorrow?" I ask.

"It's nothing. It's just I've got a hot date and I thought you might give me the evening off."

"Not funny."

"Still too soon."

"That will always be too soon."

I dry my hands on a dishcloth, turning to him, curious.

"So, tell me."

He bops about on the soles of his feet for a moment.

"I will. It's just…"

"Yeah?"

"You wouldn't understand. Not just yet. Please." He reaches out and in his eyes, I see that old hope and love.

Who could say no?

"So, where?"

"Just to meet somebody. A lead. A friend of sorts. Something I've been working on in the evenings."

"Locked in your dungeon?"

He shakes his head in irritation. "What dungeon?"

"Never mind. So, who is this guy?"

"Like I said, a lead. A contact. My new project. This guy knows stuff."

"Does 'this guy' have a name?"

Jimmy hesitates.

"I am trying to keep this as low-key as possible."

"And I am your wife. Once betrayed, forever shy. Fess up, Jimmy. Cut the bull."

"Dr. Banning. His name is Banning. Lives up the way in Neary. Has a big old place outside town. You know, on the road up the mountains past that sweet Romanesque church. Near the play park where we went with the kids last summer."

A warm day with fleecy clouds scudding past overhead. The kids had a ball.

"You cool with that?"

"I don't get the secrecy, Jimmy. Not sure I like it. Not at all. I mean, he could come over here."

Jimmy shakes his head. Is that fear in his eyes? Something pinched his face. A narrowness.

"You all right?"

"This thing is big, Zoe. I mean really big. I can't afford to screw it up, and Banning is more than a tiny bit out there." He holds out his hands. "Para-fucking-noid, and big time. I mean he really seems to have fried his brains at some point. But he has agreed to meet and introduce me to some of his fellow travellers. I need this, love. This is the one."

He reaches out and places a hand on my arm. I wince inwardly in memory of that last time, but this time his hand is gentle, cupping my shoulder. I feel its warmth through my blouse. Hot, almost feverish, but then Jimmy has never been a cold husband. No sirree.

"No funny business?"

"All above board, love. I swear. I'll be back before midnight. Sober as a judge who knows the camera is on him. Hand on heart, I swear."

I nod, almost convinced, and he smiles his melting smile.

And yet, I see an almost invisible sheen of sweat on his upper lip. I don't know that he´s lying, it sure as hell doesn't feel like it, but there is certainly something more than he is telling me. Still, I remember thinking, if it keeps him happy and the family above water and functional, these little obsessions of his are a small price to pay.

Chapter 9

Jimmy leaves around six.

He hugs and kisses the kids goodbye and pecks me on the cheek.

"Back by eleven. Swear."

"You'd better be Jimmy."

A bright smile. He kisses my lips, some heat behind the kiss, turns, grabs his keys and is out the door.

I watch him walk to the door, a spring in his step. He turns as he opens the car, aware of my eyes on him, and waves.

Even then, I was kissing the stranger.

#

I wait with a glass of red on the couch.

The glass becomes another glass. And then fills itself up again.

I am half-cut and pissed as hell.

It is after midnight and there is no word from Jimmy. No call and no sign of his sorry ass.

In the half-light of the living room with the bay windows open, I see trees swaying darkly outside, and the wind a lonely, harsh sound.

A cat cries in heat somewhere nearby, its screech that of a tortured banshee.

I think I must have fallen asleep. I return to consciousness, crumpled and woozy on the sofa. My head is already throbbing with the effects of the wine and I knead my forehead with my knuckles.

It is light. Daybreak already? Could I really have slept so long? Didn't feel like it.

I pull off the comforter. Noises outside. Voices raised.

I stumble to my feet and make my way to the window. Light outside, enough that I can see the garden is empty. I can make out the river below and the swaying trees on the hill across the incline. Trees bathed in a gray-blue light.

My hands are cold, and I shiver. The headache is getting worse.

A throbbing headache that seems to mirror the beating of my heart. Ta tum. Ta Tum. Faster and faster.

I hear those voices again. Louder. In the front yard. Loud enough to wake the kids. Where is Jimmy? I hesitate for a moment but cannot remember whether or not I locked the front door.

Even if my heart is beating like a bush drum and my head pounding, even if my legs have turned to jelly and my stomach is knotted, I know I need to check that door. For the sake of the kids. It might be Jimmy, but what if it's not? And if it is Jimmy, who the hell is he with?

I force myself towards the main door, past the kitchen, and into the hall.

The front door is ajar. Light is seeping through the open gap, a gray light, like the light I remember from the car that night.

My breath fogs in front of me. Unnatural at this time of year. I force my feet forward, one by one. I get to the door and reach out to close it.

It blasts open instead with a force like someone has kicked it and swipes me across the head.

I fall back to the ground, smashing the back of my head on the tiles, sharp and sudden pain lancing through me as I land on my wrist.

Shit.

Pain and fear. My ass is sore and I can feel the knots of terror in my stomach. Still, I have only one thought. Close that door, close it. Close it now.

The kids. Protect them.

Blood from the wound on my scalp drips onto the tiles. I scramble on my knees and hands to the door. I reach for it and swing it closed…but before it does, I catch a glance of what is happening outside. Jimmy is standing in the dim light and in front of him is a man. Not a man so much as a man-monster. Two meters tall and built, as my old rugby-playing dad used to say, like a brick shithouse.

Lowering over Jimmy. Face to face. Voices raised.

A row, I think. One that will lead to Jimmy being pulverized.

The door slams shut, and darkness fills the hall.

I try to get to my feet, to get to the phone. Call the police. Save Jimmy.

I can't. My head is swimming and blood is creating a slick sheen all around me. I am about to lose consciousness. I am standing above a deep abyss, teetering and ready to fall.

And in the moment before my consciousness dissipates another thought strikes me.

It looked like a row, but there was something in that monster's face. Something exultant.

And I think maybe I have gotten it all wrong.

They were not about to fight. They were celebrating. Faces raised to the stars and moon in howling exultation.

#

I awake and Jimmy's face is above me. His eyes are dark and shiny, like a creepy puppet in a deserted house. Hard and unblinking and full of malice.

I whimper in fear, for his face is inhuman: the lips too elongated, the teeth in his open mouth too long. Built for shearing flesh.

His head is a different shape. Still Jimmy but filtered through a warped set of filters in a program designed for horror writers.

I blink.

And it is Jimmy.

My Jimmy. Looking down at me with sympathy, a look of worry on his face.

"Thank God. You are back."

I find it hard to remember what happened. It is all a blank at first and then with a jolt of fear memory comes back.

"Where am I?"

My voice is a creaky whisper.

"Take it easy, pet. Take it slow. You are in bed. The doctor's been. Says he thinks you're fine."

He holds up a hand and crosses his thumb and little finger so there are three sticking up.

"How many fingers?" He smiles.

"Two. And fuck you too, for not coming home."

He rubs my cheek with his other hand, a gentle caress. "The doctor said you might be disoriented. You might have trouble remembering."

"I have no fucking trouble remembering, Jimmy. You didn't return, despite your promises. You were outside our house in the strange gray light and talking to a man who was more bear than man. I remember everything."

His smile is more than a little patronizing. "Do you?"

"What the fuck is that supposed to mean?" I want, no I *need*, to sound angry, but I have a horrible feeling I know what is coming next.

"The empty bottles. I mean, I am no one to judge, Zoe. But Christ. And with the kids in the house. A bit much don't you think, for the middle of the week?"

"I never. I never drank that much. And if you had only come back when you promised. I was waiting, and I was waiting."

He sighs. "Zoe, love. I was back at 10:50. I checked on my phone before I came in. I found you at the bottom of the stairs. A little bloody and out for the count. Best I can figure you stumbled on the stairs, landed on your ass, luckily, though you did bang your head a little. You'll have the mother of all bruises on your nethers. Sore wrist. Sprained not broken. Gash on your forehead. Doc Murphy trussed you up in the bandages and warned me to bring you in asap if you exhibit any signs of concussion. So, how many fingers?"

"Three. Three fingers."

And doubt is within me now. Could I really have imagined it all? I had been drinking, but so much? And then to fall. To fall like that. I could have died. Broken my neck. Could that have been me?

"The doctor´s been, then?"

"And gone."

He holds out a pill in the palm of his hand, one of those long thin plastic-looking tubes. This one is pink and green. "For the pain and the inflammation. How do you feel?"

Shitty, is the answer. Like shit on a stick. Shit warmed up.

Pain thrumming in my ass, making it uncomfortable to lie, throbbing coolly in my hand and a whole symphony railing in my head, front, and back.

"Gimme that." I grab and swallow, sending it on its way with water from the glass Jimmy hands me.

"I didn't fall, Jimmy."

"You did, love. I found you on the floor."

I don't think that is what happened."

"Shush, love." Here. He hands me another pill. This one is round and thin and somehow unnatural. It looks hollow, and translucent, as if it barely exists and light does not hit it properly. It feels like nothing in my hand. A chilled emptiness.

"A sleeping tablet, babe. Will help to clear your mind. So says Doc Murphy, and he is not to be messed with."

Jimmy's smile is unctuous and somehow too large again, but my head is in a bad, bad place.

I slip the thing into my mouth, barely thinking. Barely able to think.

I feel it coursing through me. Peace. A warmth. Like the greatest dope ever created. Pain gone. Suffering gone. Life on the upward current, flying through the sky.

Murph, you have the best of the best when it comes to strange drugs.

And yet, the last image I see as I drift away again is of a fist. A fist driving towards me. A fist aimed straight at my head. A fist that is as large as a world.

And then I am gone.

Chapter 10

It took weeks for everything to heal. Longer for my ass. Right buttock, swollen into a grapefruit of blood and bruise.

The doctors were in awe.

Never seen the like of it before, my grapefruit ass, a camel's humpback pointing in the wrong direction. Sitting was, literally, a pain in the, well you can guess the rest.

Jimmy made all the appropriate jokes of course. Told me I was officially a badass now. That I would be the butt of all the jokes in town. And so on. Made me smile, at least.

But time does indeed heal.

We recovered too. Back to normal, or what passed for normal back then.

I never did remember what really happened that night. I admit it is not impossible that Jimmy's take was true, or so I thought at the time. Maybe my memories were a fever dream. Binge drinking is not a new phenomenon. It certainly wasn't for me. No sir. Have had my share of minor embarrassments. Waking up next to the wrong guy whose name is not even a tingle in my brain and an *Oh shit* knowledge of the walk of shame ahead of me. Vomiting on the dummy, beefed up bodyguard with the Neanderthal face refusing entry to the shitty overpriced nightclub we just had to get into. And a few more I'd rather forget.

\#

Fuck it.

But, guilt or not, that was in the past even then.

I had kids to think of.

I didn't do that anymore.

#

I don't know when I decided to start following him. It wasn't a conscious decision, as far as I remember. More of an impulse.

Since that night he has been solicitous, been home a lot. Kind and good with the kids, but that dark layer deep in his eyes is still intact. Like a sheet of ice behind his iris. I sometimes shiver when I see him staring at me.

And something else has changed.

He leaves in the evenings without telling me where he is going, without me asking. It is just something silently acknowledged between us.

He is out, and I am in with the kids.

This goes on for weeks, and at first, I shrug and think what the hell.

After all, I was the one who fucked up. At least that is the established narrative. Drank too much. Fell down those bloody stairs and almost killed myself.

A narrative I almost start believing myself, despite the other memories of that night.

The door kicked open, the flailing fists.

Anyway, I was too busy with my swollen ass to care. Sitting was a chore and doing housework exhausting. I haven't been able to study in three months.

No way I could sit still and write reports and projects, so I have fallen behind. Not too dramatically. The university is understanding about the accident, but I know I have to get back up on the horse again and soon.

But I am getting better, the bruises gone, the swelling now just a hard lump in my backside. Blood pooling or some such. Working its way out.

Better, much better. Alive in this world again. A functioning human being.

And that, in turn, rekindles my curiosity. Where the hell does he go? What the hell is that little shite up to?

Gone every Tuesday and Thursday night for at least three hours. When he comes back, he is often sour and cold. Sometimes he is red-faced, as though he has run a marathon. I know it's not football training. Otherwise, I know nothing, and when I dared mention it, he cold-shouldered me and didn't speak or look at me for three days.

It sure as shit wasn't worth the effort when I was ill, and now that I am better, it seems impossible to ask. It's all too established. If I didn't need to know a month ago, why did I need to know now?

I don't have the feeling he is having an affair. He is too miserable for that.

Sometimes I wish I was having an affair. Anything to get on with my life. We are in a rut, for sure. Love doesn't live here anymore.

So, the plan: follow him and find out what the hell he is up to. A plan born out of enforced boredom; I will freely admit. Sitting (or not, in my case) on your ass will cause crap like this to seem reasonable. And anyway, I sort of believe him that it is not another woman. Curiosity, the cat, and all that.

Needs to be done.

I'll have to figure out how to follow him. He always takes the car. I ponder this for a while and then decide. Fuck it. I have to know. So, I ring the rental place in Neary and give them my credit card. It is a local Mom and Pop shop, and for an extra fee they agree to bring the car to me. I have it delivered when Jimmy and the kids are at school and drive it to the parking near the local Sentra.

So far so good.

I have the car for three days, so I sow the seeds.

"I am out tomorrow night, Jimmy."

"Are you now?" An icy chill in that voice. How dare I interfere with his plans.

"The sitter is free. All organized."

The chill disappears leaving only blank indifference.

"Fine. Where?"

"An acquaintance. One of the online students lives in Raheen. She offered to help me catch up, and I told her I'd buy her a meal. The Mongolian in Neary where we went last year?"

"Right, right."

I have a feeling he is on autopilot now, hearing but not listening. My plans do not involve him, do not interfere with his man-of-mystery evenings, so he simply does not give a damn. I could tell him I was applying for Nasa, and he wouldn't blink twice.

And that, ladies and gents, is the state of our nation.

Not giving much of a damn.

"I'll have the car, right?"

"That´s why I asked her to pick me up. I'll be gone before you get back from school. She has a load of stuff to catch me up on at her place. Then we'll go for the meal, like I said. Mary is booked. Here from three."

"That won't be cheap."

"I need this, Jimmy. I am so far behind." The big eyes, the pleading voice. I even lick my lips.

"Just don't make a bloody habit of it, right?"

"Right. Thanks, Jimmy."

And why was I saying thank you to my man, when all I was doing was leaving the house. The state of the nation, ladies and gentlemen.

Mary, a sweet old spinster the kids loved, arrived at three.

She laid her purse down on the kitchen island and stared up into my eyes.

"Feeling better, love? You look a sight lot better than the last time I saw you."

"Thanks, Mary. All better." I tap my ass. "I am no longer such a badass." I laugh. I see uneasiness in Mary´s eyes, as if she wants to say something, ask something.

I know. A woman has an "accident" at home. The undertone it carries. The way she is looking at me is only natural, I suppose. People talk, and small towns love their gossip. I like Mary though. I sense sympathy in her look. She wants to help, not gloat.

The official story is that I slipped on a loose carpet tie on the stairs. No alcohol involved. No strange men. So that is that. Mary senses more to the story, but, nice as she is, there is no way I can tell her.

A door magically blew open and showed me my husband and a stranger behaving like maniacs, howling at the moon.

Nope. Doesn't fly. Does it?

#

I show Mary the beef casserole in the oven and grab my purse and keys.

"I'll walk down the drive and meet my friend on the way. Too nice a day to be stuck inside."

The look Mary bestows on me is, at best, skeptical.

I wave from the end of the drive and then I am free.

I walk the half-mile to the Sentra and start the car. Time to get out of dodge for a while. I drive into the mountains. Sheep, purple heather, wispy clouds. I pull in to park at a lay-by with a beautiful view down into the valley and the river meandering below. I am alone. A working day, nobody about, so I lock the doors, put on some music, and close my eyes.

Sleep.

I wake from a surprisingly deep slumber to the sound of my phone's alarm hooting.

How I hate that sound.

Groggy, I rub the sleep from my eyes.

It is time. I drive down the winding, narrow lanes, seeing only two other cars driving in the opposite direction. I park about a hundred yards down from the entrance to our drive.

Then, I wait.

Jimmy is punctual.

He leaves the driveway at 7:02. In the pm. I engage the gear and set off after him. We are the only two cars on the road which might draw attention to me, but I have a baseball hat on my head, and sunglasses.

Like a real-life PI, tailing the suspect. "This is fun," I remember shouting to nobody in particular, and it was. Fun. Excitement. Solving the mystery of the mysterious Jimmy.

Ha!

A big, gormless smile on my face.

I swear, I haven't smiled like that in a long time.

Jimmy drives through Temple, up Main Street, and past the church where he takes a left. Back in the country now, flat land bordered by hedges and trees, farms, barns and silos. The mountains gray and somber in the distance, cows grazing in the fields.

Waving expanses of corn and wheat.

And still, we keep going.

It is getting dark when he pulls into the drive. This is not what I expected. Old walls decorated with moss and ornate gates leaning on towering stone pillars. A distant glimpse of something large and impressive at the far end of a long, twisting gravel drive.

Above one of the stone pillars is a triangular sign: society of the Gray Eclipse, red letters on a pale gray background. A logo of three entwined pyramids with stars dotted above.

In a semi-circle in a font designed to look almost handwritten.

The truth has come and sets us free.

That rings a bell. Something religious? Cult-like?

What the hell?

This is not at all what I had expected.

Looking back, I had suspected something seedy. Jimmy doing drugs or owing money to some heavies. Best case scenario he'd be interviewing some old geezer with a view to writing his new tome. An out to seed Loyalist paramilitary or a member of the Guards. Somebody with a story to tell or an axe to grind.

But this is way out there. This is something from way out in left base.

I drive on, pull over to the side of the road on a straight patch, and try to gather my thoughts.

Honestly folks: They are a whirlwind.

Chapter 11

I did a quick Google. Bad reception and little information.

Something about UFOs and alien religion.

Okay, okay, I remember thinking. This can still work out. There has to be an explanation.

The PI stuff didn't seem like fun anymore.

In retrospect, I cannot explain why this shook me so deeply.

What I should have been thinking was: So, Jimmy is involved with cultists or some such.

Why should that worry me? This is Jimmy after all. Religion, organized or not, plays the same role in his life as gardening. He hates gardening, but it is a necessary evil at times. Yeah, the kids are baptized and all, but that is a social thing. Joining a club, more or less. Something that had to be done, but without conviction or passion.

We might go to mass on Christmas, but that's the whole of it. Jimmy is a hard-nosed agnostic. Borderline atheist really. Well-read in science, understands the history of the church, and is a history buff in general.

So: he is doing research, has found something interesting for his next work, and is doing deep background research.

But I was worried. More than worried. Terrified.

My heart was pounding in my chest to the point I felt it was going to pop. Fear travelled in waves down my spine. I leant forward over the steering wheel, breathing deeply.

A panic attack, but why?

Something was wrong. An awful, inexplicable wrong.

What to do?

I sit there for what seems like hours. I glance at my phone. It's only been a few minutes.

My breathing is normal again, the attack over, and the fear dissipated. My legs are still weak, but stronger than even that strange panic attack is the sense of curiosity.

Fear or not, I need to know more.

Maybe it is harmless. Jimmy is sitting in that big house in the drawing room, a cup of tea in front of him. His voice recorder is on the ebony coffee table in front of him and he has notes in his lap and a pen in his hand. Talking to some old geezers about their lives back in the day.

Okay. I breathe. That's good. That's fine. Okay. More breathing.

My strength comes drifting back.

I know only one thing for sure; I need to know more. This will eat me up otherwise.

I key the ignition, turn the car around in one turn on the empty road as the gloom and shadow fall on the dancing ash trees bordering the side of the road.

Dancing in the wind, branches wave as if in warning.

#

I park down the road from the sign.

The society of the Gray Eclipse. And in larger letters underneath: Sanctuary House.

Something about the name sends shivers into my soul.

I try my phone again.

The reception is better here.

Another quick search still gives me little to go on.

A private organization. Seems faintly occult. Their website is a shadowy thing. One black page with a faint hint of gray, whorls of light and Nordic-looking runes, and a series of links that do not work, except for one that requires some sort of log-in. No scandals. No newspaper reports or funding efforts. No mentions of a founder or founders. Nothing about goals. About funding.

Totally invisible. Even Wikipedia doesn't have a clue.

Some kind of weird. Which shadowy organization has no private funding needs, barring NASA?

Well, screw this.

I need to find out more. Zoe Hearty, Private Eye is on the case again. I try to channel her strength within me.

#

The wall along the road leading from the drive is old and crumbling on top. Not easy to climb, so I walk along it and find a cattle gate about two hundred yards away. I pull hard at the parallel latch, shoving it backward and forward. The rusty thing squeaks open, and I push open the metal bars, cold and damp to the touch. I close the gate behind me and stop, listening.

The driveway to the house is about two hundred meters across the uneven, grassy field I am standing in.

Crows caw from the oaks lining the driveway to the old house. They fly above the majestic trees, dark against the lighter darkness in the last moments of this day. Looking at them, I feel lost, alone, and a little silly. What am I doing here? But then I remember the panic attack in the car and the large man I saw with Jimmy. Something is wrong about all of this, and I need to know what it is.

In the shadow of the wall, I figure I must be invisible to anybody looking from the driveway of the house. I pick my way across the damp field, ankle and sometimes knee-deep in wet grass. Cursing.

Should have brought my wellies.

Too late now. Too late for a lot of things. Let's get this done.

I get to the end of the field. The fence is wire mesh and old wooden posts, sunken in places. There have been no cattle in this field for a good long time. I find a section low enough for me to simply step over, and keeping to the shadows underneath the towering oak lining the side of the road, make my way towards the other beginning of the driveway and the lights of the Big House visible in the middle distance.

The building has been gutted and rebuilt. Two new wings are modern add-ons of steel and glass. The add-ons are ugly and discordant as hell. Red-steel triangles dwarfing the original two-story building. Designed by an architect having a bad day. A bad life for all I could tell.

I am no fiend when it comes to architecture, but this is just gruesome, discordant, almost angry.

The old house has been left with a face that looks like it has been rebuilt by a butcher. Windows that are thin diagonal slashes of metal and glass scarring the facade. A faint red light from the dark-tinged windows seeps across the lawn like cancer.

I hate it, at a visceral level. It oozes strange. It makes me tremble.

I remember thinking to myself, stop damn it. You have started thinking crazy now too. It´s just an ugly old, renovated building. Rebuilt by someone with too much money and way too little sense. But that was not it. It was so much more than that.

It was a vision of ugliness that did not seem human to me.

A faint thrum, as of a motor, trembles through the air and grinds through me. The driveway is deserted. A gravel semicircle once decorated with shrubs and plants. Weeds poke through the gravel, and wild grasses wave from the verges. Despite this, it seems empty of life in so many ways. An eerie, quiet place. Neglected rather than abandoned.

I am scared to go further. Scared too, to return.

How can I simply drive home and deal with Jimmy as if none of this matters?

From within the house, there is a noise. I want to say a scream, but if it is, it does not issue from the voice of a human. I fall back to the ground on the ass of my jeans and struggle back into the trees, hands on my ears.

The sound is like a goat being slaughtered, just amplified ten thousand times. Ear-splitting.

It tears holes in my sanity.

Nothing living should have to endure that depth of agony.

I curl into a ball and rock back and forth, my mind lost in the pain and the terror of that noise.

And then it stops. Just like that.

The silence is worse. A deafened silence. Like the world had just ended. The last moments of that sound are still with me. They sounded human. Male. A familiar sound, a familiar voice. It could even have been Jimmy.

Something happened then. I blanked.

I awaken. Could be hours later, lying on an old carpet of fallen leaves, coated in muck, shivering with cold.

I hear something. A door opens. Voices.

Groaning, I get to my knees facing the house.

The door is open and the man I saw on the driveway of our house is there, flanked by two others. They are all wearing something like a uniform. Gray coats, black trousers.

The two other men are dwarfed by this giant.

And then I see Jimmy. He is smiling. He looks happy. Normal.

He hugs the big man and high-fives the two others.

And then he stiffens. Turns. Looks at me.

There is no way he can see me. I am on my haunches in deep shadow, away from all light, and the night is pitch without a star in sight.

Still, he stares right at me and smiles.

And that smile is not right. It is not Jimmy´s smile. It is the smile of a hunter, a predator. A cold shark-like open-mouthed smile.

I will have you, it tells me. I will have you. You cannot escape me. You are mine.

I scramble to my feet, turn and start jogging back up the driveway, heart pumping, fear again coursing through me. I turn as I reach the spot in the field where I can cross over.

I can still see the entrance to the house, the red light it casts. Jimmy and the other three men are all standing there, staring at me, unmoving.

And that smile is still on Jimmy´s face.

I blurt out a cry of fear, and somehow make it across the fence, across the field, and to the car. My mind becomes blurry. My next full memory is of being in the car, driving home, hands shaking and tears pouring down my face. The sound of music from the radio singing some song about a summer in Dublin.

A happy song.

A song from a different universe to the one I am in.

#

I have no memory of parking the car. No memory of walking back to the house. I do remember the urgency I felt. Home before Jimmy. I have to be home before Jimmy. Have to.

An incantation in my head. A prayer almost.

For if he knew that it was me in the woods, if he had recognized me, who knows what could happen?

I made it.

Mary was in the sitting room, the kids in bed. I peeked my head around the door, asked her to wait five minutes. A wine emergency I said, then went to my bedroom to change into new jeans and a similar blouse. Purple blue rather than navy but close enough. Threw the clothes into the closet. Jimmy hardly ever came to my room anymore, and he had not seen me since morning.

I paid Mary, let her out the door, and was ensconced on the sofa with a glass of wine and music on the speaker when I heard the front door open. I stiffened, tingling with nerves. He could not have seen me. Could not.

I hear his heavy footsteps along the hall tiles.

Thump. Thump. Thump.

The ogre is here. He will eat me and chew on my bones.

Sweat dapples my forehead and my hands start to shake.

Keep it together. He couldn't have recognized you. Physically impossible.

Nothing to see here, Jimmy dear. Just your loving wife waiting up for you.

He appears in the doorway, blocking the light from the kitchen, his face in shadows.

"There you are."

"Here I am." I toast him with my glass.

"How was your night of study and food? Evelyn well?"

"She's fine. 'Twas fun. Don't much get out anymore, do I?"

"I suppose not. So, when did you get back? Mary is gone, I take it."

"She is. Not long ago. Just time to pour one and get the slippers on. And what about your night?" I hear the tremble in my voice.

"Same old, same old. You know the way." He yawns. Rubs his eyes. "Time for my bed, I think."

"Alright so."

"See you bright and early. Don't stay up too long."

"Just the one," I say, holding up the glass. "Finish this one and then I'm off too."

"Well, goodnight so."

"Goodnight."

And he turns and is gone.

That went well, all things considered, I remember thinking.

It was only in bed later I realized that something was wrong. Off. His back was to the light from the hall and the kitchen, the music box, and its faint throbbing blue light was on the other side of the room. There was no other light on in the living room.

And yet, I could see the pale gray gleam of his eyes peering at me through the darkness.

Like little moons. Cold as gray sand in a vacuum.

Chapter 12

The society of the Gray Eclipse.

Nothing on the website, nothing on Wikipedia.

Freaky how invisible they were.

Some blogs. A few tweets. Nothing much of anything.

From one of the blogs, a brief mention in a different context.

A society devoted to becoming and being, to enlightenment in this world and the next. The journey of the chosen and the incarnate into the Kingdom above is to be imagined as plants being transported into a new garden.

All very mystical, saying little or nothing.

A lot of tweets and Facebook postings with no factual information.

We are the chosen few, and we will be the guardians of the portals in the pyramids of the nexus between worlds.

We are the future, and the world will be radiant again.

The New King—the one that moves the crypt—is soon amongst us.

I had a feeling that the tweets and the blog entries were from people who had little or no real connection to the society. Hangers on. Wannabes.

And that homepage.

Whoever did the graphics was tumbling down from a really bad trip.

The longer you stared at the washed-out screen and runes, the more you saw, or or imagined you saw. The runes became spinning nebulae and they, in turn, became the faces of the dead. I swear I saw my granny. She smiled and then her face contorted as if with pain, her mouth opening as if to scream.

I closed the laptop cover, smashing it hard. I was sitting at the island in the kitchen, waiting for a chicken to roast for dinner, the kids bumbling around the house, homework finished.

I saw Sarah's look of still surprise, like a deer ready to flee. Poor thing. I know she can feel the tense atmosphere between her parents this week. Puts her under strain, too. She is a sensitive creature at the best of times.

I smile and wink, and she visibly relaxes.

"Just got outbid on Ebay, love. All good. No biggie."

She smiles and comes over to me, wrapping her thin arms around me. I lay my chin on the top of her head and kiss her hair. Then reach out and stroke it.

She sighs, squeezes harder, and pulls away.

"Homework done?"

"Mostly, yeah. Biology project." She waves her right hand in a circle. "We need rice for tomorrow."

"In the green jar on the counter. The one that says rice."

"Oh, yeah."

We laugh.

"Put what you need in one of the Tupperware containers so you can take it with you. There is no cooking involved, right?"

She stands there with her hands on her hips, giving me that look. "Mam!"

"Right. Right. Take what you need, little tyrant, and do as you will."

She air kisses me and spins on her heels, busy pouring rice into a plastic container with a yellow lid, her tongue sticking out between her lips.

I lift the cover of the laptop and the website is still there.

No hallucinations this time. Dull gray on black, runes, whorls. All perfectly normal. Or creepily normal. Links to a contacts page, log in, about, history. All unresponsive, except for the Homepage and the link for the password-protected log-in.

What kind of society does nothing to advertise itself, to raise money or awareness?

This shit is scary.

I close the tab and turn as I hear footsteps approaching.

Thump. Thump.

The ogre in his den.

Jimmy has a big open smile on his face, but his eyes still scare me. I cannot define it. They look the same. I have seen him in darkness since that night. His eyes do not glow in the dark like some awful doll. Still, there is a patina of something covering them. They look the same but are different, as if he is not quite the same man I married.

I don't always see it, I don´t always believe it, in fact, I never want to believe it, but I do now and more often lately.

Something in his eyes as they land on me is unsettling.

I can see him in the shadow of that mansion, staring straight at me, seeing me in a way that was impossible in the darkness. A cold, ironic look on his face. He sits on the stool beside me, reaches out for my hand and, for a moment, he is normal again. Hot bodied and cheekily grinning Jimmy.

"I am sorry, Love. I know I have been distant. Not trying nearly hard enough. It is just…it is this new project." He rubs his chin.

I look down and away. Then back up again. Still Jimmy. Okay, then. "And you have been a little distant, too. I wonder if it isn't the meds. Doc has to take a look at those. There must be something better."

I sigh. This again.

"What is it you want, Jimmy?"

"My new project. I want you to come with me on the weekend. To meet some people. We are having a BBQ. We'll bring the kids. You will like these people. Swear."

He squeezes my hand, and looks into my eyes.

"I just think we need this. Clear the air a bit. It'll be fun."

Fun with the weirdos of the Gray Eclipse? At least that is what I presume he means. A fecking BBQ with a cult, and we are to take our kids with us.

I shake my head.

Jimmy squeezes my hand harder. Just a fraction more.

"It will be good for us, love. All of us. You'll see."

Squeezing again, just one touch harder. Waiting for my nod.

And I do. I nod, but not because of him.

I am curious. This BBQ could be a good place to learn more. Always loved a good mystery, and this one is a doozy wrapped in ribbons and bows. So yeah, Mr. Jimmy Squeezing Man, I'll come to your BBQ and play the dutiful wife, but I will take the opportunity to squeeze back fella, to find out what the hell you and your best buds are up to and to get whatever Intel I can.

Zoe Magnum, freelance PI. Hitting the road again.

Chapter 13

Jimmy is full of life and even fun again.

This meeting is a big deal. He almost seems excited.

I quiz him a little about this.

"It's only a BBQ, Jimmy. An afternoon and an evening. A few beers."

At first, he blinks at me. Face immobile, as if considering. Or listening.

"We have to do this right, Zoe." He grins a toothy, ugly grin. Jesus. Is he getting old or what? "For me, please."

I am not sure what he means by that, but the enthusiasm is infectious.

So, we set out in the car. Jimmy sings as we drive through Neary. The kids are in the back, bouncing off one another.

"Give me that."

"I had it first."

"It's mine."

"Cut it out, you two." Jimmy turns around and glares at them. "No more of that crap today. Capiche?"

Silence.

"I said capiche? Do you understand?"

Slow voice. Threat laden. The kids know what that means.

Temple is just one long street with shops and pubs dissected by old alleys with houses. Quaint, but not exactly a cultural hub. Another thing that weighs on Jimmy, I know. We pass the town hall, an elegant Regency building painted an inexplicable shade of pink.

Every time he passes it, Jimmy sighs.

And that is another part of the problem. We know so few people, and in the townland of Temple, I cannot honestly say we have made any good friends either.

The village and this town should be the nub of our social life. As we drive, we see families out pushing their babies, lovers walking hand in hand, and a group of footballers, judging from the bags they carry, nipping into a pub.

A life we, in our isolation, do not share.

I guess that might explain Jimmy's enthusiasm. He is part of something. A large part of me dreads what that something is, but my curiosity overrides everything else.

So, a bundle of nerves, we drive out of town to meet the Society of the Gray Eclipse.

#

And you know what? It turns out not to be so bad. At first. Not a Gothic horror, anyway.

We pull into the driveway and park in front of the house. In daylight, the place still looks ugly, the strange angles of those windows, the towering dark glass pyramids.

But I sense no threat here today.

The air seems calm, and the day is perfect for early summer: a gentle breeze, clouds drifting past overhead, and that delicious warmth that tells you that winter is defeated and won't be back for a good long time.

The kids pile out of the car. Two dozen cars are parked haphazardly in the drive and the parking area to the right of the house.

"Kids, wait there for a moment." The car has barely stopped, and the kids are out, carrying a beach ball and box of chocolates, meant as a gift for the hosts.

Jimmy comes round the car to me as I exit and stands close as I straighten.

He grabs my arm.

"Zoe, this is important to me."

I nod warily.

"I get that, Jimmy. For the new book, right?"

He is still holding my arm and I inwardly flinch, as a dark cloud covers his eyes.

He is silent. Like a robot that has been shut off. It must have been all of five seconds.

Jesus, I think, is he having a seizure? This stillness is so unnatural.

And then he shakes his head and the light in his eyes goes on again. A smile.

"For the book, right. But these are also people I like being around. So, let's be good today, huh?" He rustles my hair. Something I loathe. "No monkey business?"

An old joke. No longer funny. Back in the city, whenever we fucked up and did something to annoy the other, the guilty party would grab the stuffed toy from the bathroom—a soulful looking, brown money with beautiful eyes—and place it in a prominent position with appropriate solemnity as a tacit apology.

So, no monkey business.

I have a feeling of late that Jimmy thinks I am the monkey around his neck. A weight without which he could soar like Icarus.

"No monkey business it is, Jim. Lead on."

"Asshole," I whisper under my breath.

#

Jimmy rings the bell. The kids are bustling with excitement. They have been promised dogs to play with. The ring of the bell is standard. A part of me had been expecting something from an old Dracula flick. A hollow knock followed by the creak of footsteps.

Pity really.

That boring modern honk does not suit this place.

The door opens, and a shadow falls on us.

"James! Fantastic that you came, man. And who do we have here?"

It is the bear. He towers over Jimmy, and Jimmy is not a small man. He is wearing blue jeans and a t-shirt. The muscles expanding from it would put even the Rock to shame.

His hair is dark, pulled back into a man bun, his beard is a dense forest, and he has small dark gray eyes that seem to reflect light.

In fact, his face is tiny. In proportion to that massive physique, it almost looks like a kid's face. Ill-formed and out of proportion to the rest of his steroid-laden self.

I stifle a laugh.

He smiles thinly with teeth that are too white.

This is not love at first sight, ladies and gentlemen.

He is smiling at the children, trying to be warm, welcoming, but there is a darkness and oddness about this man that sets me on edge.

"Zoe, meet Ramsey."

He holds a skinny hand out to me. "Delighted, Zoe. Great that you could come. Jimmy has told us so much." Long fingers, like that of an aesthete. Again, disproportionate to the rest of him. Like somebody thrown together from leftovers. Frankenstein's monster, but integrated into society. I briefly reciprocate. His fingers are cold and almost clammy to the touch.

Ugh.

My body shrinks and I struggle to keep the smile on my face.

"'Fraid Jimmy has told us nothing. About you I mean, Ramsey. You or this mysterious society of yours." My laugh is forced.

He smiles his thin smile and winks.

"Hardly my society, Zoe. I am but a cog. That is down to our ridiculous secrecy. An inherited thing. Outdated. I keep telling dad and the others. Time for our light to shine out from under the bushel. But these dunderheads never listen. But where are my manners? Come in. Let's meet the others. Get some drinks into you. Welcome. Welcome."

#

He takes us into the main house.

Nothing strange here: an old building nicely renovated and with no expense spared from the look of things.

The hallway leads into an atrium. The cornices are original and ornate. An impressive set of stairs lead to the second floor.

Ramsey catches my gaze. "The original," he confirms. "Cost a pretty penny to restore, but worth it, don't you think?"

And it was. A sweeping staircase of dark mahogany leads in a gentle sweep to the gallery above.

The kids are gone, as is Jimmy. The call of the promised puppies too irresistible, so Ramsey and I are alone.

"I really don't get the windows. You were so careful with the rest."

Ramsey looks behind us to the slashes of windows in the facing wall above what must have replaced the old Georgian slash windows.

"My Dad. An eccentric, I am afraid. Believes in the absolute importance of certain things, certain rituals, and was determined to see them realized. All a bit esoteric. To do with light and the way it falls. This is not a normal building, Zoe. I think you know that already."

He stops in front of me and turns, leaning forward, invading my personal space. An inch or two, no more, but he is also towering over me like a brick wall. And then he leans further forward so that I need to pull my head back. He lays a hand on my shoulder. I clench at his too warm touch. He removes his hand, turns from me, and says,

"Food is outside. I am famished. What about you? We can do the rest of the house later."

And for all the moderated solicitousness of his tone, I feel a threat. An ill-defined fear.

I should not be here. There is danger, for me and all my family.

#

I feel like spitting in the face leaning over me. At the time, I remember thinking I was overreacting, despite my suspicions. He had been attentive and vaguely pleasant, but I knew something visceral and dark was hidden behind the facade of this house and that its wrongness echoed within him.

Ramsey was off. The same way this house was wrong. Whatever pretense they were making with a BBQ and drinks in the warmth of the summer weekend, this was fucked up.

Ramsey smiles at me again, as if searching for my agreement. I follow the v of his body and that skinny ass through the drawing room, decorated with old lounge chairs and a sofa set and pictures on the wall of the hunt and horses. We continue past the kitchens and out the back door to the stables and gardens behind.

The place is beautiful.

Should be beautiful.

Stables to the left, an English garden to the right, and a field of grass leading to an oak forest beyond. I almost expect to see Bambi hopping through the neatly mown grass, around the little islands of deliberately haphazard wildflowers.

Very bucolic.

There are about fifty people here. Rattan chairs and a long wooden bench lounge on the patio. A canopy covers the free bar while two waiters buzz around dispensing champers and other assorted precious summer drinks.

Peach cider, anyone, I murmur to myself. Fancy, schmancy.

Still, I do grab a glass of champagne when the waiter flits by.

The kids are with a gaggle of others in a pen. The Irish wolfhounds they are petting dwarf them. I feel a moment of trepidation, but then see the look on Sarah's face. She is in heaven, not the slightest bit nervous or shy, and that allows me to be calm.

"Don't worry. The kids couldn't be safer."

A blond with augmented breasts and lots of makeup has pulled up beside me.

"Hi. Adele. Ramsey's partner. Pleased to finally meet you. You are Zoe, right? Jimmy's missus."

She gestures at the Pen. Sarah's face is being subjected to a facial tongue wash by the larger and grayer of the wolfhounds. The thing is massive. I reckon on its hind legs it would tower over Jimmy. Probably about Ramsey's height. But the beast seems gentle enough. That Sarah is not nervous is something.

"Are we sure? Those are big fellas."

"Look at the kids. They are in love."

And that is true.

The kids are as happy as I have ever seen them.

Sean is reckless. Too much so. Always has been, gets it from his dad. But Sarah is a hider. She hides herself and her intelligence. Her teachers say so and I know it.

Timid, I guess. And that timidity drives her to protect herself from the world.

Not today.

She is holding the dog around its neck now, and her laughter peals over us.

Wow.

I grab another glass and walk with Adele to where the kids and the dogs are playing. We lean on the wood of the pen with our elbows, and I sip my drink.

"Sweet kids," Adele says, pursing her lips.

"They have their moments."

Honestly, I wish she'd just go away. Mingle with the other guests. If I'd wanted to talk to a plastic mannequin, I could have gone shopping in the city.

"Ramsey and I have been trying." Her eyes are suddenly damp with incipient tears.

Jesus wept. Ramsey's Barbie doll is about to break into tears.

I reach out and touch her shoulder. A feather's touch. Feeling obliged, I guess. Social expectations, and all that. I mean I don't know this doll from Adam.

But the kids are cute. I mean seriously. Tinkling laughter, bright eyes, faces aglow. Sarah's smile is a beam that could light up a concert hall.

I remember the feeling in me then; a feeling every parent has at some point, unless they are broken inside.

A swollen heart.

Like winter waves pounding and breaking and growing stronger, beating off nearby headlands in a burgeoning storm.

Emotions all mixed up but swelling to a high point.

Love.

Pure and simple.

I loved them.

I failed to protect them.

That one is on me and is the burden that wakes me screaming at night.

Chapter 14

Fragments.

The rest of that long afternoon and longer evening.

And longest night.

Fragments.

I remember talking to Adele about life and kids, as we doted on my children. Talking to other people as the shadows lengthened. A kaleidoscope of faces, whirling and interchangeable. People laughing and talking louder as the drinks kicked in. Burgers on buns, spareribs, potato salad with eggs, little dainty quiches, Dublin Bay prawns in a garlic butter sauce.

Adele a constant thorn, never leaving my side.

And Ramsey and Jimmy joining us. Drinks together, toasting one another.

And a certain queasy unreality, like cold grease on everything.

I wasn't drunk. I had, maybe, another drink.

The fragmentation came later.

That night, inside, when they tried to break me, to pull me apart.

To crack me open like Humpty Dumpty.

They didn't succeed. Not really.

But still, I have never been whole since.

#

It was getting dark. Adele had finally left to annoy somebody else, and I was alone. I do know that my head was still clear at that point. I still had my eye on the plan. Scout the place. Find out what the hell was going on. I remember making towards the house. Ramsey and Jimmy staring at me from the makeshift bar, and me mumming a visit to the bathroom.

I sensed their stares on my back, but continued walking.

I waved at them, stumbled once. Thought it might buy me some time, if they saw me drunk-staggering. I slipped by the inevitable queue for the ladies and took a left. Deeper into the rear of the house, skirting the large kitchen and walking down a long hall. The old servants' quarters, I remember thinking. Brick walls painted white. No luxuries for the working class, natch. At the far end of the hall was the door to the extension. It was a solid metal door. Something you would expect in a bunker or a prison. Painted a gray metallic color. It was cracked open a hand's width.

I pulled the door towards me. It looked like it should have creaked, but it didn't. It opened with a supple swing. Well-oiled. Well maintained. Again, I had expected horror house movie vibes, but got none.

Reality always gets in the way of our artistic expectations.

I stepped into the room and gasped.

It seemed so much bigger inside than out: like a skyscraper in New York or London designed by a hip architect for Middle Eastern royalty with more money than sense. Enormous. Opulent. Metal and glass with facings of copper and gold and what looked like speckled marble. It soared high above me. A pyramid of glass and steel, like a missile reaching for the stars. The marble was laid in seams about a yard across every ten yards and reminded me of a catalog Jimmy and I had looked at once when we were sourcing material for an upgrade to the flat in the city: white marble with erratic threaded lines of black and lilac. Exciting, but also somehow dismal. Dark. The kind of thing where you can't help but try to make sense of the plethora of random lines: scowling ancient faces, ley lines, scarecrows in fields, burning forests. Those kinds of things.

I felt tiny. Minuscule. As if the whole purpose of this building was to turn me into an ant staring up at the eternity of the universe laid out above.

Donald Trump and his enormous ego would have found the proportions inhuman.

It might even have made him feel inadequate.

Jesus.

But I was the private dick. Veronica mars and Miss Marple all rolled into one.

I had to know. What the hell Little Lord Ramsey and my eternally errant husband were up to. Up to no good was the answer, but what kind of no good?

The floor was a shiny substance, all white, but with a texture like cork. Across from me on the other side of the vestibule were three metal doors and windows facing into other rooms off this one, I guessed.

I strode across, feeling a weight on my shoulders, as if the pull of the dark void laced with stars above had a real gravitational pull.

Step after step. Confident at first, then tired, then almost trembling with fatigue. On and on for hours.

I remember being halfway across though it felt as though I had been walking for hours, when I risked another glance upwards.

The darkness was gone, the stars vanished. Replaced by a gray swirling cloud laced with opalescent flashes like silent and diffused lightening on a gas giant, Jupiter perhaps. A strange and beautiful, if terrifying, sight.

That weight again. Heavier now. As though the gravity of the earth itself had changed. Trembling from the waves of cold that crashing over me all the aeons of time I had been walking across this strange and frozen planet of a room.

Then I heard it. Them. Voices. A voice.

Not like your voice. Or mine. No spoken words. Just pressure on my frontal cortex, a pressure on my ears.

Was it real or a manipulation? I cannot say.

Were they communicating or attempting to control me? I still do not know.

All I know is that I heard voices that were not sound. Voices that were not human and yet, as I listened, sounded to me like the voices of all the people I had ever lost in my life. The voices of all those I had ever loved.

Pounding on my ears, except they were not, for there were no sounds. It doesn't make sense. It was real and terrifying for all that. Me in eternity except for the sounds that were no sounds, the voices that were the voices of the voiceless dead, attempting to overcome me, to drown me in their discord.

I fell to my knees. I slumped forward, head on the frozen white of that enormous cavern, frozen tendrils of breath blowing from my lungs so that I was covered in a cloud of my own breath.

I dissolved into it.

#

I did dream though.

Strange opaque dreams that drove stakes through my mind's memories.

I remember rising from the floor.

I was not alone.

Behind me, helping to lift me, were beings. People. Things.

I cannot say.

I felt the chill radiate from them.

Zombies. The dead. Aliens?

What the hell do I know?

I was groggy, my mind was flickering like an old cathode ray TV on its last legs.

People (or whatever) were laying hands on me. I was chilled to the bone and my extremities were numb. I could not feel my toes or my fingers, and I could not sense the pulse of my heart.

As frozen as the dead must be.

I fell forward and was carried by arms and hands that were not arms and hands but had the appearance of arms and hands. Inhuman, I remember my mind screaming. but that too was not completely true.

I was carried to one of the rooms across the vestibule, the door opened and I was set on a table. I felt hands on me. Cold to the touch, tearing at my clothes. Pulling off my blouse. Manipulating my legs and torso to remove my jeans and grabbing at my bra and underwear. I know

I tried to fight back, hands moving ineffectually, words making no sense.

And then I lay there naked, blind to all intents and purposes.

The light was but a fog I could not see fully through.

I could sense them, though. Faces, hidden by that opalescent fog, the long, thin, humanoid bodies attached to them, leaning over me like doctors over a patient on an operating table, whispering. As though not to disturb their patient.

Whispering silently. They did not seem to need sound to communicate.

I screamed. I closed my eyes. A dream. It had to be a dream. I opened my eyes. I was still there.

I was alone, naked. A hand reached down, holding something metallic, yet not. Pulsing as though alive, sharp as a fish knife. I felt it enter me. My chest. Aiming for my heart, I thought. I screamed in torment. In agony. The hand, if hand it was, withdrew the blade. There was a long moment. The pain within me was starting to ebb when the hand, that long, elongated, gray hand, leaned forward holding something else, a sliver of copper. The copper was placed on my stomach and then expanded, broke apart into ten, twenty mobile pieces. Lines of metal like tiny nails moving in a pattern across my body until they stopped. I remember staring at them, looking down at myself as if from a grotesque distance; staring at these animated coils of metal.

I remember thinking it was like they were surveyors mapping territory, the way they moved in angles across my torso. Then they rose into the air, turned vertically, needled ends pointing at me. I understood a non-sound I interpreted as "go" and the needles pierced my skin.

They disappeared into my flesh and bones and soul, burying their way into my body and I was emptied once again.

Chapter 15

I awake to familiar faces: Jimmy. Sarah. Sean. Ramsey. Adele.

And unfamiliar faces. All standing in a half-circle around me as though in a photo documenting a tragedy from the victim´s point of view.

Staring down at me with vivid sympathy. Open mouths. Tingles of disgust on twisted lips.

I see their mouths moving but cannot hear.

I see the tears in Sarah's eyes and the way her lips are contorted and red with fear.

I see Sean leaning against his dad, half turned away, as if to flee, his natural confidence soaked from him. Sound returns.

"Zoe, thank Christ."

"Mama. Mama"

"Mrs. Hearty, are you okay?"

"Breathe now. Breathe slowly."

I begin to filter reality again, to allow the words to reach me, as my brain reboots. Inside me, the chill and silent dream remains, a stubborn chunk of ice on my soul resonating with pain, but I can hear. Process. Respond.

I am back in the world, even as the dream fades.

Dissolving into smoke in a high wind, pushed hither and thither.

As if it had never been real.

#

For a long time, I am unable to speak.

Not in any coherent fashion.

But I can listen. Understand, somewhat.

Someone has called an ambulance.

I remember Jimmy's face. Not horrified, not disgusted. Disappointed. Ramsey joins him at one stage, staring down at me.

After they shoo away the onlookers and Adele leads the kids away, Ramsey and Jimmy are left behind as my guardians.

That helpless feeling. Lying on the cold ground, the soaring heights of that crazy building, stars high above like little needles piercing my soul.

Ramsey and Jimmy stare down on me. I am paralyzed, unable to move any part of my body, incapable of speech. Then there is the pure terror at my helplessness.

There is disappointment in Jimmy's face.

A knot of pure anger throbs in Ramsey's forehead.

"Get her up! Out of here. The couch in the hall will do."

He turns to Jimmy.

"Before the ambulance gets here, Jimmy! For fuck's sake. They cannot be in here. Cannot find her here. This is our thing. Ours only."

This is my husband. This weak-willed thing, cowing before a steroid ruined beefcake.

"Zoe, can you move?"

I try to shake my head. It doesn't move. I blink to tell him no.

Ramsey reaches down, digging his arms underneath me like a fork-truck. Holding shoulders and ass, he lifts me in one clean sweep, like a parent lifting a baby. The strength of the man is unreal.

"Shift it, Jimmy. Move, man."

Following Jimmy, he carries me across the vestibule of that room that had seemed so eternal. I swim in and out of consciousness.

We make our way back through the house, into the hallway beneath the beautiful staircase.

I still cannot move. A wave of panic sweeps through me.

What the fuck is wrong with me, with my body?

I feel the sweat and the panic and the terror as a cold chill travels down my spine. Ramsey tosses me onto the old red Ottoman couch underneath the wooden banister. Tears roll from my eyes.

Jimmy reaches down and holds my hand.

"It is okay, Zoe. It will all be good. We've got you."

I try to smile up at him. I can feel his hand in mine, its warmth, and that is something. Sensation. Human touch. Something good.

I cannot be totally broken.

My husband is here with me.

I gasp.

And breathe.

And feel my body return to me.

"It's okay, Zoe. This happens sometimes. When you resist."

What the fuck?

A wave of feelings, feelings I can barely define. Disgust, betrayal, anger.

What the fuck does that mean? Resist?

I turn my face, my whole body protesting, to face them.

Two manly men standing over me, staring down. Jimmy is leaning over me, his hand warm in mine. Ramsey is a rigid mountain behind him, ramrod tall.

When you resist?

They knew. It was a set up.

They lured me here. Jimmy too. My Jimmy.

Leaning over me, a look of false sympathy on his face.

I want to spit in his eye, bite off his nose.

Fucker.

He betrayed me. This is worse. Worse than with the women.

He was offering me to Ramsey and his sick society.

A sacrificial lamb, or some type of experiment.

My body still aches. I can feel the invasion of that fish knife, those copper coils that were somehow imbued with life.

The memories invade my mind and I pass out.

Jimmy and Ramsey still staring at me with cold eyes.

Fish eyes.

Inhuman.

#

I awake in the hospital.

The sterile, tatty feel of a poorly funded general hospital. Machines beeping in the corridor and the harried feel of hard work, pain, sweat and desperation all around.

A poky little room, painted white with faded green borders: an attempt at making human what is vile and stinks of corruption, pain, and worse.

Sharing a room with someone else hidden behind a pulled curtain, coughing incessantly. Feeble. An old woman, from the sounds of it. That cough sounds serious, poor dear. Like last-legs serious.

I hate hospitals.

The nurse looking down at me, taking my pulse, is Indian and has a warm smile and gentle eyes.

"Zoe, is it?"

I nod.

Legs. Feet. Arms. Hands. All check out. I can move again, the paralysis a fading memory.

"Feeling better?"

I nod again. "I am." My throat is dry, the words little blades, but I can speak.

The nurse reaches for a glass on the bedside table, and holds it to my lips.

"Here."

I suck at the drink as though I have just reached an oasis after days in a desert.

"Can you move?"

"Yes."

"Excellent." She checks my pulse. Looks in my eyes.

"Do you remember what happened?"

I shake my head.

"Not fully. Fragments. Dreams."

"Care to tell me?"

I shake my head.

In the cold light of day, in this sterile and cold place, my dreams seem ridiculous. The fevered hallucinations of a lunatic.

She leans over me, smiling, but her eyes are serious.

"Your husband brought you here."

Her eyes are brown and speckled with gold.

She is an older woman, hair gray, slightly heavy, but still beautiful.

"He seemed distraught."

"Jimmy gets emotional."

"More than that, if I dare say it. He seemed nervous. Overly so. Jittery."

I nod. Wary now.

"Nothing broken. You are going to be fine." She smiles again. "But there are bruises all over your back and shoulders."

A memory.

The copper coils. My panic.

I scramble at the bedclothes and pull open my nightdress.

My stomach is pristine. Untouched. No sign of any entry wounds. No signs of anything at all.

Not so much as a pimple.

This is all so fucked.

"I am Nelam." She rubs my forehead, brushing back my hair.

Nurse Nelam, sweet.

"There is nothing wrong with your midriff, Zoe. What concerns me are the bruises. On your wrists. On your back. Abrasions. A couple of scratches on your left cheek. A sprained wrist. All clear otherwise, but those wounds, they kind of tell their own story."

"They do?"

"Do you remember being admitted? The doctor's tests?"

I shake my head.

"You did seem a bit out of it. Good night was it? Before, I mean?"

I hesitate. What can I say?

"It wasn't alcohol. Nor drugs. I had two glasses of champagne."

"Okay." She sighs, as though I was confirming something she had suspected.

"Your husband then?"

"What about him?"

She reaches over to me. Grabs my hand. Her hand is warm, soft, small in mine. Her eyes sparkle with human kindness.

"You know what this looks like, Zoe. All you have to do is say the word. We have people. Systems. You will be safe. Tell us what he did."

And though Jimmy didn't directly do this to me, these hazy, evil shards sticking in my mind, I am sorely tempted to shop him. It would be his word against mine. I can be convincing when I want to.

Serve the bastard right. He delivered me to that place. But I bite my tongue and say nothing.

Nelam stares at me, eyes now cold and flat.

"If that is the way you want to play this. I'll be back to check on you later," she mutters. Her face is thinner now, curdled somehow. Like she has bitten something sour. She turns her back and walks away without another word.

Her back is stiff. Her walk somehow stilted.

I could have said something. I know I wanted to.

So, what stopped me? I hear you ask. Feeble woman. You had a chance. Could have put an end to it there and then.

And that is not the case.

As Nurse Nelam held my hand, the sleeve of her nurse's uniform got pulled up. On her wrist was a gray tattoo, thin and dark and amateur, like a prison tattoo. The tattoo, about an inch high and wide at the base, was of a pyramid reaching for the stars.

#

So, poor fucked up Zoe, was the story. Wasted at the BBQ, drank God knows how much, and started talking crazy shit. Ended up in emergency with alcohol poisoning and god knows what else.

God love her.

Bless.

Sure we are all praying for her.

Course they fucking are. All the while knocking back vodkas and, gin and tonics, and all kinds of other shit, just to keep themselves on the straight and narrow. To keep the wolves of age, disappointment, and betrayal from their doors.

Much easier to do jigs of joy around the afflicted.

That Zoe. A dear soul. Can't help herself. But for the grace of God, there go we.

Something very primitive about this. Pre-Medieval defensive magic. Straight up ancient.

Say the words that you dread most, pass them on, allow their power to dissipate.

A ward for all the hurt that is waiting in the dark featured future facing us all.

Chapter 16

So, ladies, yes, I, Zoe Hearty, am your local sap. The scarecrow of pity that keeps the crows from your doors and dreams.

And yes, some doctors are worried about the state of yours truly. They think I am a few pennies short of a shilling, not all my cups in the cupboard, as the Germans say.

A fucking nut job, with addiction issues, low self-esteem, and God knows what else.

A wacko. *Barking fucking mad*, out of control. Sure what can you do but pray for the wee children she neglects?

Selfish whore.

You get the misogynistic drift, right?

So, enter stage right: Doctor Bob.

Doctor Bob is the main man.

A tall thin fellow with a protruding belly, dark bushy hair, and eyebrows to match. Middle-aged when he was born; that big-eyed hangdog look. A terrible dose of dandruff or dried skin flaking his hair and shoulder like old snow. No woman (or man or another diverse lover) waiting at home for this dude.

When I ask him about nurse Nelam, he just shrugs as if puzzled. Nelam who? Figures.

He was the one who admitted me. He is much less interested in Jimmy and my abrasions than in my mental state.

Apparently, I was not very nice to him the night the ambulance brought me to the hospital.

In his eyes, far as I can tell, Jimmy is a saint, and I am some spitting (literally, I am embarrassed to say) harridan.

It is hardly new, this narrative he has built up around me.

I am the neglectful mother: witness the drunken incident at the party and Jimmy, the teacher and football coach, pillar of the community, the long-suffering quiet man. Probably abused by this spitting harridan. Mentally, if not physically.

It is not only women who suffer from abuse, you know? I can practically read the fucker's thoughts.

Bollix.

But we all tell each other stories, and his suits his view of the world.

Jimmy is the hero, and I am broken and drifting and in need of serious help.

So, he suggests drugs. Abilify was one. Marplan another. Good shit, but it didn't help me much. Wrong diagnosis. And he wanted me to talk.

Talk therapy, I remember him saying, smiling with his yellow, crooked teeth.

Quack therapy, I remember thinking to myself.

See, back then, my memories of that night were vague and broken, at best.

Fragments of hazy memories. Like after a binge, when some time has passed. You know bad shit went down, but your gray matter refuses to connect the dots. You wish you knew, because you sense it was bad, but to no avail.

Memories of pain, of embarrassment, or is it fear?

Memories I dug up again later, but were obscured at the time.

#

I spent five nights in that shitty place. I woke in the middle of the third night from a deep and uneasy sleep. You know the kind. You wake up, heart pounding, stinking of night sweat, and an undefined fear. Took deep breaths, and listened to the old gal in the next bed named Minny Phelan snoring, a wheezy short snore, a feeble gasp for air.

Poor, gentle, kind-hearted Minny had cancer and was not long for the world.

I slipped out of bed and into my slippers. Wrapping my red night robe around me, I opened the door into the hall.

Low ceiling lights cast shadows. One blinking green light above the door into the ward, like the balefully blinking eye of an ogre. The nurses' station was through that door between wards one (me) and two. Nobody in sight. No nurses, doctors, patients. Silence too, apart from the hum of the generators and a beeping from some machine at the far end of the hall. I made my way to the heavy metal door, pushed it open, and slipped through. Another hallway and then a right turn leading to ward two. The nurses' station is on my left. A counter and the inevitable computer, two doors beyond that, both closed tight. Where the nurses hang out, no doubt, doing nursy things and shagging the doctors and each other, for all I know.

I pulled open the half door leading into the administrative space.

The computer was on, casting a faint blue glow. I sat on the low swivel chair.

The software was unfamiliar to me, but nothing special. Left criminally unlocked, didn't even require a passcode.

I was tempted to enter my name to see what they had on me, but I had other reasons for being here.

I clicked on the search icon.

An empty search field with two options came up. Staff or patient.

I type in Nelam. Then Nellam.

Names appear in a yellow-tinted table. Surnames and first names and titles.

Doctor Nell Macreedy. Doctor Marin Nelson. Mary Nkosi. Nikos Tateos.

No Nelam.

I scroll further, noticing other Indian names: Nurse Chatterjee, Doctor Munshi, Doctor Pande, Nurse Verma. But Nelam does not exist.

A ghost.

A plant.

A figment of my imagination or a spy sent by Ramsey and his gray society.

#

They released me on the Thursday after the party.

Jimmy wheeled me to the car, though I could have walked. He was being solicitous. I could see some of the nurses staring after us, wishing they were going home with him.

In the past, I would have smiled smugly.

Now, as far as I am concerned, they are welcome to have him.

I have to get strong again.

Get well again.

Then I will take the kids and get the fuck away from Jimmy and his weird-ass friends. Ramsey and Nelam and Adele and all the other freaks. I am outta here, as they say in the movies. I am leaving Dodge as soon as I possibly can.

Chapter 17

Quack therapy was not so bad.

The quack they gave me was a decent soul. I mean, he was straight out of central casting for the part: thin and tweedy with a long neck and a thin goatee.

I expected him to speak *Vit a German accent, yah!* but he was a Brit, posh, but from Devon originally. He had a nice sense of humor and long, thin hands. Soft looking hands, I could sense. Hands that I soon wanted soothing me. Holding me.

The hands of a gentleman. One of those rare ones with a trace of empathy and, strangely enough, given he was a quack, very few "issues" of his own.

Guy Wickers.

He coaxed me along.

Got me to admit stuff about myself and my mother I had never realized. Shone headlights on Jimmy and me.

Asked about my dreams.

But they are precarious and porous things, dreams.

"Zoe, to go any deeper, we need to find out what you think happened that night."

We are in his office. Books on the shelves, of course, abstract prints on the pale cream walls of his practice, furniture that is a touch above Ikea: easy chairs and Faux wood tables. All terribly modern. Nothing Freudian here, it says, nothing to see in the recesses. Just walk easy. We can medicate your troubles away.

I wish I could.

I wish he could.

I bat my eyes at him. Stockholm syndrome of a sort, I guess. He is considerably older than me. Skinny and lacking definition. Not my usual type at all. It is just the way things are between Jimmy and me. The silences. The fear. The lack of communication. Any port in a Storm, and all that.

He is patently uninterested, at least at first, professional.

But it is fun for me, and he does not seem to mind. After a while, I sense I am getting to him. For is he not lonely too?

Living in the sticks amongst barbarians. I know he is. I can feel it ooze off of him like a bad odor. A stranger in a strange country with lots of contacts, but no friends. After the third or fourth session he begins to look at me differently. A discreet, but obvious longing in his eyes.

And with no further progress towards what happened that night, what else do we have but the flirtation?

"Can't do it, Doc. What I remember I told you. Weirdness and pain. But all dreams are weird, right? Let me tell you one. An old one. I am in a cinema, right? Not one of those boring multiplexes, but an old hall. From the fifties. On the corner of Main Street and Davis Street. Jutting out almost into the street, proud and individual, more ocean liner than business. A film is on. I don't remember what, except that it is black and white. I am in a chair, deep burgundy and comfortable as sin, and the lights are down." I pause. This is truly an old dream. One the therapy has re-awoken. A recurring dream I had had in the city for years. "I am sitting with friends, a night out. Happy. And then the cinema darkens, a deeper darkness, and the tension rises."

"Zoe!"

"Sorry, Doc. Can't help the drama. Part of the story, see? It is a dream moment. You know what I mean. When the dream rises to the surface. Not just the detritus of yesterday. Something buried."

"Very Freudian, Zoe. You have been doing research."

I smile. "Well, yeah, actually." And I had. This whole process, and my time with Doc Sexy here, has given me a new interest. Actually, *an interest* full stop. All this weirdness, all the nutty things that have been happening to me, they must have a rationale. If I can break through the barrier of forgetfulness, I will remember exactly what happened, what that asshole Ramsey did to me that night.

It's all in my head.

That tolling gong I carry on my shoulder with all its rusted baggage. The detritus of time.

He shakes his head. Mock serious. "My most precocious student."

I swear, he speaks like this.

"Anyway, back to the dream. Everything is okay and then suddenly it's not. Bed sweats and twisting brain, and you know you are fucked."

"Specifics, Zoe. Show not tell."

"Right. I am in the chair and the world closes around me. My friends are gone, replaced with ciphers. Staring at me with blank faces. Behind me there is someone. A female. Leaning forward into my chair, breathing into my ears. And I cannot move. I am trapped. I can feel this in the dream. That paralysis that happens. Trying to move. Unable. And that breathing in my ears and the feeling of hands on my shoulders, reaching towards my breast, reaching lower."

I gasp. Shake my head.

"Keep going, Zoe."

"The hands of that invisible woman touch me. There. Again. Again. I cannot move. My body is fighting against the restraints. Her hands on, the faces of the audience turn, leering at me."

"I see." He leans toward me.

"And then I would wake up. Sweating and lost to the world for an endless time, my heart thumping, my mind almost adrift in the darkness."

"How often?"

"Every six months when I was younger. The intervals are longer now but it is still there. Nascent. Waiting."

"I have a feeling there is a reason you brought this to me today, Zoe."

"Despite these pretty blond locks I wear and the red lipstick I put on today to seduce you, I am not totally thick."

He smiles. I like to see him smile. Parts of me respond. Tingle. I have always had a thing for older men.

"You did the research. You worked it out."

"You are not Freudian, Doc. Consider him discredited. Dead white men, etc. You would prefer to give me the pills. I respect that."

"Medicine has its uses."

"What I've been telling you, dude. Normally I am all over that stuff, but this time, it is not for me. Not for what happened to me. Is happening to me."

He shrugs. A magnanimous male shrug. Condescending and wise at the same time, or trying to be. You know what I mean. I almost snort, but that would puncture too many of his illusions of grandeur. Like I said, he is cool and sexy, and kind.

He cannot help his gender.

And I need him.

"So, tell me, Zoe Freud. What wonderful self-diagnosis are you dying to share with me?"

"Did I ever tell you I was abused?"

A fake surprise. A tilt of his head.

"You did not, patient of mine. For it has, to date, been irrelevant to—and I use the medical term advisedly—your recent messed up state of mind. The mess I have been tasked with fixing and understanding. Your recent breakdown. In other words, my job."

"Cute, doc. Cute. Give me a little leeway here. Can you do that? I shall prove relevance, your honour."

"Go ahead." He smiles.

I was a kid. Nine or ten. We were visiting relatives, my mother´s family. A beautiful part of the country. The sky lowering above gray slate mountains, hidden lakes and cliffs tumbling to the sea."

"Poetic."

"We spent our time outside playing on the beach, in the caves around the beach, climbing the rock faces to the road above, hunting crabs and mussels, and fishing with Dad and my uncles."

"Real memories."I swear. Madleen was older. A lot. Well, in her teens. And my idol. On the local Camogie team. Destined for the heights. I remember the way she looked and smelled. Tall and tan and braver than a baker's dozen of the boys. She scared the shit out of them. But never me. She had my back. She was patient and kind, or at least as kind and patient as a teenager can be. And she let me hang out."

He shakes his head.

"We had a cottage on the coast we rented. Above that wild stormy coast. Eternal days. Summers that lasted forever. Until they didn't."

"What happened Zoe?"

"One night she came into my room. Took off her clothes. Slipped in beside me. Naked. Held her body against mine."

"What else?"

"She touched me. Rubbed me for a moment. Took my hand and made me do the same to her. I remember the feel of her pubes. And that was it. She held me close, and I slept. She was gone when I awoke. We were never together afterward. No longer friends. She chased me away, and I was glad to see the back of her."

"She betrayed you."

"If you had asked me three months ago, have you ever been a victim of abuse, I would have laughed. I am not laughing now."

"The cinema."

"That feeling of comfort and joy and powerless and sudden shock. That was her."

"So why now?"

"Something happened that night. Pills and mediation will drive it underground. I want to face the crap they did to me."

"Zoe." A long pause.

"Did I ever tell you I backpacked in Austria and Germany for a summer? Did German in school?"

"Full of surprises, our Zoe."

God, I like that, the our-Zoe thing. So, I am getting to him.

"Do you speak German?"

"I do not."

"Great language, this language of the Huns. Show, not tell, you say to me at all these sessions. Well, almost very Germanic noun is about showing not telling. Flugzeug is flying thing or tool. Fernseher is far seer, which is a crap load better that TV. Freud´s book, is called Die Traumdeutung. Genius. Dreammeaning. Simple and elegant."

I can see the worry on his face. He knows.

I am going to push his boundaries.

I just hope my wiles are wily enough.

"Hypnotize me. I need to know what happened. That pain. The meaning of my dreams. Give me back my dreams, Doc."

And that was it. My pitch.

I could do no more.

Five times I had been here. Since Jimmy and I were a broken pair, the sexual fantasies I had were of this kind and gentle man, this thin long man with the soft-looking fingers.

Gentle fingers on my skin. He rubs his cheek, unsure. I smile and lick my lips.

I know what I am doing, and I know I need this and yet my feelings towards him are also real.

This man is a protector: a real man, despite his size and lack of physical strength.

A man with genuine strength, only deep inside.

Long, long moments as he weighs his options.

And in the end, I see it in his eyes.

He will do this. He does not want to, fears where it will bring me, but he will do it, go against his better medical instincts.

For me.

Chapter 18

And so we did.

Hypnotize me.

I know that it sounds like a bad idea, like putting myself back into yet another man's power.

But I had to know.

Something happened to me that night.

An invasion.

Metal.

Hands.

Who did that to me?

#

I am lying on the sofa. It is a Friday morning in summer. Birds warble and peep outside and the oak through his window is a canopy of sun-dappled green. I turn my eyes to the cream-colored ceiling as he repeats a series of words.

His voice is a quiet wave. His tone lulls me as my eyes grow heavy.

Not everybody can be hypnotized, I remember reading. People who trust easily are more likely to go under, and if this life of mine has proven anything to me, it is that I am trusting. Gullible even.

Bet you couldn't hypnotize that bastard Ramsey even if you tried.

I go under, feel myself pulled away as if by a riptide into the ocean of my mind. The crashing waves. The stormy dark.

And then I am back in the bowels of the manor house at night.

The interiors of the pyramid lour above, its ceiling an eternity of stars. Metal invades my body. My hands are trapped in metal buckles, and I am squirming and roaring with pain.

I feel heat in my midriff as the pain thunders into my ears.

I feel their invasion.

Still, I cannot see them.

Those who are doing this to me.

Those pale, elongated faces.

Say it. Say the impossible word. Do it, Zoe. Please. Finally.

Aliens. Alright then. Aliens it is.

Digging around in my body, testing their knowledge on me. Probing and prodding me like prize meat.

Why?

Who the hell can say?

I never gave them any credence: those strange pale, pathetic people, the abducted.

Rednecks and chancers.

Looking for their 15 minutes or to make a quick buck.

Bullshit. Had to be. I mean, I believe in other life forms. The universe is a big fucking place. But the idea that they are interested specifically in Maggie May from Buttfuck, Ohio, because she is the chosen one, and her ovaries are the key to peace and love in the universe is ridiculous.

Except.

Now I am Maggie. Me.

And the pain I remember is real. Stabbing pain. Ethereal almost. A white light, like a laser might feel burning your skin if it was powerful enough. Like being zapped with electricity. Like being strapped to an electric chair.

There were no marks visible on my body, and doctor Bob never mentioned anything except the minor abrasions and swollen wrist from my fall.

So, what to make of all this.

What indeed?

I come around drenched in sweat.

I turn and my unflappable Brit with the stiff upper lip is pale. His lips are pursed and I swear I can see his hands trembling.

Jesus.

We say nothing for a long, long time. I can hear the ticking of his wall clock, the cawing of crows outside, the sounds of cars and voices on the streets below.

The clock chimes.

"I guess my time is up. See ya next week, Doc?"

"Funny, Zoe. Really funny."

"So, what says my guru?"

He shakes his head.

"I recorded it all."

He points at the digital recorder on the desk.

"Well, of course you did. I'd be mighty pissed otherwise. But what do you make of it?"

"I warned you of this."

"Did you now?" I feel my heart sink. He hears the tone of my voice. Leans forward in his chair towards me, holding those thin fingers in my direction as if to hold me, heal me, protect me.

"Zoe, it was real."

"I know."

"No. I don't mean that. The story. The aliens. That is sublimation. You must know this. But the abuse. That is real."

"So, you don't believe me."

"Shit, Zoe." His face is red with anger. "Of course, I fucking believe you. Those bastards did this to you."

"Did what?"

"Well, not that." He gestures at the tape. "But something like that. They hurt you." He stands up and walks towards me. I sit up, feeling wrung out, dizzy. He sits beside me.

He puts his hand around me, saying nothing. I lean into him, placing my head on his shoulder. It feels good, this. This touch.

This feeling of being wrapped in a protective blanket.

This feeling of hope.

"It was real."

He pulls me closer.

"It was real. No matter how it happened, it was real."

"But you don't believe it, the aliens."

"PTSD, Zoe. Christ, I do know how strong you are. I do. The cinema story shows me that. You are intelligent and self-aware, but this is the break I warned you about. This disconnect. Those fuckers were raping you. No doubt. Your mind built its own protective wall. This is the story you told yourself. Easier to credit this that to believe that the man you loved for so long is an abusive rapist and belongs to a gang of abusers. Jesus."

I put my arm around him and feel tears rolling down my cheeks.

"I need to call the police."

I shake my head. "No!"

"No?"

"Jimmy is coming to pick me up." I glance at the clock. "In ten minutes."

"You shouldn't go back."

"I have to. I have to be with the kids."

He sighs. Pulls his arms away and turns to face me.

"If you go back, be careful. I am going to get you out. I swear. We'll figure out a way."

"You will?"

"I swear."

"A lot of men have made lots of promises to me recently."

I lean in to kiss him and he turns his mouth from me, but I know he wanted to kiss me back. I can see it in the glint of lust in his eyes.

"Keep that up and my licence will be out the window."

I mock punch his arm.

"I won't be the one officially complaining. Will I?"

The light in his eyes is warm and tender, a warmth that I don't remember Jimmy ever showing me. Not even on the best of days.

"We don't have anything for the police."

"The recording?"

"It's of a crazy woman. You said it yourself. I am not fit to bear witness. I believe in aliens."

"Then just leave him."

"I will. I promise. But I need time."

He is rubbing my neck, and that feels fine. I glance at the clock.

Time to go. I wrestle myself away from those caring arms and into a standing position.

"I have to go."

Just then, there is a sound of loud voices outside. Marcy, the receptionist, and Jimmy. I hear the thunder of his feet as he approaches the consultation room and Marcy shouting 'stop!'.

The door is blasted open and there is *my* Jimmy. Tall and broad-shouldered and powerful.

His face is red with anger.

"Are you done here yet, Zoe? I have to move."

"Mr. Hearty? What the hell?"

"Stow it, doc. Or do we even call you lot docs?"

"Mr. Hearty, I need you to leave. Now."

Guy gets to his feet, god bless him, and walks over to Jimmy. He looks so small, so frail. Jimmy bosses him by inches and multiple pounds of muscle.

"I need my wife, dip shit. If you are finished anal-ysing her, that is." He puts one of his meaty hands on Guy's shoulder. I recognize the look in his eye. Seen it too often before. It might be early, but he has had a snort of something and at least one drink. I thought he was supposed to be working today.

He is in a Jimmy frame of mind and that spells danger.

"Mr. Hearty, we are not finished with this session. Zoe has made real progress today. I need you to back off. Marcy!"

Jimmy grips Guy's shoulder. I see the wince.

"Marcy, call the police."

Jimmy smiles a shark's smile.

"You really don't want to do that, fella."

"Is that so?"

"It is, doc quack. It is really. Zoe, move."

And to my shame, I do. I could have stayed. Maybe I should have stayed.

I didn't and now I am here.

#

The car ride home is not fun.

I can see Jimmy´s right hand on the wheel, though I am turned away from him.

A vein throbs between the middle finger, and the index finger and his hand looks red. Holding tight to the wheel, holding on to his anger.

"So was it good? Useful, like?"

I feel him turn to me. I sense the smile. Half-apologetic. *I have messed up again, Zoe. Please forgive me.*

Usual crap.

"What the fuck was that, Jimmy?"

"What was what?"

"You were rude. And you threatened him."

"I told you. I need to get home."

"It was, yeah."

"Was yeah what?"

"Good. Useful."

"So, do you remember more?"

Even facing the window, I could feel him staring at me.

"I do, Jimmy. I most certainly do."

"That´s good."

"Is it?"

"What do you remember, Zoe?"

"I'd rather not talk about it."

I can feel the heat from the other side, building inside him.

"Christ, woman. You owe me this. We need to talk."

I can feel his eyes, not on the road, boring into me.

"Jimmy. Eyes fucking straight. I'd like to get home in one piece."

"Fuck this, Zoe. If we don't talk, then where are we?"

"You tell me, Jimmy." A quiet voice. So quiet I am not sure I even said anything. "You tell me."

We arrive home. Jimmy is broody now. In a mood. He slams the car door shut and walks off to the shed near the river, arms swinging.

In the house, I make dinner and wait for the kids to come home. We spend the afternoon moving around one another, but I am short with them. Absent.

Still lost in my nightmares.

Jimmy appears for dinner, says little, gets up from the table before the kids are finished, and stomps off to his study.

I put the kids to bed, and read them an old picture book, *Em and Little Blue.*

A story of night terrors and how the little boy, Em, defeats them. The kids are too old for this story, really, though they do not complain.

I think the story is more for me than them.

I grab a glass of wine, that old thirst driving me. The need to forget. To gorge. I knock it back, grab the bottle, and go to the living room. I watch something on TV, something about houses, that I don't take in.

My head is filled with night terrors and the only weapon I have is the alcohol.

That and the thought of a gentle arm around my shoulder. The idea that I have somebody on my side. A real person, a kind person, a man who is gentle and cares. Who will stand up to the bully and defend me.

A fine thought indeed.

Chapter 19

It always comes at night.

The dreams.

The troubles.

Whatever this is.

And Ramsey.

I hear the car. My window is pulled partly open; the night is hot and humid and my bed a damp jungle with night and alcohol sweats.

A ray of light crosses the ceiling.

Car light. Nothing gray, nothing alien, thank the lord.

My head is groggy with the wine and an incipient hangover.

Shit.

My heart is a runaway train.

"Shit! Shit! Shit!"

I struggle out of bed. I am still dressed and can't remember making my way to bed.

The nightside clock tells me it is 3 in the morning.

Who visits at this ungodly hour?

Of course, I know the answer already. Ungodly people.

I make my way downstairs, but only after checking on the kids. I stare at them for a long time. Twin beds. Gentle snores in the yellow glow of their night light—a frog called Jumpy, for obvious reasons. Here my heart is at rest. Here I am at peace in a way I once never imagined possible. Even at a distance, I feel them, touch them, as though my skin is wrapped around them, my body an immaterial thing. I can hear their hearts beating. I know the warmth of their sweaty bodies, can see them twitching in that beautiful quiet sleep that seems reserved for children. Or so we imagine, as adults.

You must know this. I was their mother. I was proud as their mother. Proud to be their mother. And it suited me. I know other women who tolerated their offspring. Not me. That was never me.

I loved them. I lived for them.

I would have died for them.

#

I close their door behind me, softly, so as not to wake them.

The heat of their bodies is like a shield around me. The house is dark, that night darkness that makes everything strange and uneven, but there is nothing alien here tonight. No creepy lights or chilled air.

I tiptoe down the stairs, flashlight in hand, and sneak towards the back door, past the kitchen and the pantry towards the side of the house facing the river.

It is a sticky, humid night in high summer. I hear a fox bark, a nightingale sing, and the sound of hot air sighing through leaves mingled with the murmur of the river.

And voices.

Near the water. Down by the shed.

My legs are weak and feel like jelly. I need to pee, and I gulp back a burp laden with vomit. I need to run away and ignore this. To go back to bed.

To close my eyes, massage my sore forehead, and sleep.

Sleep the sleep of the damned. A gust shakes the branches of the nearby oak. The ambient sounds ring hollow. Night sounds.

An owl?

Then a high-pitched scream like someone calling for help.

A fox.

I stop every ten steps, fighting my fear. My heart is a gong ringing in my chest and a chill film of sweat clings to my body.

Thank God, I am still wearing my jeans and top. I would hate to be caught out here undressed.

It can only have been moments, but I feel like I have been walking in a jungle forever. In a world not my own.

And then I hear them.

Voices.

Ramsey's deep bass. Jimmy's more modulated tenor. In the shed.
Raised voices.

Passionate. Involved. Full of lust, though not in any sexual way.

And for the first time, I know I have lost my husband; he has a new
love, and his love is not me. Not us. This is different to the affairs; that
was sex and pleasure and conquest. This is completely different. I have
lost the totality of him. His heart, now elsewhere.

"Ka wills it so."

I crouch beneath the lone window in the long wall of the shed. The
window is cracked open.

Ramsey's voice is a deep rasping growl.

"Ka wills it so."

"And what of Banning and the others?"

"Ka wills it so, Brother. He has spoken through the prophet."

I hear Jimmy's sigh.

Jimmy has always had a front. Been a tough guy on the face of
things. His size has helped.

But he is not a strong man.

Yes, he has been successful, but his strength was built on weakness.
On a certain cunning. On a certain ability to ingratiate and abase
himself. I sense Ramsey is no different.

Big, strong men with meaty fists. These are not the leaders.

But what they say next tears the legs out from under me.

"This doctor knows too much."

"He knows nothing."

"He has been in her mind."

"Don't be so dramatic, brother. Zoe's memory is shot. Even if she
could remember, what would she tell him?"

"Ka wills it so. The prophet wills it so. It falls to us to deal with it."

"We do not need the attention. You have to know this. Not so close.
Not when we are so close."

I fall to the ground.

My head throbs from the remnants of the wine, and my body is weak
from the fear of this sojourn into the dark side, from the realization that
I have stepped into an alternate world.

A place where monsters and aliens coexist with you. With me.

I sit there with the sticky wind of that dark night, a warm fan in my face, sweat rolling in fat wet drops like obscene tears down my forehead, sweat coating my buttocks.

Cold sweat. Nothing to do with the weather.

Guy!

They are talking about Guy. My husband is talking about Guy, and his new guru is egging him on. Whatever they are planning will not end well.

God!

I push myself backward.

Against a loose plank on the grass behind, knocking it into another.

Shit!

Silence from inside the shed.

A long moment of disbelief, as if the world has stopped.

They know I am here.

Or someone is.

But they dare not acknowledge it.

Christ!

I am sitting on my ass in the damp while they are hiding and listening in the shed. And none of us can acknowledge the existence of the other, like some Norwegian sex farce where everyone has been caught with their knickers hanging down, but nobody can call quits.

I still cannot believe what I just overheard.

Ka wills it so.

I have a feeling that whatever the fuck Ka wills cannot be good.

They suspect Guy. They believe he knows what happened to me and that has put him in danger, in their firing line.

What can do I? Get the hell out of here, slide on my ass away from this deadening silence. Call him, warn him, without Jimmy hearing me.

And then tell him what?

The honourable Guy Whickers, esquire. Posh and logical and kind.

Guy, I will say, my husband´s buddy who is a believer in aliens, says that Ka wants you hurt. Maybe dead.

Sounds logical.

Sounds sane.

It is only me, the sexy loony who tried to kiss you recently.

Fuck!

No! No, it doesn't sound sane in the least, but what are my options exactly?

And so, I do just that, I back up on my ass until I am far enough away to stand without being seen and then hightail for the house, half expecting to hear the sound of feet charging behind me, half expecting to be knocked to the ground in a rugby tackle.

But they do not come after me.

I reach the rear of the house, pull open the door, grab the phone from its charging station in the hallway, and sprint up the stairs, locking myself in the bathroom.

Still no sound of pursuit, no sign of Jimmy.

I hesitate a long moment before dialling the number, saved months ago when we set up our first session.

"Come on. Come on" I bark at the ring-tone. "Pick it up, Guy."

And he does.

And he is quiet as I explain what happened, what I heard.

When I am finished, there is a long moment's silence.

"Guy!"

"Okay, Zoe. Still here."

I breathe a sigh of relief, letting go of a breath I did not know I was holding.

He hasn't hung up on the crazy lady, hasn't renounced us. Me. The memory of his hands wrapped about me is a lit fire in my mind. I feel a tingle as I think of him.

Unprofessional on his part and desperate on mine, yes, but the world is too full of strange at the moment. I am happy to have someone on my side. I need that more than anything right now.

Guy is a rock in an ocean of roiling shit.

"So, what do you think?"

He laughs, and the laugh is gentle and almost humorous.

"I think they are full of shit. I think that I have a nice set of golf clubs, one of which I can spare to wrap around their fucking necks if they come anywhere near me. I think I have to get the police involved, and I think you need to get you and the kids out of there. And then you can tell the police what you heard. That'll scare them right off."

Clearly enunciated and earnest in that Brit voice of his.

A balm to my roiling, feverish soul.

Pack up and go.

Christ.

Now?

Seriously?

#

Sitting here now, recording this for you, I remember thinking, why the hell not?

Our marriage had been a joke for a long time. A knock-knock joke where nobody answers, then the door creaks open to reveal a hollow scarecrow of an ancient dream constructed of dried saplings, ready to combust.

Guy, and I know this at a deep and fundamental level, is a strong man. A good man. Not needy and big-boy greedy like Jimmy the devourer. Guy is an adult, a centered grown-up with a moral code. It might be too early to say it, but we would be good together. His gentle honesty would be a balm to the edgier parts of my nature. He has never said it, but I know. He likes me. A lot. He would never have risked that breach in professionalism otherwise, holding me so tight.

His dark brown eyes, liquid with care and light.

For me, this is the colour of hope.

"Zoe?"

"Yeah!"

"What?"

"I cannot stay here any longer." My voice catches. I haven't said the words, but I know how true they are, how they have been welling for so long, distilled through my body, hidden and unseen, but getting stronger and stronger as they age.

I hate Jimmy. I hate him for who he was and the pain he has caused me. Banging those sluts to feed his needy ego, I hate him for the moments of violence, for the arrogance he carries with himself as though it is his birthright, when the polar opposite is true. I hate him for his failures, and for stealing my hopes from me.

I love him as the father of my kids, but that is not the basis of a marriage.

I imagine him, holding court at a cocktail bar, drink in hand. Older. Bragging to his equally lusty buddies, "Sure, tis only Zoe. She will forgive me. She has to. Stuck with me she is, boys." He still looks good, still hot and sexy, but there is a fragility about him. I see this now. It is all an act. We can never know one another, not really. But now, when I look at him, I focus on his eyes and not his ass. I see the confusion there, the fear. The knowledge that he is getting away with this against the odds. The self-loathing. The boy who pissed his pants when his mother locked him in the naughty closet.

Why do I only see this now?

I cannot save him. He is lost. I tried. I really did. Gave it my best. Gave birth to two little angels. Two sweet bundles of life.

That was the best he could give me. That was all.

I wipe tears from my eyes.

"Get us out of here, Guy. I cannot bear it any longer. Take us away. Away from here." I hear the hitch of fear in my voice.

I am not a fearful person. Not normally. But what of this is normal?

I hear him sigh at the other end of the phone. A sigh, not of frustration, but of relief.

"I will."

"Can you get us tonight?"

"What about Jimmy?"

"It´s best if we do this quick. One sharp cut. I don´t want to give him time to think, to wheedle. To hurt us. I'll get the kids up. If Jimmy tries to stop us…"

"I am not quite as helpless as you might think, my dear lady." He laughs. The laugh lends me confidence. "And I will bring my golf club." In a quieter, more urgent voice. "This is for the best, Zoe. You need this. I'll be over in an hour or less, when I have sorted a few things out. I'll book a room at Melody´s. Two rooms, I think. You and the kids will need a bit of space to work this through. I'll stay as long as you need, but I don't think we should complicate things too much just yet. Will that be okay?"

I felt as though I could almost reach through the phone line and hug and kiss him.

Chapter 20

We never stood a chance.

It is so easy to see that now.

Back then, I did not know the depths and the reach of the power arrayed against us.

I could not know.

How could I?

All I had known was Ramsey and his wife and the strangeness of that Gray Society.

I knew nothing.

A naif.

I had not even seen Banning.

Had not been touched by the quicksilver that was the forked tongues of the apostles of Ka.

I could not have seen the danger. I need to believe this. Nobody could. If I had, I would have gotten them away so much quicker.

And I was scared and shocked.

Broken in many ways. Broken by my Jimmy. A victim of his need and greed, the bravery sucked out of me, the independence, the ability to react quickly to danger.

I am not the first to whom this has happened, nor will I be the last.

I stayed.

I put them in danger.

I will never forgive myself till the day I die.

#

Guy never came to collect us, and Jimmy never reappeared.

Not that night.

Jimmy was off on a bender, or so the story goes, and did not show up again for two nights.

Guy was a different story.

#

I knew.

Before I heard the truth, I knew.

I woke the kids, made them get dressed, ignored the "Where is Daddy, Mammy?" stuff.

Packed bags and kiddy essentials. Dolls and favourite books and enough to change into for a little while.

Distance.

We had to get some distance. I had to be able to think straight.

I know.

Looking back now.

My infatuation with my therapist, allowing him to enable me to leave, to run away again.

On the face of it, it looks textbook.

Running away again into another man´s (controlling?) arms.

Spin the bottle and play all over again.

Maybe, maybe not.

But there was trauma at play and the forces driving Jimmy at this stage already beyond such hackneyed reasoning.

There was malice afoot, a tornado of shite, and I was caught in its swirl and struggling to get free.

#

Like I said, Guy never showed.

I sent the kids back to bed.

I could still have left.

When I think back now, I cannot understand why I didn't. But I was different then. Still dependent. Still lost.

Everything that had happened had been too much.

So, to my shame, I did nothing.

114

The kids woke late the next morning, a Saturday, and said nothing, did not even ask after Jimmy. His absence was their normality. We sleepwalked through the day, me helping them with their drawings and Lego, sprawled on the floor, trying to keep my inner munch-like scream from tearing their ears and mine apart.

Guy was not answering his phone. Jimmy had left his phone at home.

We were adrift, cut off. And we could have, should have, escaped.

I was such a fucking coward.

Guy was dead, of course, though I did not know it then.

Chapter 21

I am standing staring out the kitchen window when I see Jimmy outside, walking up the lane to the house.

He is wearing a blue Loewe T-shirt and jeans. He is clean-shaven, his eyes are not the usual returning-from-a-binge scarlet, his hair is combed and his skin clear.

He strides up the lane, past the hemlock we had to cut back last year. His arms are swinging and his lips are pursed as though he is singing a song or whistling a tune.

I gape at him.

"No fucking way, Jimmy. Not this time. Not this fucking time."

He stops and stares as if he has seen me through the window.

I know I should at best be a blur as seen by him from without, but it feels like his eyes are a dental drill boring their way into my soul.

Dark, those eyes.

Full of hate and despair.

I feel a sudden cold chill rise over me. My legs grow shaky, and I can feel a hole form beneath me where recently solid earth had stood.

He reaches the front door, takes out his keys, and on his face is a smile. Anybody else might say a normal smile. I know better, and I imagine rushing to the hallway and smashing the door closed in his face, bolting it and calling the police, but I am frozen in place; a courgette raised shoulder high in one hand and a knife in the other, like some perverse riff on Lady Liberty.

I hate myself for my cowardice. I hate myself for my dependence.

I just hate myself sometimes.

He pushes the door open. It squeaks a little like it has done for the last few months, though neither of us has bothered to fetch the wd40 to fix it.

That little parable about sums us up.

"Daddy´s home!" Jimmy bellows.

Without irony, I imagine. Jimmy can be funny, can be quick and cutting, but self-irony is not a particular strength.

Irony that the kids also do not share, and why the hell should they? They run screaming with delight to him, bounce off him, pull at him, their returning king. I can hear relief and happiness in their voices.

I had not told them why their father was away, and we hadn't really discussed what happened the night I woke them, dressed them, and sent them back to bed. I can imagine that they had both been afraid he was gone for good. My silence on the issue cannot have been healthy, but fuck it; I am only human.

He drags them both into the kitchen, Sean wrapped around his legs, Sarah piggybacking his shoulders.

"Honey, Jimmy´s back."

Again, I get no sense of irony in his words, or maybe I am too upset to recognize it for what it is.

I feel my hand tense around the knife in my hand and I find it hard to turn. What is the etiquette in situations such as these?

I have no idea what to do. Guy did not show up, is not answering his phone, has not been seen since Friday according to his secretary, and here comes my fine man, all clean and dandy, after being gone for the weekend. Without a word. Without a call. Again. The last time I heard his voice, he was plotting with Ramsey in our shed.

I imagine I can smell the blood from his hands. Is Guy gone? Driven out of town like in one of those old westerns I used to force myself to watch with Da. Is he hurt? Jesus, dead? What the fuck have Jimmy and his moronic cult gone and done? What am I supposed to do about it, and how the hell am I supposed to live with this man?

"Zoe? Everything okay?"

I force myself to turn around. It feels like I am turning for a half a century, the fear like a powerful stasis, friction keeping me from moving at a normal speed.

But when I finally do raise my eyes to him, there he is.

Not a monster, but a man.

My fine, bold, sexy man with that big goofy grin on his face, the Jimmy special—designed to melt the hearts of lovers and mothers and all of the others. A wide-open, cheeky-boy grin, slightly crooked that says, "Trust me. I've got nothing to hide, and I'll have your back. Though, I might tickle you or throw ice water down your back if you aren't careful, if you are not looking. Just for fun, mind." *Devilment*, as my Gran used to say.

Hair slightly awry, eyes glowing with humour, earnestly wanting to be liked. And I always used to fall for it.

No more.

But he is signaling innocence and that I do not get.

"What's up, love? You not happy I am back?"

A quizzical lift of his right eyebrow.

"What's up?" I can hardly breathe, my fear suddenly a flame thrust of anger. "What the fuck is up? Is that what you just fucking asked me?"

"Zoe! The kids. Take it easy."

"Language, Mama," says a clearly delighted Sarah from her perch on those shoulders above me. Looking down on me with pursed lips, only partially serious, not yet sensing the mood. "Naughty Mama. A Euro for the naughty jar."

Sean cackles in agreement. "Naughty jar, naughty jar."

I toss the courgette and knife onto the cutting board behind me and throw my hands up in the air.

"Whats up?"

"Yeah, what's up?"

"Gone again, Jimmy. You took off without a word, with no way for us to contact you." I can feel the hitch in my voice and feel the rising heat in my cheeks. Anger fighting the frustration and tears, the thought of Guy driven away, perhaps hurt or worse, the fear I felt on seeing my spouse strolling up the driveway, my damned fury at the nerve of this fella to just stand there in front of me playing the innocent, and for all I know with blood on his hands and in his heart.

How dare he ask me what is up?

"Zoe!" A perplexed look on his face, almost wounded. God this man can act. "Zoe." A hand reaching towards me with splayed fingers. "Sure, we talked about it last week."

I shake my head. No! I know what is about to happen, what he is about to do, but I am as helpless to stop it as a child on a motorway with a truck ploughing towards me.

"No!"

"Zoe!"

"No"

"We agreed."

"Bullshit we did."

Squeals of delighted chagrin from the kids.

"I told you I would be gone. School off. Kids with you. Men being boys on their own. You know, the fishing trip? More background for the book."

That smug look of worry on his face. I wish I still had the knife in my hand.

"You were out by the shed with Ramsey."

"We needed the kayaks. Sure, I left you a note on the console. Underneath the vase."

A smug, victorious smile.

And the wind is already gone from my sails. Am I really the fantasist? Is this a dream? A psychotic dream. A nightmare. Brought on by too much or too little medication. Too much booze and not enough love.

The doubt sets in as it always does. Could I be wrong again, mistaken as always? Poor Zoe. Does her best, but you know…

I struggle for the words to put him down, to tear the edifice of his self-serving lies apart, but we have never been equals in this. He could tie knots around me in argument and logic, twist my thoughts and ideas, bend them to his will. And always I struggle and promise to do better. Rhetorically and emotionally. Keep my cool, stab him with the pinprick of reasoned and reasonable argument.

And always I fail.

I begin to flounder—in words and deeds and ideas. Bouncing within his lies like a jelly. Like I am speaking in an unfamiliar, foreign language.

I know what happened, and yet the doubt, the deep insidious rot that is self-doubt, sprouts roots in my head and heart.

Could I really have imagined all that about Guy and Ramsey, have forgotten what we had actually planned?

Could I really be that stupid?

In the past, I might have bought it. There have been days when I did. No longer.

But this is not the time to show that the power of Jimmy is not what it was.

I need to dance clever now.

Be careful.

For my sake and the sake of the kids.

So, I smile, wipe my hands on my apron, lower my eyes, and give the whole apologetic Zoe spiel. Daft bugger forgot again, but sure what can ya do? Heart is the right place and all that.

I do what I have always done. I bend my will to his and pretend it is mine. But this time, for the first time in a long time, I know who I am.

I cannot be fooled any longer.

No more.

This is no longer about love and saving a marriage. I accepted all those compromises and humiliations for the sake of the kids and because I could not see a way out.

I still don't.

But I no longer accept his reality.

I am not what he wants or needs me to be.

There is no saving this marriage, but I can save the kids. I just need to figure out a plan.

#

Why not just take off?

Hit the road, Jack, and never look back.

Yeah right!

To go where?

To do what?

Guess who has control of our bank accounts, guess who bought the house with his own hard-earned money.

"Of course, it is ours, Zoe. The way I see it, this is just easier, see. Cheaper, as well. It'll be fine. Trust me."

Words again.

Words that swamped me with the kind of detail I was never really equipped for. My parents certainly did not encourage me to be self-sufficient, to be an adult about money. School certainly never did. And I wasn't particularly inclined.

Stupid, in retrospect.

But that is 20/20 vision for you.

So, I am broke, and estranged from my not very loving parents. I have some friends back in the big smoke, but nobody I can count on for something as enormous as this.

I am on my own, on my Sweeney Todd. Me and the kids, absent Guy.

The police, I hear, are looking for him, and about time. His car is gone and nobody seems to have seen or heard of him for days.

I hear all kinds of rumours from the gossiping soccer moms at the school gates. Having an affair and forced to flee an irate husband, depressed and lonely, in hock to some paramilitaries whose only revolution these days is beating up other drug dealers and the drugs they bung up their own noses.

The gossip is malicious nonsense, of course.

But I can feel a real sense of frisson in the gossip.

Finally, something worth talking about in this quiet and almost invisible town.

A story, a potentially juicy scandal, and at the base of everything, just a little fear.

This does not happen here.

It just doesn't.

People, adults, with established reputations, a doctor for God's sake, with his own practice. These people do not just disappear. Or run away with some bimbo. There has to be more to the story.

The stories did what stories always do—expand in detail and depth. Until the car is found.

Hidden down a side road out by the corrie lakes in the mountains.

I have been there with Jimmy and the kids. Families, hikers, and joggers park their cars at the layby above the lake. The view from there into the valley below, between two peaks, is mind-blowing. On a summer's day, you can see across the whole rich depth of the valley below to a distant set of ragged peaks. On a winter's day with clouds and fog, you can just about see your nose.

The walk leads down the side of the mountain, an easy hike even for the kids. It meanders a little, a twenty-minute walk at most, cutting through damp fields of heather and gorse. Around one final bend lies the lake, its waters gentling lapping, set in an amphitheater of mountains—like a jewel.

But not a jewel you would buy for those you love.

A deep, non-reflecting onyx, the water in winter like iron, like coal. There is a gentle current, and the water is chill and clean but the depths—an abyss.

Divers have lost their lives down there in the darkness, and the locals avoid swimming in it like the plague.

Both haunted and cursed, they maintain. For deep in its depths is a fairy fort, not inhabited by nice Disney fairies, but beings that curse your cattle and steal your children and leave affliction in their wake.

Old stories, born of a dying world and a fading tradition. But the place still demands respect. If you stand next to its lapping shoreline on stones that have been worn down by the flow of water over millennia, and you hear the wind screeching down the surrounding wall of rock, and you feel the wind in your hair, it is impossible not to feel a chill in your spine.

I hated the place, but Jimmy would insist, especially in summer.

"A nice walk. A swim. Don't be such a ninny, Zoe. The faeries will not bite the kids."

Guy's car is found parked down a dirt track less than two hundred meters from the layby. The police report no traces of violence, but his clothes are found piled neatly on a small stony headland of rocks leaning into the lake on its western shore.

There is no note. No explanation, but a conclusion is quickly reached. The police are not treating the death as suspicious. Unfortunate, yes, a tragedy, of course, but not one that needs any further action. Divers search for the body for two days but few hold any hope that Guy´s body will ever be found.

"Them waters have swallowed up more than just the Doc over the years, I tell ya. And it rarely spits out what it swallows. Dark waters those, Mrs. Hearty."

And that was that. The end of the story.

Suicide.

A middle-aged man living alone, a psychiatrist who snapped under the generic pressure of life and the crises he had to deal with.

You never can tell. You never do know. "Didn't that lovely cooking chap top himself too. A shock. But you can never tell what grows in a person´s mind."

Guy´s parents came from England. There was a nice non-denominational ceremony in the grounds of the Church of Ireland chapel in Deeny forest, on the banks of the Nire. The celebrant was a local humanist who had agreed to hold the ceremony in the church. A pretty redhead, a patient of Guy's, sang an old song, a dirge about falling snow and green shoots of life. Of death and resurrection and we all walked behind the celebrant to the river and sang "The Parting Glass" together, before casting white roses into the fast-flowing river.

> And all I've done for want of wit
> To memory now I can't recall,
> So fill to me the parting glass,
> Good night and joy be to you all.

A sizeable crowd of locals had gathered to show their respects.

The sun was warm on our shoulders. I walked beside my handsome husband, Sarah holding my hand, Sean holding his father´s.

Not a real funeral service, of course, in the absence of a body, but a moment of closure for the parents. I still remember people looking at us, at him, how tall and handsome he looked, how self-possessed. Some of those looks were warm and appreciative, others less so. Looks of jealousy and desire.

Little did they know the heart of the monster that beat inside.

Looking back, I understand why. He was good-looking, but we also looked good together. The outsiders from the Big Smoke with the two adorable kids, the nice house in that great location by the river.

Young and already semi-retired.

A dream life.

Until you live it.

Chapter 22

We get back early evening from the commemoration service, and there the dream ends and the nightmare renews.

I open the door. The kids are bopping around like hungry puppies: bored and restless after the stiff solemnity of church and the ceremony outdoors. Jimmy pushes past me into the house and disappears into his den, as is his want lately. I feed the kids, the three of us making sandwiches and fresh juice in the kitchen. I watch some cartoons with them on Disney+ and then cajole them into getting ready for bed. After a chapter of the Faraway Tree, I kiss them goodnight, and the warmth of their hot skin as I hold their cheeks makes me want to cry.

I can feel the buried tension in them. The unspoken question: "Why is Dad acting so strangely? Is it something we did? Tell us, Mam." I feel their tears, as yet unborn, beginning to well deep in the hollows being carved behind their eyes, hollows born of ill-defined guilt. Is it us? What did we do? Why is Daddy so strange? Are we to blame? Why does he not love us anymore? What did you do to him to make him like this?

Unanswered questions born of fear.

And I was incapable of answering.

What would I say?

"Children, children," ruffling their hair. "Please don't fret, my darlings. Only, I think your beloved father, the man you look up to, might just be a thug, a murderer. Or an accomplice to murder and mayhem. A hanger-on, as it were, to a gang of weirdos who freak me the fuck out, and whose motives are way suspect."

No, that would not do as a nighttime tale and pep talk. It would not do at all.

125

When I leave their room, tonight as every night since Jimmy got back, I shudder in the dark of the hallway.

In darkness, but for moonlight from the ceiling windows and the window on the southwest wall, I feel alone. Estranged and in my home.

A place that is no longer mine, or perhaps never was.

In this silence and darkness, I feel like bushmen must have felt under the stars in Africa over thousands of years—the emptiness of the desert all around me, the sound of the wind, and the distant howl of predators. The utter loneliness of it all. Except the bushman had the skills to navigate his environment, and I do not.

This strange world I find myself in is a mystery and a puzzle. A deadly puzzle, one I am not equipped to solve.

I feel like one of those disposable side characters you meet in disaster movies. The pretty, yet innocuous blonde, a little plain and always in the background, who gets squashed, mauled, or eaten first.

You know what I mean.

And that is what my house feels like.

A dark place in the day after the disaster.

Since last weekend, I never see him at night anymore. He goes to work in the morning, comes back in the evening or late at night. If he does deign to show up, hours after the school closes and the kids are home, he is sullen and withdrawn. Mostly he locks himself in his den. Sometimes when I look at him, carefully, for I do not trust his temper, he seems nothing less than a stranger. Somebody who is not the person I married.

Tuesday, late it was I think, he was walking past me from the kitchen back to his den, a sandwich on a plate in one hand and a glass of milk in the other, and I glanced up at him. His eyes were dark for the light in the hall was not on, and his lips were downturned.

But, and this is what struck me with cold terror for one long moment, he did not look himself. I know, I know. It is a phrase and it is lightly used, but here I mean it as a literal fact. He looked like a different version of himself. Older. Worn.

But that is still not everything, not enough at least. He was like a copy of himself, his own non-identical brother. He seemed thin, his shoulders sloped forward, his nose longer, almost beak-like. He looked avian and dangerous in a way I had never seen before.

The word 'vulture' came to mind.

My skin crawled and something in my brain, some part way deep near the cerebellum, had me almost gagging, almost running.

Something about this new Jimmy freaks me out.

Anyway, this home no longer seems so much like a castle. More like a freaking dungeon with Frankenstein's monster, or whatever it is that Jimmy is becoming, wandering the creaky halls below.

I know. I know.

Drama, Zoe. Don't gild the lily. Enough already.

We get the message.

No! No, you don't.

The changes are real, not the by-product of a fevered imagination.

Real and happening to me in real-time, but so slowly I have barely noticed. In that way we never notice until one day you look at your relative, a younger cousin perhaps you see every day in school, and blink and ask yourself, "When did he get taller than me?"

That kind of gradual yet abrupt change.

A new and alien Jimmy being born in front of my eyes.

#

I tiptoe down the stairs after turning on the low lights. The last thing on earth I want now is to wake the sleeping monster.

Let him do his thing and I'll do mine.

So, I go tiptoeing into the kitchen and back into the pantry. I reach past the pastas and over to the right behind the sodas.

Aha!

A still half full (half empty, if you like, but I am not that kind of girl) bottle of Penfolds. Australian, I believe dear people. Cabernet Shiraz, no less.

A smooth, medium-bodied red wine accentuated by ripe cherry and plum notes, black pepper aromas, and soft, silky tannins. A food-friendly wine, also great to drink on its own.

Well, I sure as hell do intend to drink it on my own, by its own. And the next bottle on the shelf too, if I still cannot sleep.

I retire to the drawing room, my dears, and pull the curtains and put on a Spotify list, full of lovely songs I used to sing when I was young and buff and full of cum, as Jimmy was wont to say.

When we were in love and together.

And I cry.

Not wail.

Not whine.

Just tears. Rolling down my face.

For Guy.

For lost possibilities.

For time lost.

Mistakes made.

For Jimmy as he then was, or as I imagined him to be (not the fucker he now is).

For me.

For me and the children and this half-life we are forced to lead in the shadow of the ogre.

And then I hear the sound of a door opening.

The ogre, the vulture, that creature of darkness I have created, is on the move.

Do I run or do I hide?

#

I freeze.

The sound of his steps stomping towards me. Somehow wrong.

Like he is marching to war on poorly shodden feet. Hard-stepping, but also a sound like dragging.

Like he cannot perfect his goosestep.

He slams open the door so the handle bangs on the wall and stares at me from the darkness surrounding him in the hallway.

I drop the glass of wine I am holding and it falls to the ground, probably staining the Persian carpet beneath the mahogany table. It bounces and smashes into hundreds of tiny pieces.

Jimmy is standing there, a dark form against the darkness, barely lit by the table lamp to my right. I feel him staring at me, though I cannot see his eyes. I sense as much as see him rubbing his forehead with the knuckles of his right hand.

"Jimmy?" My voice catches in fear, I can barely think, move.

Rooted in terror. A trite phrase until you experience it. I am trapped by his louring presence, by the almost physical roots of the terror which have wrapped themselves around me and are binding me to the sofa. I feel like I might be swallowed whole and sucked into the earth beneath the house.

"The music is too loud."

His voice. It is gruff and thin at the same time, as though piped through some sort of ancient wooden instrument in a museum.

Discordant to my ears at least and not much the Jimmy voice I know.

"It is too fucking loud."

I scramble for the remote.

"I've got it, Jimmy. I'll turn it down."

My voice seems hollow, my hands are clumsy. I feel my bladder loosen and my hands tremble.

"Make it stop."

His voice is quieter now, a piping hiss, and that is even worse.

"I grab the tiny remote, but my hands are shaking so much it slips out of my sweaty hand onto the sofa and lands between two cushions where it disappears.

I watch it go, in disbelief.

Everything is so out of kilter, so strange. Time and movement, and again even gravity itself, are different.

The remote disappears into the space between the pillows as it has so often before. Seeking the dark places down there it seems to be eternally attracted to.

I have made love on this sofa listening to this music. Jimmy and I. Him taking me from behind as often as not, and that remote has always managed to disappear.

Sex with Jimmy. A distant, sad memory.

I can feel him moving towards me, though I keep my eyes focused on the gap where the remote disappeared. I do not want to look up. To see him.

"Make it stop."

"Shit!"

"I've got it, Jimmy. Chill your bases, would you?" I reach into the gap, my fingers touching the cool metal of the remote. All the time I feel Jimmy's presence in the room, moving closer.

I hold it aloft like a magic wand, point it at the box on the table, and zap. The little pixies within turn the music off.

"Happy, now, Jimmy? Bad music be gone." My hands are no longer shaking. I am feeling a little more myself, and yet I still keep my eyes averted.

I do not know how or why, but I knew, even back then, that to look up was to falter. To be cursed.

If I looked at Jimmy, I might never look away again. I could be frozen in place. Turned into stone.

So, I keep my eyes on the magic remote in my reasonably steady hand and wait for him to leave.

He moans again. A moan of pain and discomfort.

Shit, I think.

And then my blood freezes.

"Make it stop."

He is closer now. I can feel his shadow over me, the volume of his weight. A louring presence. He moans again and the pain in his voice causes me to wince.

"Make it stop. Make it stop."

And I know then that I am in trouble, for his voice is strained and high-pitched, like nothing I have ever heard come from Jimmy's mouth before, like nothing I have ever heard from a human mouth before.

#

I keep my eyes down and try to push backwards and sidewards on the sofa.

"Soft now, Jimmy. Soft."

My voice sounds desperate, but then why wouldn't it?

I feel him edge closer.

Another high-pitched moan and then something like a scream, only quiet.

A quiet scream but one dug up from the depths of his body.

There is that comedian on telly who does the little man in a box voice. It sounds like that. Like a scream from deep within which is drowned out before it reaches the surface.

It sounds fucking unnatural is what it does.

I start to push forward, ready to bolt out of there.

Whatever the hell is wrong with my once beloved and now incredibly strange husband is no longer any of my business.

Get the kids. Get the car keys and get the hell out of here.

"Make it stop, you witch."

Shit!

That is not good.

Anger now in that voice. I make to get to my feet but feel his hand on my shoulder. Hot hands, literally burning, as if a fever is raging within him.

In trying to move, I can not help but look up.

His other hand is still rubbing his forehead with his knuckles, there are tears flowing down his cheeks, his nose still has that thin, avian cast. But it is the eyes that turn my legs to lead.

Colder and deader than ever before.

I imagine for a moment I feel something move behind them, a soft blink, but then they are shuttered. Pale as ash and twice as dull.

A smile creeps onto his face.

"You did not make it stop, whore." The smile is grotesque—Heath Ledger doing the Joker. He leans in over me, pushing me back. His face is close to mine now and I can feel the carrion stink that is his breath, as though he had fine-dined on rotting meat in the last few hours.

I move my head, one hand trying to push myself to my feet, the other trying to shift his hand from my shoulder. I try to pull it away and he shoves me back, hard, into the sofa and kneels so he is straddling me.

I turn my face away from him, from his stink and his weirdness.

"Bitch. You deny us. Deny the people of the stars. The chosen ones."

His hand shoots out and grabs me by the throat. He is leaning over me, eyes obsidian and cruel as he squeezes.

I struggle, my hands tearing at his wrists, trying to pull his hands away.

Dark eyes. Ageless. Ancient but not wise. Cruel.

I feel my eyes close as I gasp for breath as my body struggles against him, bucking and shoving.

He is too strong. Too much. Too heavy.

And then I am no longer there.

#

The room is pitch black when I come to.

I gasp and cough, and when I try to breathe, there is nothing but a rasping sigh and a harsh flame in my throat.

I cough again and the flame is burning coal.

Disoriented. Afraid. I can feel blood on my lips and dampness beneath me.

Have I wet myself?

I stink and it is the stink of piss and terror and despair.

What the hell just happened?

It takes me some long moments to remember, and even then, I am not sure.

Could I really be lying here because my partner brutally assaulted me? My husband. Father of my kids.

Is this my life?

I push myself to my feet and stumble—still gasping flame from a painful throat—to the bathroom. A wave of greasy queasiness scythes through me and I have to swallow the hot bile to keep from puking.

In the mirror, my right eye is blood red and there are red dots like popped blood vessels in a string of beads across my face. Red weals ring both sides of my throat. I can barely breathe. Jimmy strangled me. He might have tried to kill me. I have to believe he tried to kill me.

I blink shame-fueled tears from my eyes. One part of me still wants to deny, to hide, to tell myself that this has to be a dream born of my fevered mind and the red wine. I know it is not.

Jimmy was crazy or possessed or whatever. Screw that: Jimmy *is* crazy, possessed and whatever.

I have to get out of here. I do not even know why I am still alive. My hands are shaking like I am just coming off a bender. My guts are roiling and I have trouble swallowing. Why did he not finish what he started? It doesn't matter. Not now. If he didn't finish me this time, there is no reason for me to believe that he won't next time.

I have to get out of here.

So how?

Jesus Zoe, get your thinking hat on.

Jimmy is still in the house, I have to guess. Is he still on the warpath? Who knows?

The kids. Jesus.

No!

I run out of the bathroom and up the stairs, two at a time. Jesus wept. Please God, no.

He can't have.

He wouldn't.

Despite the pain of my bedraggled body, I fly up those stairs like Superwoman on steroids.

I make it to the hallway. Silent, dark. The same strangeness I had felt earlier. The same sense of disconnection.

But the kids are here, and they need me to protect them. To save them, if I still can.

The door to their room is still closed. It looks safe to me. A portal to a place of safety. They must be okay. They must.

I push open the door and smell them: the night sweats of young children, their sweet breathing humidifying the air. I take a deep (painful) sigh of relief.

Okay.

Jimmy the monster has not been to visit them. Not yet.

#

I sit on the side of Sean's bed, inhaling my children's sleeping nighttime smells like a soothing balm.

I need to think. To plan. Get the kids out of bed. Get gone, finally.

Will that work?

I don't know.

The same issues remain. Where do we go? Where will I get money? And how will we survive alone in the future?

But this is not the same as before. Our situation now is desperate. All in capital letters.

He could have killed me. Perhaps he thinks he did. The kids were at his mercy. He would not have been the first narcissist to want to "assist" his family in ending their lives before ending his own.

And when I think about it for a moment, I realise that he ticks so many boxes: his fragile ego, his failure, at least as seen according to his own lights, his lack of real empathy, his violent tendencies.

You see them so often on the telly. Those monsters who should be protectors who murder because they are weak and self-obsessed.

I can imagine you are looking at me now, faces aghast and disbelieving. Considering everything I am accused of. It is not the same. It isn't. Wait and see.

Okay, Zoe, I remember thinking, trying to calm myself. This house, this home—it has become something like a mausoleum to our dreams and it is only the kids that have been keeping those dreams alive. Fine. The life we had is over, time to start anew, far away from my deranged husband.

Get out of here then and do not consider the costs or consequences. Mom and Dad, like it or not, here we come.

The kids must sense something in my hushed voice when I shake them awake. My fear perhaps. They cannot help but see the state of my face. Sarah stares at me with big eyes as I grab a large camping rucksack and once again stuff her clothes, a few books, and her cuddly toys into them. No time for considered packing. God knows where Jimmy is or when he will come looking for me, for the kids. God knows what he might do then. Sean rubs his eyes as I pack for him. He opens his mouth, his pink tongue between his lips as if considering what to say. He closes it again without saying anything and wraps his arms around me. His face is sleep dewed and bewildered.

I hug him back and then do one last station of the room.

Fine.

Packed.

Can't afford to take more. Sarah has gotten dressed. I don't even bother with Sean. I throw a sleeping blanket from the bed over him and lift him. Sarah grabs one of the handles of the rucksack and I lift Sean into my arms. He wraps his arms around me and leans against me as we make our way side-by-side down the stairs.

I remember the surprising weightlessness of that moment, a loss of tension, the steam escaping from the pressure cooker.

Relief.

A way forward.

Something like movement. Hope.

Dashed less than a minute later.

Jimmy is in the hallway near the front door, facing the wall. On the commode in front of him is a framed picture of the four of us that had fallen to the ground a long time ago. We had been talking for ages about getting the glass repaired. Jimmy has a hammer in his right hand and is suckling a long nail in his mouth.

He turns when he hears us and stands there, one hand on his hip the other holding the hammer down by his side, tapping against his leg.

He spits the nail sideways onto the repaired glass of the picture.

"Going somewhere?"

He raises his right eyebrow.

The hair on the back of my neck rises. I picture those hands around my throat again and I gasp and a rasping, burning cough follows.

Sarah has stopped and is looking between us, her eyes wide and round.

She feels the charge between us. More sulphuric than electric.

"Just taking the kids for a spin."

"Bags packed and all?"

"I thought we might visit Gran and Granny for a day or two."

"Did you now? Did you indeed?"

"I did, Jimmy. Kids haven't seen them in a long time, you know."

"I do, Zoe, love. I do know. But that is on them, isn't it? Isn't that really on them? Not really a reason to leave in the middle of the night, I would have thought?"

Not a question and though his tone is reasonable, quiet even, I can feel the edge behind the words. He starts tapping the hammer harder against his thigh, an almost rhythmic sound, that grows steadily louder, at least to my ears.

135

I stare at it. The hand. The hammer. The noise he is making that sounds both like a clock tolling and the sound of violence. Metal beating flesh.

A warning.

A foreshadowing.

"You know what, I really don't think you should go. It is late. Tired driving, and all that. And you had some wine earlier, no? We can talk about visiting the kid's grandparents tomorrow. Wouldn't that be better, guys? Safer and easier on everybody?"

Ta-thump- Ta-thump.

I say nothing. My mouth is dry, my tongue rasps like desert sands. I want to speak, but can't.

Ta-thump- Ta-thump.

Louder, almost a shout.

"Don't you think?"

Startled, Sean starts sobbing quietly into my t-shirt. Sarah is staring down at the ground.

"It will only be for a few nights, Jimmy. Only a short while."

The sound grows louder and beats in my already damaged skull like a gong in a bell.

Ta-thump. Ta-thump.

Like the beating of my heart, like the passing of time, like the last moments before death.

He moves towards us and I start to edge backwards. He is close enough for me to see his eyes. What I see there almost makes me crumble with white panic—a wave of coldness sweeping my body and setting my skin into clammy goosebumps.

His eyes are lit by the ceiling light. Around his dark pupils, those cold dead things that had tried to murder me earlier is something new, a frame of yellow dots, like a rectangular chain of lights, tiny flickering lights.

A frame of lights that do not belong in human eyes, a frame of lights within which I can see Sean and myself as dim reflections.

I knew then that was no longer Jimmy. That nothing of the man I had known, for better or worse, remained. I did not know what that meant, or what it could possibly signify. How the hell could Jimmy not be Jimmy? All I knew was terror—not for me and my life, but for the children.

I look around for something I can use against the blows I know will come. A shield. A weapon. I drop the packed bag and pull Sarah backward, pushing her behind me.

Nothing I can use. No weapon. Nothing of any use to protect us or stop Jimmy.

I expect us to end. Here and now. The pain of that, the knowledge that I have failed to protect the children is a knife that makes me sigh in pain.

The kids are both sobbing, aware of the ill-defined threat that pulses between us.

Then Jimmy stops advancing. He stops and cocks his head to one side, like a dog listening to a signal only it can hear.

And for long, long moments he does nothing. Just stands there frozen.

And then he leans forward, his body arched forward, his nose long and thin, his eyes agleam with those yellow lights.

"Okay!"

I breathe, for the first time in what feels like minutes.

He straightens and smiles, and he looks like Jimmy again.

"Okay, Guys. What do you say Sean? Sarah? Time for a little holiday? A road trip to Gran and Granda?"

"Jimmy?"

He smiles at me then, an almost Jimmy smile, all the scarier because it comes from a Jimmy who was so different just a moment ago.

"We'll all go." He reaches out a hand and rubs Sean's head. I pull back, I can't help it. The abrasion around my neck begins to throb again. I begin to panic. If he comes with us, we'll never get away, be rid of him. Never.

"No need, Jimmy." I try to smile, but I know the smile is at best a grimace. The smile of one who has been paralysed with fear.

A frozen landscape.

And yet my heart is playing death metal drums and my hands are damp with sweat. Jimmy leans forward. Not far. No more than a few inches. He is so close now, louring over me. I look up into his strange eyes and edge backward, trying to keep Sean from wriggling free, more aware than ever of that fucking hammer in his hand.

Think, Zoe.

Think hard.

We cannot have him with us.

"It is alright, Jimmy. Really. We'll only be gone for a few days, and I already told them we were going alone. Without you."

He pauses. Head cocked to the left as if listening to instructions, like some ham actor with a microphone in his ear. That or a news anchor.

Seconds pass.

"Sure, they won't mind, Zoe, love. It's been a while."

That hammer, tapping off his thigh.

Metal on flesh.

"No! Jimmy." I hold up my free hand, palm out as a shield. Mother's love. "Jimmy, love. I have to do this now. You have to let us go. Just a few days. Just a little time out. I can't let you come. I just can't."

And there it is. The truth and nothing less. I do not trust him one whit. I am scared shitless and I am leaving. My leg is trembling, I need to piss and my stomach is a twisted knot of roiling ropes. I just hope that there is enough of the old Jimmy left in him to let us pass unharmed. To not explode with violent rejection.

A long pause. I risk a look in his eyes. Those faint yellow lights in the ring around his iris are glowing, spinning slowly, like a big wheel seen in distant rain in a city at night.

I close my eyes and look away, for there is only madness there. For me. For him. For the kids.

A long pause.

"You could leave the kids here? I'd follow tomorrow. Give you a chance to sort things with your folks."

"No, Jimmy." A long, strangled sigh escapes me.

Oh, Christ.

"Jimmy!" Tears well in my eyes and start down my cheeks in great fat rivers. I hate myself for this. This lack of strength. My inabilityty to out-talk or out-think this man.

I am like frozen Jello, and the kids need much more than that.

"No!" Now I am being loud. And it feels good.

"Excuse me!"

Tap, tap, tap goes the hammer.

Tap, tap, tap.

"I said no, Jimmy." I wipe my hand across my face. It comes away damp, but those traitor tears are gone.

"No. I can't trust you alone with them now. You have to let us go. You have to."

"Or what?" A grin on his face both amused and brutal. "Or what, Zoe?"

"You'll have to stop me. Put me down and keep me down." I am almost spitting in my frenzy. "And I will not go without a fight."

I realise the truth of this as the words leave me. Terrified? Of course, I bloody am. But I will fight tooth and nail if he tries anything, hammer or no. Literally tooth and nail and hand and heart. "I will bite your fucking nose off if you come any closer. I will hurt you and bad before I let you touch these kids."

A snarl in a voice I hardly recognise as my own.

Jimmy shakes his head, rubs his forehead with the knuckles of his free hand as if in disbelief.

"I am taking the kids, Jimmy. They are coming with me. No ifs and buts about it. Do you hear me?" Sean is still howling on my chest and I can feel Sarah's quiet sobs. The fear in them.

A long silence, his head cocked to one side, listening to the radio messages in his head only he can hear. I hold my breath as if underwater.

"Okay."

I sigh.

"Go then. Take them." He moves to the side. I suck air into my empty lungs.

"I'll be in touch, Jimmy. I swear. If not tomorrow, the next day. To hash this out. To come to an arrangement."

A laugh.

"To hash it out. That's good, Zoe. We'll do that. Hash things out."

Another laugh, harsher.

"Get the fuck out then, you bitch. Go!"

"Sarah, love. Grab the bag with me."

I feel rather than see Sarah's hesitation, caught between the two lodestones of her life. How to choose? Not the time for that, I am afraid.

"Sarah!" My voice too loud and Sean starts howling even louder. "Sarah! Take the handle now."

And she does. Blessedly, she does. And Jimmy waves an ironic hand at the door. Our gracious lord letting us leave. As we pass by him, as I am forced on the way down the hall to turn my back on him, the fear returns.

Almost concrete in its expectation.

A hammer thudding against my head, bone cracking as I sink to my knees and he is standing above me his arms raised for one more devastating blow, and the last thing I see are the kids and their fear knowing, fearing, they will be next.

But then I am at the door. I turn the knob and pull it open. Jimmy, as far as I can tell, still hasn't moved, and I have no intention of looking to see where he is. I usher Sarah through the door into a mild and soothing breeze. An owl hoots in the distance and the sound of a car driving too fast echos along the mountain roads.

Out, get out.

Almost there.

For a moment, I think I have forgotten the keys, but I feel them stabbing into the palm of my hand. I have made a balled fist.

I grabbed them from the console in the hallway on the way past. I shuffle with Sean, sobbing rather than bawling now, and Sarah to the car. Press the dongle. Get the kids settled in the back. Toss the luggage into the boot. All done with my back to the house and the still open door and Jimmy.

Things I have done a million times that seem to elongate with both time and importance.

Some sort of black hole I am wading through.

In the car.

Finally.

Foot on the brake, press the button. Another moment of fear before the engine growls its continued existence. Hand on gear. Car in reverse. Press the accelerator.

Almost there, Zoe. Almost there.

Gear into drive.

Forcing myself forward. One step at a time. One action at a time. Every single step one more on our path to a new life. One without fear.

And the car is turned and we are ready. Only then do I glance back at the house. Jimmy is in the doorway, silhouetted by the light from within. He is speaking on a cellphone and I swear I can feel his eyes on me, and worse, much worse, a smile on his face.

I press the accelerator and drive out and into freedom.

Chapter 23

Freedom.

A new life.

For a short time, it almost seems in range.

Almost.

We have music streaming. Some oldies stuff the kids like because we used to bleat it out loud and proud when we were on our occasional road trips. The kids are singing along, though I can tell their hearts are not really in it.

The road is almost empty, still far from civilization and the motorways, but further every minute from my man Jimmy.

My ex-man.

The past. A forgotten place. Not yet, perhaps, but soon.

For the first time in a long time, I feel light. Free. Unshackled.

I can make it work, first with my parents, as uptight as they are, and then with the rest of our lives. Reset, rebuild, keep the Jimmy fellow at a great distance and move on from his poison; and from whatever the hell else has gotten hold of him recently.

Free as a bird, or at least a low-flying bird, driving half a tonne of steel, plastic and aluminum.

Until the light appears.

The shadow light.

I sense it first in the distance, a vague glow in my rearview. I look away. No! Not now! Please!

I glance at the kids in the back. Quiet now, dozing. Sarah´s head turned away from me, Sean in his baby seat, his mouth open in a little bow.

I avoid the mirror until I no longer can. The glow is stronger, like a perverse sunrise on this deserted stretch of road in the middle of nowhere, in the middle of the night.

I can out-drive it, I think. We did, Jimmy did, the last time.

I shake my head as my heart sinks and the tears well again.

We never did. Jimmy did not.

Whatever he once was, however imperfect, that is not the man I just left.

We never did.

I do not need to look in the mirror again, for the night is growing brighter, though that too is wrong. The hue is changing. What was once clean and dark and pure and earthly is tainted.

Light from a zombie's dream, gray, and yet not, for it casts no real light. More like a taint on darkness. My breath fogs the window above the dashboard, and I feel the kids stir uneasily in the back. I press the accelerator. I have to.

I glance in the rearview again. A car behind us, still distant. Moving fast. Swallowed by a bend and then visible. Lights on high.

Shit.

I press on the gas, aware that I am no longer fully in control of this beast. Not at this speed, in the dark, on these roads.

Maybe. Just maybe, I am panicking for no reason.

I breathe deeply, sucking air into my lungs as I relax a little on the pedal, focusing on the bends in the road ahead.

It'll be nothing.

A car on its way some place, just like us.

The gray light, a phantasm of my fevered imagination and my almost fractured body.

I risk a glance.

A few hundred meters behind us on a straight stretch of road and the high lights still on, catching up fast. It can't be Jimmy in the little Toyota, too much power, but those lights, that driving; I cannot mistake that for anything but aggression.

And all the while I feel the cold of that gray light, that non-light, seep into my pores. A deep chill like standing in an industrial

143

refrigerator after the door has closed and the ambient heat has gone. A deep freeze.

My breath is fogging the windows so much I can barely see, and the car behind us, closer now, so much closer, starts honking and doesn't stop.

One loud shrill blares into the night.

The kids wake up.

Sean starts to cry.

I steal a glance at Sarah. She has her brave face on, but her hands are twisting the blanket on her lap into tight knots.

That sound—driving a nail into my already fragile brain.

Tonight. It is still tonight. It has been too much.

Too much.

I almost died.

I almost escaped.

Too much.

My mind drifts.

It drifted. I know it did. I caused the crash.

I can't explain why, even today. Could I make excuses? Perhaps. I had been strangled and the pain was still not dealt with, never mind the horror of the event itself. I had been in a toxic relationship fraught with violence. I had lost a friend.

Those high lights. Blinding. The ooze of gray filth that is the light. The deep chill that surrounds us. That blaring shrill sound from the car tail-gaiting me.

I risk one final glance in the mirror. I imagine I see Ramsey leaning over the driving wheel, one hand pressed at an angle with his elbow up against the horn. A wide evil grin on his face like the smile of a shark as it bears down on you.

And then we were gone. I was. The car was.

That cold contraction deep in my groin, that wave of fear like a tsunami.

I am no longer in control.

The car is its own master, and a violent one at that.

I hold tight to the wheel. Fight it. To gather hold of it, to set us back on a safe course.

And then there is nothing, or almost nothing. A feeling of moving too fast. My body being tossed, forces pressing against me and me resisting until I no longer can. That shit-awful feeling of falling, of careening and out of control, as we spin off the road and down into trees.

A drop. A headlong rush.

Dark monsters that mean death are all around us. Trees in daylight. Beautiful and uplifting. Deadly now.

We are plunging headlong.

Too fast.

I remember scoping the tree, a thick oak, knowing we could not avoid it. One tiny second. A millisecond only.

A moment etched like diamond scraped on glass in my brain.

The violent thrust of my body out of all control as we crash into it.

And nothing, as the dark returns.

Part 2
Avenging Angel

Chapter 24

Awareness is a subjective thing.

I read that once. A series of moments we knot together into a cohesive whole, all the while telling each other lies. One moment after another, unconnected and random, seen and processed by yon beast on two feet trying to make sense of who she is in this empty, vast, and unholy place.

This cold universe bleeding into inevitable darkness.

A series of photos we turn into a moving video, a story we pretend takes the sting out of everything we do not understand.

It breaks.

The movie.

It is fragile as we all are.

Perhaps more fragile than we know.

And what happens when it shatters?

#

I wake in darkness.

For a long moment, I do not know who I am. I am cold and in a frenzy of pain and heat all at once. My head is a mess of pain. I can feel and smell blood all around me.

I lie like that, face in the dirt for a long moment, trying to piece together what happened.

Our car careening.

The white lights.

The car tailgating us.

The kids.

The kids.

A sudden rush of adrenalin sweeps through me. I lift my head, tasting blood on my lips and my tongue. My left hand pierces me with a rod of driven pain, a spike into my chest and I almost collapse again.

No!

The children, woman-child. Find them.

I stagger to my feet, breathing hard.

I remember the gasping pain that I had breathing after the strangulation. That is still there, worsened. My hand. A tightness stabbing my lungs, so my breath is little more than a wheeze. My left leg, tender and painful as I try to stand and worse again when I put one foot forward.

Dark here, wherever here is. Trees all around, blocking out the stars above.

Faint moonlight seeps through the canopy. Vague and subtle, like the devil, like a lie about light. Enough though for me to know that I am no longer in the car.

That the car is nowhere in sight.

How can that be?

I was driving. I know I was, the kids in the back strapped down. Me too. I am religious about wearing that damned belt, and yet here I am in the middle of nothing with no sign of the car, the kids.

Whisper it: we crashed.

My heart pounds at the thought but not with pain.

No, sir.

Whatever braises, bruises, and breaks my old body has suffered tonight that is nothing next to the thought of losing the kids.

Sarah. Sean.

I need to get to them.

Broken.

Not only my body.

My train of thought. My memories.

Car. Blinding light. A loss of control.

Nothing. Emptiness. A hole where I know there should be something but is nothing.

A concussion most likely, but I experience it as a tear in my reality—as though I am a piece of paper torn in two—there is the me before, and then the me after, and a great, gaping hole between.

Was I thrown?

I scan the area around, twisting painfully.

No sign of a car, and surely I could not miss that, even in this gloom. No smell of burning—God forbid—or metal or petrol.

No sense of anything except trees and leaves and the things that move at night.

A howl far away, a banshee cry, a wild cat in heat. The sound of wind rustling through trees.

I feel nothing here of man, except me.

And so, I start off, pain dragging on my steps, one—and only one—thought in my head.

Find them.

Find them.

Find your children.

#

Hours of pain.

My body wracked and feverish.

Moving without aim, and lately without hope, barely able to remember my name.

Zoe.

Sarah.

Sean.

In the moments of clarity when I can still think and move, I imagine I am traveling in circles, lost in the cold wastelands of a Viking Hel.

And then I hear a voice.

A man's voice. "Over here." A long pause. "Over here, Zoe. Don't be afraid. This way. This way."

A voice with a northern inflection.

His voice.

My new companion.

My savior, if you wish, my guru; though I did not know that then.

At first, I think of hiding—what if it is Ramsey or Jimmy?—but the pain is unbearable and my throat is almost closed to the point of being painful to breathe. The pain in my chest means each breath is an intense stab. My only thought is to find the kids, and I know I will not be able do that alone. Anyway, I knew from the timbre of that voice, it cannot possibly be Jimmy nor Ramsey—those deeply macho men-children.

This was something different, something new.

I try to call out.

"Help!"

But that is beyond me.

Like a twig floating downstream, insentient to all intents and purposes, I follow the sound of his voice, leading me out of the maze that is this cursed forest.

Leading me with the strewn crumbs of his voice to life again.

I wish I had stayed where I was. It would have been easier. The burden should not have been mine alone.

Chapter 25

The car.

I see it now in a clearing in faint moonlight. Almost agleam. Unreal. Unnatural, as if painted there: broken car in the moonlight by Zoe Hearty. A deeply cynical work, by the way.

The car had smashed into a bent old pine. I glance up to where we must have come off the road. An incline leading north to a flat emptiness between two rows of trees offset against one another. The bonnet is smashed into a bow, but there is no steam or sense of heat. All the energy that had once been spent in this place is gone. Evaporated. You know the feeling. It´s like visiting a deserted house.

"Cold as a grave," I think, as a wrench of fear worse than all the physical trauma slides through me.

The kids?

He is near the bonnet, staring in my direction.

As I stare at him, he reaches into a pocket of his long trench coat, pulls out a zippo, flicks it, and lights a cigarette. He stands there, broad-chested, overweight, pulling on his smoke like some noir detective from back in the day.

"They are gone, Zoe. Not dead. Gone. Trust me on this."

He holds his free hand out as if to reassure me.

The words take some time to sink in, the meaning. It is like trying to interpret a foreign language. And when they do, I sink to my knees. The world shrinks, an enveloping wave of darkness smothering me. Shrinking and pressing down on me until nothing but a dot of light remains, like in one of those old cathode ray tubes, and then even that is gone.

#

I remember very little of the following weeks. Leary told me afterward that I was fevered, raving most of the time.

A fucking space cadet on a whale of a bastarding mission in interstellar space, to use his exact words.

That's Leary for you.

Why swear once when you can fit two into a fucking sentence, and yet he is not totally uncouth, not without a certain turn of phrase and flight of fancy.

Typical jaded copper with his heart battered and bruised and yet still somehow intact, still capable of empathy for the right causes, for the dead and the battered and the put upon. For those who have been beaten and broken. For the unwilling dead he still dreams about, calling to him for release from their pain and humiliation.

And in this we were soulmates; we were both dream haunted.

My dreams in those weeks were bright with fear.

Of being chased by monsters with long bodies and gray skin and long pincers for hands. I ran alone through darkness, forests full of skeletal trees, devoid of leaves; their branches hands of despair reaching out to me. Monsters with Jimmy's eyes. Clever fast monsters flitting between trees in a primeval forest, their voices inhuman—screeches like cats in heat or cicadas clicking and buzzing as they locked in on me.

Monsters whose sounds, despite their strangeness, reminded me of Jimmy's voice.

Running and running and running away from the monsters, towards my children.

In a forest full of witches and demons I call out to them as I run. It does me no good. Their voices are lost to me, and mine is drowned out by the screeching and the clacking that are the Jimmy monsters chasing me. In another dream, they are in a cottage in the woods being fattened by a witch, the witch is a bitch with the face of Ramsey. I still remember their hopeful faces looking up at the sky as the Ramsey witch sings in the kitchen, and I know they are there, waiting for me, hoping, praying, crying. Trying to persuade themselves that I will save them. They believe this. They do. What choice do they have? They have to. They love and trust me. Until the moment when they are fat enough and Ramsey drags Sarah from her cell in the dark pantry and ties her with metal chains to the stake over the fire and slits her throat with a butcher's knife, all the while whistling to the tune playing on his Spotify stream in the background.

Also Spoke Zarathustra. And afterward; *The Blue Danube,* all to the sobs and screams of my beautiful young boy in his metal cage, mourning his sister and frightened beyond sanity. The smell of the abused flesh of my oldest daughter fills the room as she cooks on those devil's flames.

Normal dreams you can wake from.

You wake startled, heart pounding in the depths of the night, the sweat pouring from every pore. But you wake and you lie awake and you rationalise and your heart starts to slow.

Until you are back in this world.

Until sanity returns.

Or the world makes sense again.

For me, it never did.

I don't think I have ever really awoken from the horror of that night and the portent of those dreams.

#

He told me how close I had come to dying. Worse. Of being lost forever.

He told me everything.

He showed me my enemies.

Those lost gray souls. Those betrayers of this world. Race traitors, I think the fascists would say, but it wasn't so simple. Back in college and ever since, I have loathed those racist shits. The smug and the broken. The last vestiges of the "White Man's Burden." Mostly stupid, but always grasping and needy. The obvious kind and then later the subtle kind. Those pretenders in their white preppy clothes with houses in the suburbs and a subtle but definable message. I am more. Privileged. Who I am is better. I always have been. Can't help it. I was born to it.

You know what I mean. Not the guy with the shaved head and tattoos. That rowdy we can all hate and ignore. Not him, but the blond you meet in Ikea, whose daughter is in your daughter's class.

I am soo not racist but... If we can do it, lift ourselves up from the dirt, why can't they? And slavery, it's all so yesterday. The Irish were once black too.

You know what I mean. You have met them too, been there when they spew their bile at some party, babbling away, lost in their own self-love.

That was not me. I swear. I was never racist in that way. Neither actively nor passively. Live and let live, say I. Usually.

But what then would you call Ramsey? Adele? The others in the society? To betray not your nation, your race, but your kind, your soul, to renounce who you are, to give yourself away, or to be given, taken, and to welcome it. To hold humanity up to a mirror, find it wanting and say we should become something else. To give yourself to an alien force. To allow yourself to metamorphose, I suppose, though there is truly no human term. To be subsumed. Overpowered. Overcome. As if we were cocoons waiting for a new being, a being not ourselves. A being neither alien nor fully human like Jimmy had become.

To sell the world to the highest (or only) other bidder.

But I get away from myself. I'll explain that later.

I was patchily conscious in between the dreams. Leary fed me and cleaned me and held me. I remember little. Struggling against him, screaming, my mouth hoarse with my screams and only a dim awareness as to who I was and where. Lying in bed, the fever raging through me, too weak to move my head, too weak to speak.

I was in the forest. I collapsed. I had dreams. I awoke screaming. I wished I was dead.

I was not granted that boon. For a reason. I am the harbinger. I bear the warning, and if you do not listen, then we are all doomed.

#

The light is like a brutal assault as I try to rise from the depths. I have a feeling of struggling, hitting out. Of being held.

"Drink, Zoe, drink."

I open my eyes. My vision swims and sways and I blink away the mist veiling my eyes.

He is holding a glass of water to my lips. I open my parched lips, drink a little, cough as it hits the back of my throat like a frozen shot of vodka. God, that is good.

"Easy, Zoe."

"Who the fuck are you?"

He laughs.

"Call me Leary. And I am a friend, if nothing else. The one who brought you back from Hel. Beaten to shit you were, young lady. All mended. At least as good as we are going to get for now."

"You should have fucking left me there."

If the kids were dead, I could not bear to live.

Another laugh, almost a growl. Something bearlike. Comforting. I know this might sound strange, but I never doubted for a moment that he was on my side, one of the good guys.

I guess that is just the way it is, sometimes.

"You don't want that. You are too strong, too important for that whiny little girl shit."

"Really? And who the hell are you to know what I want?"

"I guess, as your saviour, I am granted some deeply brilliant insights into your character. And then there are the kids. Just a wild guess, but you probably want to see them again."

That made me sit up, or at least push myself up onto my elbow.

I remember the scene at the car. He had said that they were gone. Not dead, gone. And a tsunami of bright hope sweeps over me. They are alive.

We are in a small bedroom. White-washed walls. Low ceilings. One square window in the middle of the far wall. An old farmhouse cottage that has seen its best days come and go. Leary puts the glass down on the night table. He is perched forward on a paint-chipped wooden chair leaning forward over the bed, hands on his knees, belly front, and center. He sees me taking in the room.

"Home sweet home, Zoe. At least until we sort out this shit and get your kids back. I am renting it from some doper in town whose Da used to farm this place. Told him I am on a retreat, come to reconnect to nature, and do some mediating through painting. Dipshit bought the cock and bull story, hook line and sinker. Or he doesn't give a fuck.

Money under the table and all that. I mean, do I look like the meditative type? Makes no odds, we are safe here, love. And hidden."

Love? A little patronizing, granted, in that elder lemon way of his, but there is kindness in his worn face. He cares, for whatever reason. About what has happened to me, to the kids. And whatever I am to him, or he is to me, our goals are aligned. I feel this.

Naive, you might say, the typical Zoe failings: trusting men, falling for their macho bullshit, putting my fate in their hands.

Leary was different. You'll see.

He is a tall man, broad-shouldered, with a huge belly that is almost an assault on your personal space when he is talking to you. His face is a testament to the violence he has endured and meted out, and his cauliflower ears are testament to a youth spent in the rugby trenches. A copper. A bull of a man with hard knuckles. A tough man with a good heart. Ugly as sin, but with a gentle smile and eyes that twinkled when not lost in the pain of the past.

He told me. We had met once in the city. I had been mugged, and he was the responding detective. "Below my fecking dignity, a murder dick such as meself, to respond to such as that, but I was nearby."

I remembered: withdrawing money from the ATM late at night, the echoing emptiness of the streets in the year of the plague. Two stoners with their picket-fenced teeth and smirks grabbed me and made me withdraw more money, man-handled me and touched me up as my fear grew until it threatened to swamp me. The glint off their blade as they worked themselves up, becoming ever lewder, ever more dangerous. The old woman who reported hearing my screams, and Leary the first on the scene, though he did little more than scare them off and tip a hat to me as the uniforms arrived and he left.

But it was him. My saviour then. My saviour now.

So, what was he doing here now?

I pushed, he told me his story.

He had retired, his money made by hook and by crook; he was no angel. He left the city and bought an old lighthouse with a jetty along with the small fishing boat that came with it. The lighthouse was medieval, almost a castle, but had been renovated and then deserted in the great crash. He had his boat, his castle, and his free time, the dream realised. For a fortnight, until he got bored and the whiskey could no longer drive away the ghosts.

So, he set up shop as a private dick, and the jobs, banal as they were, kept the demons at bay. Until a case ran him smack bang into the Society.

And that was when he first noticed them.

A missing person's case. A young girl, a teenager. Katlin. Seventeen and blond, pretty and naive. The desperate parents hired him. The mother red-eyed and drawn. The father a straw man, hollowed out by grief that could not yet accept the likely reality. Their only child gone, her mobile phone left behind. They feared the worst but had to know; the police had nothing after months of trying.

Leary left them. Dry-eyed, for he had seen too much of life to cry, but they had touched him—as the parents of the missing and the dead always had. He called in a few old favours and got access to the phone. The cops had checked out all the phone numbers, of course, but it was in the browser history that Leary found the thread that would lead into the labyrinth. The homepage of the Society of the Gray Eclipse. That weird page that had sent me on a spiralling nightmare trip. Leary said the same thing happened to him. He had stared at it for what seemed like hours. He knew—call it an old cop's gut instinct—that The Society was involved with Katlin's disappearance.

"I locked up the lighthouse. Even then I think I knew I would not be back. I followed the society's trail here. Follow the money, as the old saying goes; the fuckers made that hard on me. It led me here, to Banning and Ramsey." He looked me in the eye. "You've met them."

"I know Banning only by rumour. Ramsey is a dick."

"They all are." He shakes his head. "You have no idea, Zoe. Not really."

"So, tell me."

He lowers his eyes, and turns his head.

"Trust me on this. I will. Not yet. It is too raw."

I stare at him and he turns back to me.

"I'll show you. I swear. We'll go together. It is the only way. You wouldn't believe me otherwise. Jesus, half the time I don't believe me."

His laugh is forced and uncertain, and I see dark clouds gather in his eyes. Anger? Fear? Both, I decide.

"Did you find her? Did you find Katlin?"

He says nothing for a long time. He is staring at a spot somewhere above my shoulder. I am about to repeat the question when he turns to me again.

"I did. I wish I hadn't."

Another long pause and more turmoil in those expressive green eyes.

"I rented this place and set up surveillance, of a sort. As well as a one-man band can, you see. First at Ramesy's place. The manor house."

"I've been there."

"I know. I saw you. Back then my only interest was Katlin. Ramsey led me to Banning's ranch. Nothing. I followed them, staked out their places. More nothing. Acolytes and hangers on but no Katlin. I was about to throw in the towel, but I gave myself one last week. I was outside Ramsey's place with a flask and my binoculars, it was late at night when I heard a scream. I ran to the house. Jaysus, I remember thinking to myself, they are slaughtering the poor thing. Terror, a high-pitched squeal. A woman. I knocked on the door. Banged the fucking thing almost to the ground. Ramsey opened the door in a t-shirt and jeans, bare-footed. The screaming had stopped. He looked me up and down as if I was beneath him. Arrogant prick that he is."

"What the fuck do you want?" Ramsey growled.

I took out my old badge and held it out to him. Never did hand the thing back and nobody came looking. He took it from me, turned it around in his meaty paws without really looking, and then tossed it back to me.

"Sir, I heard screams. I believe I have reason to inspect this building."

"I don't hear anything," he said, cocking his head as if to listen.

"Sir, I know what I heard."

"I don't suppose you have a warrant, Detective?"

"I have probable cause."

"I don't think you do."

"Sir, if you could just show me around the place, I´ll be on my way. Otherwise, I'll call in the cavalry and they won't be best fucking pleased."

"The pig."

"What?"

"What you heard. The pig. Out the back." He gestured to the rear of the house. "It is slaughter day."

"Sir, what I heard was human. Are you going to let me in, or should I make my call?"

Smiling, he stepped aside and waved me in. I got a full tour of that strange house, and then he took me out the back. Behind the stable they were all milling around, wine glasses in their hands, animated and for all the world like a gathering of fashionistas at a cocktail party. Fancy dresses, jackets, ties. On a stone slab in the center lay an enormous pig, its throat slit and blood still dripping into the large plastic bucket below.

In another time, they could have been a coven of Satanists around their common sacrifice, and that, I have come to realise, is not so far off the mark.

There she was. In the midst of that loud, giggling throng gathered around the butchered animal.

"Katlin?"

He nods.

I made straight for her. Ramsey put a hand on my shoulder to pull me back. I slapped it away, turned, and thrust my face at his until our noses were all but touching.

"Did you just lay a hand on a policeman in anger, Sir?"

He shook his head, a small smile on his face.

"My mistake, Officer. I was just going to offer you a drink."

We stood like that for some long moments before the tension in his face eased and his shoulders relaxed.

"I need to talk to somebody and then I'll be gone."

"Take your time, Officer. Mi casa es su casa."

"So, you found her? You found your Katlin."

Leary shakes his head. "There is no simple answer to that, Zoe. It was her, but the girl those parents knew was gone. I showed her a letter they had given to me for her to read, should I ever find her alive. She looked at it, at me. Didn't even bother reading it. Her eyes were what got me, dark, almost inexpressive.

"With lights around the pupils? Little pinpricks of things."

He looks at me in surprise.

"My husband, Jimmy. He exhibited the same weirdness."

"Katlin dropped the letter on the ground with a purse of her lips. Started to walk away from me. I tried to explain, but she kept looking at me as if I was a buzzing insect, one she would gladly crush. I put a hand on her shoulder at one stage, to try to persuade her to come back with me, to come home. She hissed at me. Like an irate snake, her tongue sticking out. I backed away from her then. God help me, I did. *I do not know you, I do not know them,*" she said, in a voice that was thin, strangulated. Almost too high to be human. *Leave me now. Leave!* There was blood on the back of her hand and her face had turned a pale ivory. A fucking zombie statue. Scared the fucking bejapers out of me, I swear. And that's when I knew for certain that the voice I had heard earlier was human after all."

"What did you do?"

"What could I do? I wasn't a cop anymore. I left, tail between my legs. I remember Ramsey's grin as he closed the door on me, like the fucking Joker. Ear to ear. I fucking hightailed it out of there. Rang the cops with an anonymous complaint, but nothing ever came of that. I heard afterwards that Banning got his lawyers to sue the local police for harassment. The locals were looking out for me, the impostor, so I had to keep my head way low."

"And the parents?"

"I could not tell them what I had seen. I could barely tell myself. I got a friend in the department to ring them. He spun them some cock and bull story. There had been a drowning down by Ardmore. A woman lost at sea. The body never recovered. A witness actually saw it, but the woman who was swept away was never identified. In our bullshit story, the Jane Doe became Katlin, and the parents had some sort of closure. A funeral service. A chance to move on."

"But you stayed here. Why hang around?"

"I thought about leaving, but I couldn't. Katlin and that whole thing had rattled me. I had to find out more. So, when the heat died down, I did some digging on those fuckers. Then I saw you and the kids at Ramsey´s house. I knew that I had to do something. I couldn't let you become the new Katlin."

Chapter 26

"What happened to my children?" I ask him then, heart pounding. I cannot bear to hear the answer, I cannot bear to not hear the answer.

"Ramsey took them back to your husband."

I gasp in relief and he reaches out to me and holds my hand.

"I arrived too late. After the crash. I am sorry, Zoe. They were already gone."

"You are sure?"

He nods. "You don't remember anything? The crash, what happened after?"

"The white light, Ramsey tailgating us, spinning off the road. Then nothing. I was nowhere near the car when I came too. What happened? How did I end up where I did?"

"We may never know for sure. Most likely you were concussed and wandered off. You were in a terrible state."

I glance around the room, at the bare lack of amenities. The almost squalor. There are bandages around my chest, my arm, my leg. My fever is gone and whatever pain I have is a dull background throb.

"So, Nurse Nightingale, who did all this?"

He smiles. "Not me. I am not the nursing kind."

"You can't have brought in a local doctor?"

"Don't worry, Lass. I may not be local, but I do know lots of people in lots of places. A perk of the old job, see. Called in a favour. A doctor who would be in a much worse place but for me. You don't really need to know who he was or why he was helping, but help he did. You were lucky all told. Lots of bruising, some of it severe, nothing broken."

I shiver, but not from fever or pain. All of this, it is overwhelming. Like being swallowed in a stormy sea, head spinning, trying to breathe, to keep my head above water.

All the time feeling riptides dragging me further away from shore.

The kids are alive and with Jimmy.

Jesus.

The Jimmy I barely know, that strange monster that is the new face of my Jimmy.

Leary's story about the girl. About Katlin, about the strangeness he witnessed at that odd country house. Her eyes. Like Jimmy's. I still don't know for sure what that means, but it is nothing good. The kids are alive. They are with Jimmy, but that does not mean they are safe.

Far fucking from it.

"I have to go and get them back. Sarah and Sean."

Leary nods in agreement and purses his lips.

"You must know by now your husband is one of them. One of the sect. He and Ramsey are the ones who report to Banning. Only the two of them. Lieutenants, if you will. And from what I have seen, those two sick fucks cannot be trusted with children."

"Will you help me?" I hate the sound of my voice, the neediness, the lack of strength. I hate having to put my fate in the hands of yet another member of the prick family. Balls and a penis giving you an unalienable right to be a dick. Except, Guy was different, and in his own way, I sense Leary is too, for all the roughness of his battered exterior.

He shakes his head, but in disbelief, not in refusal.

"Did you not hear my story, Zoe? Do you not know what it means? I ran the fuck away, Zoe. Me! In all my years on the beat and then as a murder dick, I never ran—despite the blood and guts and violence. But then again, I never felt terror as I did that night when Katlin hissed at me, and her eyes, those dead eyes, started to spin. I swear I almost peed myself. I ran like a fucking coward."

"Anybody would have. You can't be held responsible for that."

"I left her behind, Zoe. Katlin, too, but I think it was too late for her. I mean the woman whose voice I heard. The scream that called me to the door. I left her there. I ran and left her behind"

There is a sudden dampness in his eyes. He wipes it away with the back of his right hand.

"I left whoever that was and beat feet. I haven't slept all that well since, you see. That scream wakes me at night still and I cannot get it out of my head. I just can't."

He leans forwards and squeezes my hand again, forcing a weak smile on that worn face. "Call me old fashioned, but the damsel in distress shtick works every time."

"Fuck off."

He laughs then, a genuine laugh, enjoying my rather limp riposte.

"I will not fail this time, Zoe. You are my second chance. Of course, I will help. We need to get your kids back. I need the redemption, so I am all yours, but we also need to be a bit damned clever about it. These are unscrupulous shits we are dealing with."

#

Leary says we can't just rush in like headless chickens.

He leaves me to rest. My dreams are free of monsters and Jimmy.

Instead, I hear the voices of my kids, calling to me, but their voices are hopeful and warm and lacking fear.

I have an ally.

Leary has my back. I will be with them soon

I awake to a gray dawn, sparrows singing in unison outside and flitting between two rowans, ripe with red berries. A dog barks nearby and I can hear music and the smell of bacon cooking.

I push myself up in bed, wait for a dizzy moment as the blood flows back to my head. I feel used up, bone-tired, but mostly pain-free. I struggle to my feet and, apart from a slight tinge in my ankle, feel nothing when I walk to the chair where my jeans and jumper have been placed. Washed and folded, I note. A homely touch for that gruff bear of a man.

"Zoe, that you?"

"Be there in a sec," I shout.

I am fit. Strong again. Certainly strong enough to confront Jimmy.

Leary is in the low-ceilinged kitchen sitting on a three-legged stool he dwarfs. Sitting there, leaning over the table, like a giant in a house built for hobbits.

I have to laugh. He is reading a newspaper, a slice of toast in his hand, an empty plate lined with grease, and a half-empty cup in front of him on the scarred wooden table.

"I see you have recovered some form," he stares at me sternly, but there is laughter in his eyes too. He can't be unaware of how ludicrous he looks. "The lighthouse was bigger," he mutters. "I swear on my mother's grave."

And I laugh again.

He smiles then and points at the old aga oven set against the sink in the far wall. "Bacon and eggs in yonder pan. Plates in that cupboard and grab yourself a cuppa. I figured you would need all the food I could shovel into you. Fatten you up a bit, after all that trauma."

I gobble the food down like his giantess wife, not tasting, just shoveling to fill the empty growling cavern that is my stomach.

"Hungry much, were you?" His smile is gentle, and I swear it almost makes him handsome. Almost.

I nod, still swallowing.

"You ready to face the day soon?"

"I am," through a mouthful of food.

"Time to find out where the kids are."

That causes me to pause. I stare at him as I finish chewing.

"You said that Ramsey took them to Jimmy."

"I did, and he did."

"So, then we know where they are."

"We can go to your home, stake it out, but we can't be sure they will be there. Things are moving quickly now. The society is preparing for something. I have heard enough chatter from them to know that."

"You bugged them?"

"Ramsey's car is all I could get to. But they are up to something, and it is coming fast."

I push my chair back and get to my feet.

"We have to go then. Now! Go get them."

He holds a hand out to me and lowers it in a gesture for me to sit, to be calm. How does he expect me to do that right now? Seriously."

"Zoe, think for a minute. Please. You have been out of it for almost a fortnight. As far as Jimmy and Ramsey know, you are out of the picture. The crashed car has never been found. The cops know nothing. As far as anyone else is concerned, you just legged it. Abandoned your family, taking a time out. Whatever. That means they are relaxed, Jimmy and the rest of them. Their guard is down."

I sit down on the ridiculously small chair opposite but cannot help glaring, my face hot with anger. "I want the kids. I need them back. It's been too long. You don't know what he is like?"

"I am not asking you to wait. Not really. But I also need to nail those fucks. I cannot have them ducking back into the woods to hide. You see?"

"Not really, no."

"We can't just go storming in. We'll stake out your house. Today. See if your children are there. Bide our time and then get them out of there when Jimmy is asleep or out of it. Fuck it, I'll take him down myself, if I have to. But..."

A long pause.

"What?"

"I can't afford another voice haunting my dreams. I have unfinished business, too."

"You want to find out who she was? That woman you heard."

"I need to. She was as real as you are. Zoe, I want to help you. I do. But I need to do this too. Whoever she was, I have to find her, bury her, and let her say goodbye to her parents or her husband and children. Do you get it?"

And I did. His need to avenge the dead was his prime motivation. He would not rest until he had found out who she was and what had been done to her.

"So, we break into my house and kidnap my kids?"

He laughs again.

"That's about the size of it. It's like this, Zoe. Our first priority is the kids, of course, but I want to know more, about the society and their plans, about who she was. That woman. So, we get the kids and while doing that, I'll see what I see."

"Jimmy has an office. His den. If there are secrets, that is where they will be."

A large, slightly uneven smile on that pocked, heavy, yet somehow awkwardly handsome, face.

"Grand. So, then, that's a plan I suppose. Would you like another cup?" He shakes his empty cup at me and smiles quizzically. That simple, ordinary gesture of kindness almost sends me into tears.

Chapter 27

Leary's ride is an old banger. Some sort of Renault high-top van. I never did care much about cars, so don't bother asking me the name.

Untidy inside. Scratched hard plastic and worn seats. Has lived a hard life and been around the block more than once. Suits Leary somehow.

"Close your eyes and imagine it's a fecking Mercedes. That's what I do." His grin is infectious.

He drives carefully, one hand on the wheel. Surprisingly relaxing after Jimmy's manic, macho driving style. In the back seat is a duffel bag filled with what he, somewhat euphemistically, called tools.

He had unzipped it as he put it in the car to appease my unspoken curiosity: one handgun, what I take to be a taser, a crowbar, hammers and chisels, an electric saw and a set of what could only be lock picks.

He smiled at my reaction.

"Like the Scouts say."

"Be prepared."

"That is indeed the fecking saying. And I hope we are. I sure as shit do!"

Nervous and excited, and I get that; so am I. All going well, I would get the kids away from Jimmy. The plan then was the same as it always was: to hightail it out of Dodge and flee for refuge to my, ahem, loving parents.

"There has to be another way," Leary says.

"I don't see it."

"Jimmy knows—and thus the society knows—where your parents live. They could still track you down."

"I have nothing. No money. Not even a car now. It's my parents or nothing."

Leary glances at me, his eyes guileless.

"There is the lighthouse. They don't know me, and they sure as shit don't know where I live."

I stare back at him as he turns to face the road. His profile is Roman, though he has a small roll of fat around the collar of his shirt. Broad and still muscled despite the beer belly.

You could do worse, I say to myself.

A refuge that is secret, and Leary wants nothing from me, as far as I can see. Get on my feet there, get a job, and be rid of my abusive partner once and for all. Enough time to think at least.

"I'll think about it," I say. Though I know from the lightening of my heart that the decision has already been made.

#

We never did have neighbours we got to know well. The nearest were a good bit up the road and rather insular.

Back then, that was a bit of a shame.

Now it is a blessing.

We have been outside the house all day and waited until night fell. No car. No lights in any windows. No sign of Jimmy or the kids. And still, we wait, though I have ants in my pants.

Finally, could be ten or so, Leary turns to me and shrugs. He gestures towards the house. Wordlessly, we leave the car, sneak down the driveway and make for the back of the house. Leary does not bother with finesse. He smashes a window at the back with the crowbar and shrugs as he throws a guilty look.

I suppose I should care.

My house and all that.

I don't give a shit.

He beats away the jagged edges and with gloved hands clears away the windowsill.

"Lead on, Milady." He grins and I can see the adrenaline rush lighting his eyes, though, honestly I am not sure we are breaking and entering.

"Are you sure you didn't find my keys?"

His grin is almost evil. "Perfectly."

"Danger hog."

I hop up on the sill and maneuver myself inside. I drop to the floor and move to one side. I pause, listening, still crouched. Silence. Emptiness, except for my breathing.

That sadness that always enfolds empty places where life once was.

Leary lands beside me. There is moonlight enough for us to sense, but not see by, so Leary turns on his flashlight.

"Lead on, Macduff. Show me the kingdom."

"Gobshite."

We scour the house, taking our time. The kitchen. Clean and stale. No fresh food. Everything points to desertion. The living room. Jimmy's music box is gone, otherwise nothing much but the accumulation of dust has changed. Upstairs and the bedrooms. I can't help the tears that well when I enter the kids' room, but even here I feel little of their presence. Their things sure, the Yu-Gi-Oh cards and the Princess beads.

But their comforters are gone—they were with me when the car crashed—and there is no sense of their presence. Their smell, their breath.

I wipe away the tears.

That leaves only Jimmy's den.

We tiptoe down together. I have the taser in my belt. Leary has the pistol in his, with his bag slung over his shoulder.

"So, this is your husband's dungeon? I expected it to be a bit deeper."

Smartass.

We are at a lower level, set off from the pantry and to the right of the kitchen. Three steps down to what was meant—I think—to be the utility room, but had been transformed by the previous owner into a bedroom.

The pantry was large enough for shelves and a washing machine and dryer.

Jimmy's dungeon, down in the deeps.

Standing in front of the wooden door, my heart starts to beat fast again. I have not, I realise, been in here since Jimmy claimed it for himself.

How strange is that?

Sometimes I want to kick myself.

For all I know, he could have a dozen murdered and stuffed corpses in here.

I was a fool.

A fool in love, but a careless fool.

"I don't suppose we have a key to this, either?"

I shake my head.

"Above my pay grade. Jimmy´s sphere of influence, not mine."

Leary´s look says it all. "Jaysus, Zoe. He really did a number on you."

That look cast a light through me like a beam. Was I that person? The budgie in the cage? Gaslighting, isn't that the hip term.

Doubt, domineer, control, destroy.

"Shit."

"What?"

"Shithead. Shit situation. Just shit."

I kick the door.

"You were strong, Zoe. Whatever he did to you, you took it on the chin like Frasier and you survived to fight again. Look at me."

I do. And I see the warmth in his eyes. Strength like Guy had. Kindness.

"Okay."

"You want this?"

He hands me a heavy hammer and I grab it.

Beating down the door to the dungeon is the best therapy I have had since Guy.

#

I remember an old friend of ours, a stockbroker, telling us an anecdote in a posh cocktail bar near the sea. All of us warm with alcohol but not yet drunk. All of us focusing on being more interesting than we really were.

Like us, he was not a Brahmin, not from their caste of wealth, so he had to work on construction sites in the holidays. Good solid work, decent money.

All through college, I was on a scholarship, of course, but every little helps. The best job, I mean the best job, the most exciting fucking job, was as a demolition man. Not high-tech stuff, mind, or explosives. We are talking sledgehammers and drills.

The rush man. The joy when a stubborn wall you have been pounding on for hours falls. When it just pauses and then ponders its gravitational situation and then, bam; you jump in the air and the fucker is literally dust rising.

Best job ever. Beats many an orgasm, I tell you.

A wink and a smile. Rich and rugged and still a man of the people.

You get the idea.

Bullshit, of course. The fortune he made afterwards. The women he shagged. His demolition days were a great story at a cocktail party. Nothing more. Probably bullshit to begin with, who knows?

But it did feel really fucking good when the wooden door to Jimmy's den broke open.

We were adventurers blowing open the gateway to the Devil's dungeon. It cracked open at the hinges after five hard swings. We cautiously pushed aside the remains to get into his lair.

Inside was darkness but for the one pale light on the far wall.

Leary knew more than I did then. Suspected even more. My Jimmy had changed. I had lived through that. I had seen the weirdness inside him. I had accepted his difference and internalised it, but never verbalised, never attempted to put a name or a design to what was happening.

I was a burgeoning Alice. Little did I know, and way too little did I fear, the shitty wonderland that lay ahead.

I was about to find out.

For whatever reason, I found myself on tenterhooks, tiptoeing into the room. A vestige of Jimmy's control over me and this space in our house.

"I don't want you ever in there without my say so, Zoe. Is that clear? Is it?" And that look in his eyes, part contempt, part pulsing anger.

There was a camp-bed against the far wall next to Jimmy's desk, which had his large monitor and his laptop. Horizontal trays that contained papers and pens and other assorted rubbish.

"What exactly are we looking for?"

Leary rubs his chin. "There is a plan afoot, Watson. Ramsey let slip that much. Something that has him all hot and bothered. The end of days, he said at one point. Fucking plonker."

"Nothing more concrete?"

"Paranoia does make them careful. I'll give them that. Anything we can find about their plans. Anything that can point us to Banning."

"Banning?"

"The brain to Ramsey's muscle. Used to live in the mansion with the others, but the fucker disappeared off the face of the earth a few weeks before you went to that party."

I close my eyes to banish the memories of that night—the rape of Zoe. The pale faces. The metal knives, the hands like fire.

"You okay?"

"Sure."

"A location then, with an X marks the spot and the file marked top-secret plans. Or whatever we can find." Leary stuffs the laptop into his duffel bag and rummages through the drawers in the desk. I do the trays. Mostly writing. Some school stuff: lesson plans, timetables, rules and regulations.

Nothing of use.

A sudden reflection on the table causes me to glance up at the far wall. The pale light is gone and in its place is a harsh red glare, like a traffic signal.

"Leary."

He looks up and sees the light, too.

"Shit."

"Not good."

"No."

"You done?"

"Yep. You?"

"One drawer left."

"Hurry. I don't like this."

There was a sudden change in atmosphere in the room. It took me a moment to work out why. Through the far window, the dark, moonless light had changed.

In the distance, a faint gray light like fading ash in a dying fire encroached.

"Leary. We have to get gone."

"Almost there. Just a second."

I feel the night start to get colder as the light draws closer.

"Done." Leary slams the last drawer shut. Shoves a slim folder into the bag and zips it.

"Something is coming."

My stomach knots in fear and my legs grow wobbly. Sweat beads Leary´s face, his breath is a misty fog in the cold.

He puts a finger to his lips and points to the front of the house, away from the approaching light. I nod and we move, quickly now, almost running.

The front door. I turn the handle. It is, of course, locked.

"Fuck."

The spare key.

I reach for the empty vase on the commode. The key rattles as I lift it. I upend it, hands shaking.

"Come on, come on," I mutter. The key slips from my shaky, freezing fingers and falls to the ground. Leary´s hand on my shoulder is a quiet reassurance.

He bends to pick up the key. Slips it into the lock and pulls the handle. The gray is everywhere now, like a film of burnt ashes. I want to be braver, to stop shaking, but I can't help remembering the car and the way this light seems to invade and pervert. It destroyed jimmy. It led to the crash. It led to the rape.

It is the *other*. Literally the bane of my existence and it is back.

The taser is my right hand; Leary has his Glock in one hand and the bag over his shoulder.

"Run for the car, Zoe. I think discretion is no longer an issue. Right?"

His calm smile is betrayed by the look of panic in his eyes.

But his presence is calming.

He has my back.

We start to run down the driveway in single file.

An inhuman snarl from somewhere in the front garden.

Then a long answering howl in front of us near the road.

I stumble against Leary, who has pulled up suddenly. We are near the gate, ten meters from the street and the old wall that lines the road.

Again, that snarl. It sounds like a rabid wolf. And an answer echoing from the road.

Leary turns to the sound, gun pointing into the gray.

"Get behind me, Zoe."

I catch a brief glimpse of something dark moving between two bushes on the grass and ease myself behind Leary.

He fires. The light is blinding.

The noise of the gun almost makes me drop the taser.

He drops the bag and faces the garden at an oblique angle to the path.

"Get the flashlight. Do it. Quick!"

I bend down fast as I can, keeping my eyes focused in front, my hands still shaking. I open the zip and fumble for the flashlight.

There. It is one of those large, almost industrial size torches with a handle. I flick a switch and point it at the garden. Hibiscus, Mountain laurel, Rhododendron. Growing mostly wild and uncared for.

A movement behind the hibiscus. Fast. So fast.

Charging towards us, flying almost. Dog-like but malformed. Legs too long. Body too straight. Moving almost upright. Like a mutant human. It howls, a sound that too is more human than not. Its fangs (teeth, I think, shivering in disgust) are as long as my fingers. It eats up the distance to us.

Those eyes.

White as any rabid dog or B-Movie zombie.

Leary shoots. The bullet hits it in the chest. I see the spurt of blood, but it does not slow down. Leary fires again. Another hit, but the thing does not skip a beat.

Another growl.

From behind me, behind the wall.

I dare not turn, need to hold the flashlight straight, can't afford to distract Leary. I do risk a glance over my shoulder. Another nightmare, running towards us, this one definitely upright, claws outstretched, mouth open in something like a silent scream. I feel my heart pounding. I have to do something, or we are finished. Leary is still engaged with the other one. I twist sidewards, reach over my shoulder, and aim roughly. It is less than five feet away, its howl deafening. A rancid stink of unwashed fur and shit washes over me. I wait. Another millisecond and then I fire the taser.

Two taser darts hit the thing square in its hairy chest and it pauses, slows down, shakes its head. This thing is different from the other one, more humanoid, but the fangs are, if anything, even longer. It shakes its head again, points a claw at me and smiles.

Then Leary blows its head off.

Chapter 28

We are both breathing heavy when we get to the car. Leary slams the door, throws the car into gear, floors the gas pedal, and pulls out onto the road; the engine protesting at the sudden violence being done to it. The tires screech as he does a u-turn and we burn rubber as though the demons of Hell were on our tails. Which, in a sense, they are.

My heart is a jungle drum, my hands palsied, and I feel a tangled knot of terror in my stomach.

To top it all, I can barely see —my head pounding with something like a migraine.

"What the fuck?"

"I know. Jesus wept."

We do not speak for a long while.

It's not that we have nothing to say—the thoughts are spinning around in my pounding head, like tachyons in a particle accelerator— it's that we cannot fathom how to say it. What the hell just happened? What were those things? This whole wonderful tour of duty has thrown up shock after shock after shock, each one driving me deeper into this nightmarish wonderland, but what the hell was that?

Seriously.

What?

"That was fucked."

The road is empty of cars, the headlights are cutting a thin path through the darkness. Darkness that is a balm after the corruption that is the gray light.

Leary's hands on the wheel are steady but his jaw is clenched. I see a twitch on the side of his mouth.

"I knew one of them, Leary. I have fucking spoken to him."

Leary shakes his head. He blinks. I know he is holding back on me, has been from the beginning, but I figure it is time we got it all out.

It had all gone so quickly. Leary's third bullet was a fortunate headshot which finally dropped his creature. He had managed to turn in time, with barely a moment to spare I figure, to take out mine.

I had stood there afterward, breathing heavily, adrenaline pumping through me as though I was a holed balloon, staring down at it. A dog-like humanoid. The left half of its forehead was a pulp of shattered bone. It lay spreadeagled on the concrete path, a halo of blood and bone and brain around it.

And as I looked it transformed.

I blinked. I rubbed my eyes. Blinked again. No difference.

The thing was no longer a thing.

It was human. Eyes, ears, nose and hair. All the requisite and normal length, all standard sized and of average appearance.

And I knew him. It. Whatever. We had met. He had been at the party. Adele had introduced him to me. A tall, dim-looking man in his early twenties with a thatch of unruly blonde hair and dull, gray eyes. Lightless eyes with that darkness that Jimmy, even then, had developed. Bruce something or other.

I screamed. I leaned over and vomited on top of him. I felt my sanity, my sense of who I am and always have been, diminish as a wilderness of chaos and anti-matter threatened to envelop me. In no world that I could accept, would such a thing exist. It just would not, could not.

A man cannot become a beast in darkness. Werewolves and fairies and all that sci-fi channel crap does not exist. They simply do not.

I felt my legs sag.

Leary had grabbed me by the arm and hustled me to the car.

"Leary? Come clean with me." I say in a soft voice.

He tilts his head to me, eyebrow raised, lifts his right hand from the steering wheel, and places it over mine. Only when I feel his warmth do, I realise that my hand is chilled. Fingers like frozen stalagmites of ice.

Frozen, yet fluttering like leaves in Autumn.

Now, his hand lies lightly on mine. Its warmth is a comfort and I can feel my headache lessen. The sound of the car is a comfort, the darkness, the sheer normality of all of this. The quiet peace of driving on empty roads at night.

"I will, Zoe. I promise. But you had to see this for yourself. You would have run a million miles if I had sprung this on you earlier. I know I would have in your place. Run and never looked back, except to call the police and nut doctors and warn them to bring tranqs."

I smile, faintly.

"You saw what they really were, didn't you?" There is a note of doubt in his voice. How could there not be? He needs my confirmation as much as I need his explanation.

"I saw it, I heard it, I smelled it. And then it transformed. It became him. Bruce his name was. I met him at the party."

"Jesus, Zoe. That is a bitch. Someone you met. Christ."

"So, spit it out, gumshoe. What the hell is going on?"

"This is how they infiltrate us. This is how they come amongst us. Smoke and mirrors, until we do not know which way is up."

I start to object. This cryptic bullshit; I am tired of it, the lack of knowing, the ache I feel for my kids, the sheer abject terror and absurdity of all this. I am exhausted and terrified at once and I still feel like puking.

"We will be home in five minutes. I can show you better there. Please. Give me this one chance.

I snort in disgust and close my eyes. Just a moment, I think, to ward off the pain in my throbbing head. Just one moment. A wave of blackness hits me and that is the last thing I remember for a good long time.

#

"You up yet?" Knocking drives away my sleep.

My eyes are gummed together and my mouth feels like an ashtray; though, I no longer smoke.

Sunlight, bright and warm, is pouring through the mean window on the opposite wall.

Late morning, I guess.

I must have passed out in the car.

Shit.

I crawl out of bed, limbs weak as a foal. The pain in my head has eased. Small mercies.

Leary put me to bed again, fully dressed, bar my shoes.

Him taking care of me is getting to be a habit.

One I could get used to.

"Coming," I say. It sounds like a toddler learning to speak a foreign language. Even I don't understand what I just said. I stare at my reflection in the mirror. Eyes red as if from crying. Skin pale and drawn, hair wild and askew.

I take a few minutes to fix the nigh impossible. I stop when the smell of food drives me from the room. My stomach is loud and complaining, remembering the indignities of the night before. Screw it, I am at least borderline presentable.

"You feeling okay?"

Leary is on the hobbit chair at the table, looking towards me with kindness in his eyes and a vague smile on his lips.

One ugly fucker.

But my ugly fucker.

I nod.

We eat. Without talking. There is only the sound of my ravenous slurping.

After one loud and decidedly unladylike burb, I slump deeper in the chair, stomach pulling me down, and waiting for him to begin.

#

"I don't even know how to say this, Zoe. I came here looking for Katlin. I told you all that."

I nod, gesture impatiently for him to continue.

"From the beginning, it bugged the shit out of me. The fact that the Society has nothing except that one website. No Facebook representation, nobody tweeting. Who the hell doesn't do that nowadays? So, after Katlin blew me off, after the police ended up with nothing, I did a trawl. A deep trawl, with the help of some contacts in shadier milieus. People who can find out even your darkest secrets. People I often wish I didn't know."

"So, what did you find out?"

"That is what is so strange. The society barely exists but, in one form or another, has been around forever. It still has almost nothing online, but it shows up all over in history books."

"What?"

"Okay, some of this is speculation. Some of it is fact. And a lot of it feels like sheer bloody fancy. But if you can come up with a better explanation, then be my guest." He pauses, breathing hard, face red. I say nothing. "Okay, here is what I think. We know they are alien. You do accept that, right?"

Everything in me screams. I want to throw my cup at him and stand and stamp and shout. To force him to stop being such a goddamn fool. To stop spouting such utter bullcrap. To get to the truth.

But I do none of that.

For this is the truth.

Aliens, and not the good kind.

The shitty ones.

They came with the gray light. They infected Jimmy, won him to their cause. They raped me at the party. They were responsible for Guy's death. They have my children.

So, aliens. Fuck it. Isn't that what the science bods always said. It was inevitable that there would be other life. Somewhere. Guess it's here now. The real question is: what the hell does it want?

"I have to, I suppose."

And there it is. And that feels like a weight lifted off my shoulder. An acknowledgment of the impossible made possible.

"I was back in Dublin, doing my digging. Living in a hostel near Connelly. I was stirring up a hornet's nest and they must have cottoned on to me. The beast came for me as I was walking home after a night in the pub. More like a bear that one with sharp fucking claws. Massive. The scene went down a little bit like last night. It attacked, I nearly shat myself, but I had my gun and I was lucky. It managed to tear up my shoulder, but I shot the fucker in the mouth. Blew its jaw off. It lay bleeding out on the ground when I saw it turn. Turn back. Whatever. A bear of a man with a long unkempt beard and a ripe smell, but a man. Only a man. That is when I knew for sure. Whatever this is, it is not human. Whatever the aliens do, changes us."

"What happened?"

"Dumped the body in the nearby canal. Found a quack doctor to patch me up. Kept digging for info. Found some cyber-geeks who could help me. They were the ones who showed me the light. Does the name Ka mean anything to you?"

I feel a twinge of pain.

A sore memory.

"Ramsey kept repeating it. The night Guy disappeared. He said Ka wanted it done."

"That was careless of Ramsey. Out of character for him, but that´s good news for us."

"Leary, can you get to the point?"

"Give me a moment. I need to show you something. He stands up and goes to the small dining room off the kitchen. I hear him rummaging in the old wooden closet. He returns with a fat folder under his arm and a sheepish smile on his face. Like an embarrassed teenager showing me his rare stamp collection. He lays the folder on the table and gingerly opens it, as if it were rare and valuable revealing printouts of A4 size. Dozens and dozens of them. If Leary was anybody else, I would have loud warning bells ringing in my head. With him, it just seems strangely eccentric. He thumbs through the dozens of A4 pages inside and pulls out three.

"That is a picture of Ka. An ancient Mesopotamian and later Egyptian God," he pauses. "And this is Apollo, and this one, Neargal."

"So?"

He passes them to me. Colour printouts from web pages: text and pictures formatted badly, kooky and UFO centric, very much amateur day at the races. You know the kind. Stuff you read with a smile on your face, something you might joke about later with a friend over wine. An intellectual level that makes tabloids seem like Booker Prize winners.

I feel like smacking Leary upside the head and telling him to cop on. He cannot be serious. He spreads the rest of the papers out on the table and starts to arrange them, looking up at me occasionally with an expectant look. And then I see it too. Time after time after time.

I still want to throw something at him.

"Come off it, Leary. For fuck's sake."

He holds his hand out to me, fingers splayed in a placating gesture.

"Listen. The Society of the Gray Eclipse. You were at their headquarters. You've seen those triangles on the logo. He leans forward over the table and the papers strewn about, and stabs a finger at one. "There." Pushes it aside. "And there." Again. "And there."

In picture after picture of deity after deity of the ancient world. Ancient Greece. Apollo, wielding his arrows of disease on a terracotta vase. The Mesoptamian god he called Neargal painted on the wall of what looked like a tomb. Dozens of images of ancient gods. And some images that are more modern. Grainy, black and white pictures of what I take to be the appearance at Fatima; two children stand in front of a cottage, the pyramids like graffiti almost hidden in the right-hand corner of a whitewashed building. Pyramids—on all of the pictures, both modern and ancient—that bear an uncanny resemblance to the logo of the Society of the Gray eclipse. And everywhere too depictions of men who are dressed like astronauts, tall thin men with long fingers and pale eyes wearing open-faced helmets and, what could be, spacesuits.

"This proves nothing, Leary. So, the Society borrowed an ancient symbol. I have watched shit like this on Discovery too. Talking heads, talking bullshit, nonsense which actually sounds intelligent until you listen to how hollow the words are. All smoke and mirrors. Empty voices."

"Smoke and mirrors, Zoe? Very apt. I believed that once too. But can you still afford to be in denial after you have seen with your own two eyes what those people are attempting to describe, Zoe? What they somehow intuit, but have never seen? That is why I think their explanations ring hollow to your ears. Mine doesn't. You have seen it up close and personal."

I lower my head and suck in air. I know he is right.

"I have seen with my own eyes," I repeat in a quiet voice.

For it is all true. I have seen them, alright. Up close and personal, like Leary says. They have taken my life from me. Leary reaches across and taps me gently on the shoulder.

"I fought against accepting this a lot longer, trust me. What person of sound mind could believe in this nonsense? I tried to persuade myself that I was delusional. Given all that, what I have seen and experienced, what you have seen and experienced, there can be no doubt. We have no room for that. We need to save your family and soon."

I nod.

"Okay. An ancient society. Alien gods. I'll buy it all. But what does it mean? How does it help us? It is like one of those Templar, intergenerational, conspiracy theory, heap of crap memes. QAnon for an older generation. What good is that?"

"It helps us know them, Zoe. What they want."

"Who?"

"Why the aliens, of course."

Shit.

"And what do they want?"

"What do evil aliens always want?"

I shake my head.

"World domination, of course."

"Shit."

"Yeah."

"But they usually just show up, say take me to your leader, and blow crap up."

"That's Hollywood. My geeks in their technical dungeons on the dark web whisper other possibilities. Look for the timelines. Just look. Draw the dots."

He waves at the printouts. I pick them up and shuffle through them. Mesopotamia, Egypt, Greece, Europe, The New Worlds. The Greek Plague devastating Athens, the Antonine Plague leaving Rome a shell, the Black Death wiping out sixty percent of Europe, the devastation of the Americas that coincided with European arrival: empty, desolate cities all over the continent. A once thriving culture all but extinguished. The Flu Pandemic in 1918 just after the appearance of Fatima killed more than the number that died in the Great War. The pyramid symbol carved or painted on statues, in grave goods, on walls, repeated again and again along with the images of the gods of disease. Until modern times, then the Society of the Gray Eclipse starts building a web presence and infecting husbands.

"It makes no sense. If they had wanted to eradicate us, they could have done that a long time ago, surely?"

"I don't know, Zoe. Really. Even the wackiest weirdos don't know. It is all just conjecture. I'll tell you what I think, but it is just an idea."

He looks at me for permission to go on, as if embarrassed. This really is not Leary, a nerd with wild ass conspiracy theories. No wonder he looks so self-conscious. Should be wearing a tinfoil hat.

"Well go on then. Cut the tease."

"They didn't come in all guns blazing because they couldn't. They were not strong enough."

"A space-faring race couldn't deal with the ancient Egyptians?"

"Look here. Do you see it?"

He shoves a handful of his printouts at me.

"The same faces."

"The same half dozen faces. Again and again. For thousands of years."

"It is hard to tell. Really?"

"You know what you are looking at Zoe. They are the same."

And he is right, in drawing after drawing, picture after picture, the same men, tall and thin with slit eyes, towering over those around them. Pale men with the faces of aesthetes or fanatics. Standing near to or behind the gods depicted on murals, on walls, on friezes. Uncannily similar, not as a race, but as individuals. Representations of the same beings. Over hundreds and hundreds of years."

"There can't be more than half a dozen."

"A scouting party. The first arrivals. Small in number. Powerful technology, yes, but not such that they could wipe out all mankind. They can live forever, at least compared to us, whether that is technology or biology is irrelevant. They were the first."

"Okay. Kinda makes sense."

"Think of them as a Klingon scout party, searching for a possible place to settle."

"Settle?"

"Space is big. Even close to light speed, it must have taken thousands of years. Tens of thousands. You set off like that you are leaving home forever, right? And you can have only one purpose, and it isn't to jet off to the beach and text 'missing you' back home with your holiday snaps and selfies. You are on a serious mission into the dark unknown. Think Conquistadors. Think the Mayflower."

I have a different image: of men and women on the Oregon Trail, the wagons, the dust the cattle, the danger, the blood. The set of their jaws as they stare westward, knowing that whatever is ahead has to be better than what was left behind. Aiming into the wilderness and the unknown and the hope of a better life.

"To settle new planets."

"Only thing that makes sense. Fleeing from something else, perhaps. Other species. A world they fucked up. Slavery. Who knows? Running to a better life. The Huns were running from some other screaming bastards coming up right behind them before they crossed the Volga and did for the Romans. The history of the earth. Practically a rule of nature. The weak run and find something better or perish. Beware those caught up in the tides. Why should it be any different up there?"

He points skyward.

"Okay. I'll buy it for now. They do exist. They are among us. I have seen them. But, if you are right, surely their fleet must have arrived by now." I point at a batch of pictures dated back to the late nineteenth century. "New faces appear again and again. A wider variety. Why are we still here? I mean humans. We are their rats to poison, their natives to destroy. Surely, they could have figured out a way to get rid of us by now."

He shakes his head.

"I honestly don't know. Not a clue. I have been spinning my head around that for a long time. They are riffing on disease and destruction, that much is obvious, but yeah, I agree. An advanced race could surely have found the ultimate cure for humanity a long time back. And that, young lady, is where we come in."

"We do."

"We get your children, find out what the hell they are up to, and do our best to make sure they don't do it."

I hold my hands together as if in prayer as he waits for me to say something. This is so much. Too much. How does a sane person process any of this? I feel like I am lost in a maze where reality has developed new and confusing rules and the controller of the maze can change things willy-nilly.

So, I believe in aliens now, I guess, and shape changers and conspiracies to destroy the world as we know it.

Why the hell not?

If nothing else, Leary is Leary, and he would not be telling me this if he didn't believe it. That much I can follow and trust, that can be my thread through the maze.

I smile at him in acknowledgment. We are in this together, my smile says, and I don't consider you a total raving loon. At least not any worse than I am.

"Did you find anything in Jimmy's room? On his computer."

"Nothing much. Some writing in what looks like code. I tried to break it. No luck so far. Other stuff. Some drawings. A few photographs." His look is gentle. "I burnt those. They wouldn't have done you any good. Nothing we can use at the moment."

I can only guess what was on the photos: trophies of Jimmy's conquests, the floozies he had and did not want to forget.

"So, what is our next move?"

"Their headquarters. That strange old Manor house. The only way I know of to get back on their trail."

I feel a buzz of excitement. And a rush of gratitude that I have Leary with me.

I am not sure I could do this alone.

"We storm the place, yeah? Guns blazing. Let's go now." I am only half-kidding. The yearning is driving me. He laughs.

"Like the goddamn marines. Hoo, yeah!"

"Shut up."

I punch his arm.

"Tomorrow night, Zoe. And in the cover of darkness. I have things to do tomorrow. Things to do."

He winks at me—international man of mystery, and no matter how long I nag him, he refuses to tell me what.

"Wait and see," is the last I hear from him as he waves me good night and gets up from the table, and walks to his room, leaving me alone with my thoughts again in that shabby old kitchen.

#

The next day drags. I am caught between terror of the future and terror for my kids. I want to get my children back now. Screw that, I need to get them back. Their absence is like an aching hole in my heart. Leary was right. Our best chance—perhaps our only chance—is the big house. Stake it out, break in, find information, free the kids if they are there.

And that means waiting. Not rushing in like headless chickens.

Yeah right! Tell that to a mother who is childless.

And another thing.

That place terrifies me in my depths. I have broken out in worry hives. They have spread all over my arms and my stomach is acting rebellious. Churning and empty at once.

Call me a coward if you will, but remember, this: this is fear not of the unknown but the known. I know what can happen in that godawful place.

But Leary is right. This is our only option. We have no other plays. I cannot stomach the thought that the kids might be there, that those fucks could be experimenting on them.

After supper, still exhausted, I lie down on the couch and doze. I wake after a few minutes, heart pounding like drums in my ears and drenched in cold sweat.

I had seen them there. Sean and Sarah, lying on tables, pale thin hands holding metal, cold merciless eyes staring down at them.

Like you would look at an insect you were dissecting.

Jesus.

Leary is right.

It didn't even register the night before. Isn't this what the fuckers always do. All those stories. I was beamed up by aliens—seriously, I was—and they examined me. Sent probes into my nose and up my bumhole. All that kind of crap I used to mock.

Well, I am not laughing now.

I rush to Leary's room. He is lying fully dressed on his bed, his stockinged feet hanging over the bed, eyes closed, snoring gently. I shout him awake. I want to storm the place immediately, break in there, save the kids. Now, Leary, now! I am beside myself, screaming and shouting, slashing at him with my long nails. Why won't he understand? But Leary talks me down like a horse whisperer. Gentle voiced. Hands on my shoulder. Pulling me close. Tells me to try to be patient. We have to wait. Hide out for a day or so. Let the heat settle. Who knows how the cops will react to the deaths on your property?

He brings me back to my room and lays me on the bed, gives me a pill which sends me into a free fall of dreamless sleep. In the morning after breakfast, he grabs his car keys and leaves, saying he has things to attend to at his lighthouse on the coast and would be back as soon as he could. He is gone for under four hours, time I spend pacing and fretting, with all kinds of waking nightmares rattling around my head. When he returns, I understand why he wanted to delay.

Weapons.

A large traveling bag full.

Three pistols, a double-barreled shotgun, and a small Uzi.

He catches the look I throw at him and shrugs.

"When I was on the force, I did not always hand in what I confiscated from the scumbags." The smile is cheeky again. Back to himself

"Figured, you never know when things might come in useful."

"To start your private war?"

"You complaining again?"

I shake my head and laugh at the look of mock affront he is wearing.

Body armour too, the Kevlar type you see on police shows, and other assorted knickknacks. A ton of ammunition, of course.

"Are you sure you are not a member of some militia out of Montana, or the IRA? Jesus wept."

"Sure, I was only storing it all in my bunker. With the canned food, in case of the Zombie apocalypse. Just as well, huh?"

"I guess," I say, more to myself than him. Thinking, it ain't zombies, but the situation we are in is fairly frigging apocalyptic indeed.

And again he insists we wait.

For night. For the witching hours.

I know he is right; we might only have one chance at this, and we need to be as prepared as possible.

I ask him to give me a handgun, and we spend the afternoon with me learning how to use it. We eat a fast-food takeaway from the village, both of us lost in thought. Not speaking. The food is bland and mostly tasteless, but I figure I will need the strength, so I force it down.

"We should leave at midnight, Zoe. Try and get some rest."

I pace and pace the room, in darkness, with no light except the pale radiance of the moon through the gauze curtains.

Walking back and forth. Hands crossed over the chest. Head low and facing the ground.

Anger and terror the fuel that is driving me on and on.

Sleep? There is none.

Of course not.

I do my best, in my broken way, to keep the worst images from my mind. I focus on my feet on the cold stone and the silvery gleam of the moonlight on the windowsill.

Anything to not think about the kids and what lies in store for us.

Just after midnight, there is a knock on the door.

I am so lost within my frozen self that I barely hear.

Leary pushes the door open, pops his head in, and smiles, a rueful tight smile.

"You ready?"

"I am."

"Grand, so. Let's get on."

And we do.

Chapter 29

We park about half a kilometer away from the entrance to Sanctuary.

Sanctuary, what a title.

Who said aliens don't have a sense of humour?

Leary drives about three hundred yards down an overgrown lane. He turns off the car and we step out into the sudden darkness. The moon is low and hidden beneath the trees, which are sentinels on both sides of the narrow lane.

I wonder briefly where this path leads to. A deserted farmhouse with the family long gone, their memory but a faded whisper in these wooded hills? Perhaps it leads to an old mill or mine and the ghosts beneath the ground still dig for treasure like demented dwarves.

A dog howls somewhere in the distance and I hear a cat calling in heat.

Otherwise, the earth in all its splendor is silent. The night is a solemn and cold thing, and for a long moment I imagine I am alone.

And that feeling, that solitude, is a wonder of the good sort, only possible in the gentle cover of these rustling oaks towering above me in the darkness.

For a brief moment, I am on my own. Leary is a figment of my febrile imagination. The kids are safe and well and tucked up in their beds and snoring gently in their snuggled-up sleep.

Jimmy is sitting in the living room with his feet on the table, listening to Nickleback on the surround sound, with a smile on his face and his phone open in front of him, texting somebody.

Still a bastard, mind, but my bastard.

But that was in the alternate world. The one I had known once but left behind. The one where wonder meant a beautiful sunset as the sun disappears behind distant peaks, great sex on a tropical beach, and later, the feel of my babies in my arms as I whisper one last goodnight to them.

Their warmth and gentle breaths. Their trust in me.

I should have appreciated it then, that world, for all the genuine wonders it contained.

Here, in this darkness beneath the trees, in this twisted wonderland—the one in which I have been chasing aliens down the rabbit hole—there is no space for wonder, only terror.

I laugh out loud, a startling sound in this relative silence.

Leary turns to me, startled.

We are a long way from the house and still he holds his finger up to his mouth, urging me to be quiet.

I laugh again, but I do keep it down this time.

"What?" he growl-whispers at me.

"I was thinking of a song. It´s gotten inside my head now. Bit of an earworm."

He shakes his head, but sighs too. "Jaysus, Zoe. This isn't the time."

Guess he is as wound up as me in his own Leary way. His 'big man calm' and 'I know what to do' vibe undercut by churning fear.

I say nothing, but stand there, one hand on my hip, knowing even now I´ll get him to bite.

He moves closer to me, leaning forward so his face is close to mine. He looks ridiculous in his too-tight open-faced balaclava and dark sweats.

Like a Navy Seal who actually has the body of a seal.

"Fuck it. Right, so. Go on. What song. Let´s hear it."

I smile again.

"White Rabbit."

"Shi-it, Zoe. Jefferson Airplane. Here and now?"

"Can you think of anything more appropriate to where we have to go?" I gesture at the darkness in the rough direction of the alien house.

"Nope."

"Do you remember the lyrics?"

"I most certainly do." A soft smile now on his face. A smile I have grown fond of.

"One pill makes you small, Go ask Alice," I sing in a whisper.

"And if you go chasing rabbits."

"Know you are going to fall."

"Fuck, I think you've infected me now."

"See. Psychedelic eeriness. Especially tonight."

"Alrighty. Let's go chase ourselves some goddamn rabbits then."

"And try not to fall."

"Amen to that."

And we climb over the nearest ditch and into the damp long grass of the neighbouring field. As we make our way slowly across the wide expanse of waving grass in the moon glow, I hear him humming to himself.

And I sing along. In my head.

"Chasing rabbits, and trying not to fall."

#

Leary is a wonder.

Have I told you that?

Was a wonder, I suppose I should say now.

But that comes later.

For his next trick, he pulls a pair of binoculars out of his rucksack. The same rucksack that contains his handgun, reams of ammunition, and a freaking Uzi.

"Night vision, so they are. But you can get this shit anywhere." I still note the smugness of the smile on his lips. Have to be careful of the hero worship. Don't want to stoke his ego too much.

Still, it feels pretty damned good to be with someone who seems to know what the hell they are doing.

We are on a hillock in the neighbouring field to the house. From where we are kneeling, we have a perfect view over the trees into the driveway, the parking area in front of the house, the main door, and adjacent pyramids that are the wings.

The places looks deserted, feels empty, in a way I find hard to describe.

The main building looks like it has been abandoned for years. Like dust has built up and rot set into the floorboards. The foundations have started to sag in the middle and made everything that bit smaller and less even.

I imagine it creaking inside: night sounds that belong to more than just the shifting, unhappy madam that it has become.

Pure fantasy, of course, for how can it have turned into a haunted house in the short months since I was last here.

But sometimes fantasy and reality meet in those interstices in the world where violence has been done and the unreal sighted and reported.

Like now.

Leary lowers the binoculars and glances over at me. Shakes his head.

It is late, or rather early in the morning. Everything is boarded up, the car park empty.

"There ain´t nobody home, Zoe!"

There is a long pause, as if he is debating with himself.

Caution versus the need to move forward.

"The fuckers may have pulled up and gone, but maybe we should wait and see whether anyone shows up. That is the more sensible course. I don't know that it is the right one."

I know what he is telling me. He may not sense the evil haunt in the house, but he knows. Deep down, he knows.

He knows that the kids are most likely not here.

He knows that if this place is empty, empty as my house was when we visited it, then Sarah and Sean could be gone for good.

God knows whether I will ever find them again or not, find out what Jimmy has done to or with them.

This is our last and only hope of getting them back. We do not know if they are alive or, God forbid, not. We do not know, but we can imagine.

Time is running out.

"We have to go now. I cannot afford to wait."

Even as I say it, I can feel my stomach lurch and my legs turn to jelly. My hands are shaking as if palsied. Sweat breaks out on my forehead and upper lip.

I really, really do not want to go back into that place. It is a place of fear and darkness.

"Fuck!" It sounds like heresy in the silence of the night.

"Guess we are not playing assassins anymore." His voice is mock scolding as he puts a gentle arm around me. I remember feeling like I was sinking in on myself, like a solid body dissolving in a vat of acid, or ice melting in warm water. I was tortured, abused, raped in that building, and now I need to find the bravery within myself to go back. For the sake of the two people I love in this world above life itself.

To honour the vow that I swore at their births to protect them.

We stay like that for a long time, seconds, minutes, or hours. I do not know. It might as well have been an eternity for that is what I suffered.

Except then it was gone.

I force my hands to be still.

I suck air into my lungs in great breaths, gird my stomach, and make steel of my legs.

Not literally, of course. That would be daft. But you get the idea. I dug deep and found my courage.

Leary knew when I was ready. Of course, he did.

"Shall we?" His voice mock-serious, but tinged with an edge.

"We shall. We shall indeed. Lead on Macduff."

And so, he did. Down the hill and into hell.

#

The grass we are trudging through is heavy, laden with dew, the ground uneven and treacherous. Leary is breathing hard and cursing under his breath.

We are moving too fast for the ninjas I guess we are supposed to be, and the old fella feels it.

But fuck it.

We are doing this.

The tips of the pyramidal extensions gleam in the moonlight as if imbued with a chill power, yet the darkness around the house itself, in the shadows of the eaves, is absolute.

As is the silence.

Our feet slipping through grass. There is only the rhythm of our moving feet.

No other sounds.

Except the sounds of our breaths, amplified. We are astronauts sucking oxygen in spacesuits in a distant and inhuman world.

An immense, eerie, empty world, for the world itself is of a different construction in the bleak shadows of this awful place.

We reach the graveled areas in front of the house.

Leary bends over, huffing.

"Fuck me," I hear him say.

And I understand. The hill was steep and the going heavy, and the night pitch but that is not the sum of it; it is as though the house itself has a gravitational field stronger than the rest of earth. Movement here, near the house, is harder, slower.

Leary is already struggling with old age and a massive gut. He needs denser gravity, like a kick in the head.

With Leary leading, we duck into the darkness that surrounds the house and, in Indian file, move towards the rear of the building. I dare not look up as we pass the pyramid.

My mind screams at me to run, to turn. Not to risk that horror again.

But my mind is a fickle, treacherous thing and I will those feeble thoughts away with all my newfound powers of determination.

Zoe Hearty, warrior queen. Yeah, right! But at least I haven't cut and run yet.

And then we are past that accursed extension and at the rear of the estate; the stables and other outhouses visible in the distance, as dark artifacts in the little light we have.

Leary nods to a window near the back door. A cat cries from far away and I jump. Shit.

We get to the window. Locked of course.

Leary gestures me to stay and walks the length of the back of the house, rattling doors and windows.

When he returns, he shakes his head. Everything locked, as expected, and silent as a tomb. I point at the window and shrug. He gives me a thumbs up. We had discussed this, but he hasn't seen any sign of an active alarm system.

Either strange, given how paranoid these society fuckers, or disillusioning. If they believe they have nothing left in this building, then why protect it?

And Leary does it again.

Out of his duffel bag comes a lock out tool.

His smile is comfortingly smug.

"I was in the boy scouts, what can I say?"

It is a tall, thin flexible piece of rounded metal, a semicircle with a handle and a pincer at the far end. He inserts it between the narrow gaps at the side of the door.

"A miracle of a thing," he says happily. And it is, for he maneuvers the grasping pincer, and with a simple wrist movement turns the handle of the door within.

"Two pounds of torque. Like stealing candy from a baby."

I whistle quietly. It really is impressive. But that does not stop the circle of cold fear, panic almost, that begins to circulate in widening waves through my stomach.

Leary shoves the door in and steps into the darkness. I hesitate. A long, long moment. It is with a conscious effort that I push my right foot forward over the threshold and place it in unholy ground.

#

God, it stinks. I almost gag.

Rotting flesh, spoiled food or worse, and a deeper smell that is almost sulphuric.

Like an old chemistry lab which has seen its fair share of failed experiments.

Light from the moon eases through the two large windows in the rear wall and we both have flashlights, so we can see well enough. We are in the large kitchen, part of the servants' quarters at the back of the house.

Leary taps me on the shoulder and points to the open door leading deeper into the house. I follow behind him. The place is a mess. Fallen and broken furniture and rubbish strewn everywhere, pantry cupboards open, stains on worktops, a buzzing from the sink that sounds like a legion of moving flies.

Cockroaches on the ground. Stains on the walls too. In the light of the torch, these look more like excrement than blood, but who can tell?

I bump into Leary. He has stopped near the open door.

I follow his gaze to a heap of gnawed bones near the door.

"The dogs must have been hungry," he says, but his voice is quiet.

"Those are not human."

"Doesn't look like it. But I'll let you decide, what in the name of Jesus, human means recently."

His face is stretched, pale as a Samurai's warmask and almost as fierce.

"They are long gone. The society. It doesn't feel like there is anybody home."

"No, I guess not."

"And no frigging dogs."

"Nope. Thank the lord." I hesitate. "Leary, I don't get it."

"What?"

"When I was here last time, at the party, this place was different." I try to put into words what I barely understand. "A rich folk's pad. Well kept. Classy furniture. Nice wallpaper. Wall hangings. All very chic. This is… it's crazy, Like bedlam. Dope heads in a tenement on the Northside would be ashamed."

"I know. I was here too remember. Ramsey showed me around."

"So, what gives?"

"The center cannot hold."

"Jesus, Leary. Not Yeats."

"No? Seems not inappropriate right about now."

And it does.

Lines of the poem come back to me.

"The blood-dimmed tide is loosed," I say.

"What rough beast, its hour come around at last, slouches to Bethleham to be born."

And I do know what he means and feels. This is the hour of the rough beasts. They are waiting to be born, have been born already. Those alien pricks.

Whatever has happened in this house in the last months has been an abomination. Inhuman, in every sense of that word.

And my babies are not here, or if they are, they are silent and entombed.

I start to cry. I feel a knot in my chest like a fist. I have trouble breathing. Tears explode out of me, great gasps of pain and anguish, like vomiting fear and grief.

After everything that has been done to me, to the kids, this place is showing its true nature, and its nature is like the straw on that camel's back breaking me in two.

I can't take this shit anymore.

Leary wraps his arms around me and whispers soothingly, and his arms are warm and comforting.

It takes long minutes before the panic subsides and I can breathe again.

"It was the bones."

"I know," he kisses the top of my head.

"They are so small."

"Shush, Zoe. They are animal, not human. I swear."

"I have to get them back."

And there it is again, that image from a dream, of the kids in a cottage—or was it a barracks—in the country being fattened, prepared, for something, their lives in such peril.

To be eaten.

Or worse.

To be turned like those monsters we killed in our house.

Fear enlarging their pleading eyes. Mam, come and get us, come and save us.

Tick, tock as time goes by and it feels like I am on a treadmill, running hard, as fast as I possibly can, but getting nowhere, no closer to them.

"This place is a shithole, but an empty fucking shit-hole. We just have to look hard enough, Zoe. Scour the bloody place. We will find something here. We will. They have left something behind. We'll find out what these fucks are up to and where they are now; then we will get your kids. We just can't afford to lose it now. Agreed?"

I suck in deep breaths and my heart slows and the pain in my chest lightens.

I push him away from me, and bend over, hands on my knees.

A few minutes later and the panic is gone.

I straighten, stare up at him and say, "I am getting sick of this, Leary. Can you not just get your shit together and keep it that way for once?"

He looks at me with real kindness, his eyes moist, and he places one big mutt of a palm on my cheek and leaves it there for a few seconds.

It feels both warm and cooling at once.

Comforting.

"Let's do this then."

#

We scour the place from top to bottom.

Broken or upset furniture, a harsh smell of urine—almost like a stinging gas—smeared walls, random bones, empty pizza cartons, beer cans, and even more smeared walls.

It looks like the place hosted spring break for a bunch of psycho convicts and drug dealers.

The extension—that pyramid-shaped room that had freaked me out so much the first time I was here—turns out to be nothing more than a modern folly: lots of high glass letting in star and moonlight like a foyer in some city hotel that is trying hard to be modern chic, three or four bedrooms on the far wall, marble flooring.

Nice, in its own way, if completely inappropriate for the rest of the building. Not scary at all.

If it wasn't so derelict, I would expect some gentle piano music and a smiling concierge behind reception.

Bland and boring, apart from the stink and the dirt.

And yet I remember the effect it had on me—like walking alone through the universe in an infinity of stars and time.

"The magic is gone," I say to Leary quietly as we stand together looking up at the stars.

"Magic?"

"They are so far ahead of us technologically, it might as well be."

"Fair point."

"So where have they taken it? Where the fuck are they?"

Our search proves pointless.

There is nothing here except despair and a nagging headache from the poisonous air.

Exhausted, we sit shoulder to shoulder on a sofa near the main entrance. Saying nothing.

I feel the earth opening beneath me, a cavern of despair. I see no way forward, but I have let myself go once already tonight. Twice would be indulgent.

Leary is silent.

I can feel his exhaustion as a wave of negative energy around us.

He will never admit defeat, but this situation is dire. No records, no paper, no laptops, no files. Nothing. Spoiled food and excrement.

Could be a metaphor for my life lately.

I laugh.

"What?" He sounds peeved.

"Nothing. Just thinking." I slap him on his shoulder. "Get up off the flat of your arse, you big lump. We ain´t done yet."

"We should try again. Try harder. Must have missed something."

"We should. We will."

"Right so."

And he is about to stand, hands on his knees, when we hear the sound of a growling engine. Diesel car or van, approaching and fast, tires trundling over the gravel outside.

"Jesus."

Lights from outside sweeps through the narrow windows, lighting up the hall and the wooden staircase.

"They came back?"

"Christ, I hope so. If it is cops, we are fucked."

We move now, like a well-oiled machine, two minds acting as one. If this unexpected visitor is police, then we are done, but if it is someone from the society, then we are back in business.

Perhaps.

We move from the sofa to the dark space beneath the wooden staircase. I position myself to the rear, gun in hand and trained on the long hallway that leads to the kitchen, while Leary has the shotgun leveled at the main door.

He glances over at me and smiles.

"Knew something would come along."

"Hope it's the right something, Butch."

"Right you are. We don't need a last stand just now. And Sundance…"

"What?"

"Remember to aim."

I give him my worst stink eye and smile.

One way or another, this is it.

#

A key turns in the lock.

That gets my heart beating again and, despite the nerves, I sigh in relief.

Unlikely the police would be so polite as to unlock the door if they were after us or even after the society.

The door swings open, and in the pale back shadow of the moon, a man steps into the room.

Unmistakable.

That pumped-up body.

That 'don't fuck with me' stance.

Ramsey.

Standing in the doorway like an advertisement for stupidity and steroids.

"Is he alone?" I allow myself a faint whisper.

Leary shrugs.

I check out the passageway behind but hear nothing, see nothing.

Ramsey sniffs the air, like some bloodhound with heightened senses.

He senses something, us I presume, *that* he had not expected. Something, for want of a better, less ironic word, alien.

And how the hell can he do that from that distance?

He steps into the room and from the light of the high windows I see the glint of metal in his hand.

A long, wicked looking blade. His Samurai sword.

"Are you here, Witch? Is that your foul odor I sense?"

His voice is flat, dull.

Like somebody narrating in a foreign language they do not fully understand.

"Zoe, Zoe, Zoe. My favourite Witch Bitch. We've finally caught up."

I glance at Leary. He looks back at me and raises an eyebrow.

"I never did think you were gone for good. I told Jimmy. I did. Said the Witch Bitch is not dead. No, sir. She will be back, I said to him." He laughs. The sound is hollow, like echoes in a drum. Ramsey, or whatever this thing is, sounds fucked up and on something serious.

"Come to me, Witch Bitch. Time to put an end to all this nonsense, don't you think?"

Weapon held two-handed in front of him, he edges into the room and makes for where we are hiding.

Ramsey is looking at me. Despite the darkness and the fact that he is silhouetted in moonlight, his eyes are aglow—a creepy gray-blue light that is the colour of death and ash, the exact same hue as the unearthly light that followed us in the car.

"Come on down, Witch Bitch."

His eyes are on mine. In mine. My heartbeat is a concussive drum.

"Witch Bitch, Witch Bitch, Witch Bitch."

A pounding sound in my ears as I step towards him. Am pulled towards him.

The eyes dragging me forward.

It is like being harpooned, stabbed, and pulled at once.

The sound of his voice drowning out any of the righteous protests my brain is attempting to raise. Another step. I lower the gun. Three steps, four, five.

"The kids need you, Witch Bitch. You know they do. They are waiting for you. To hold their bitch mother again. They are crying out for you, you know; I can take you to them. You can be together again."

His voice is suffused with glee and a hunger that is almost palpable. For violence. For blood.

To feed.

I know I am walking to my death.

To my willing destruction.

But in the glow of those eyes and the hypnotic fervour of that voice I am helpless.

Mowgli in the python's gaze.

I have the crazy notion that he intends not to eat me, but to swallow me whole and consume me over time.

Crazy, yes, but this is the wonderful wonderland I have fallen into, where even the worst nightmare seems possible.

And isn't that exactly what these alien beings do, swallow and transform us. They changed Jimmy. They turned those people we killed at my house into monsters.

They devour us and then spit us out in whatever fashion they choose.

I fight the pull with all my heart and soul, but to no avail.

And then I remember who I am fighting for.

An image of Sarah appears. Sean is there too. In front of me. Hazy and imperfect images of them, like corrupted video files.

Ghostlike. Flickering.

Jumping up and down. Waving me back.

Screaming.

Terrified eyes. Pale and haggard faces. They have lost so much weight. They look ill and worn and exhausted.

My babes.

And, as if from far away, as though from tunnels deep within the mass of the earth, their voices. Calling out to me. Thin and hollow

Stop Mama. We need you. Stop.

Don't go to the monster.

Come to us instead.

In order to save them, I must first save myself.

Break this spell. Stop my descent towards Ramsey's craziness.

And just like that, with that simple realisation, the spell breaks. It is like ears popping on a descending airplane—you know what I mean— that sudden hard pop back into the reality of sound.

From behind me, Leary's voice comes hard and urgent. "Jaysus, Zoe. Get your ass out of the way. You are in my line of fucking fire."

There is a sound of something fast approaching from the rear of the house, an unnatural skittering sound, and far away in a normal world, I hear a dog bark in a distant field.

And yet I move forward, through the fading mirage of my wonderful children.

Towards Ramsey.

I am but a dozen paces from him. He must think I am still in his thrall for he does nothing.

And still, I move forward.

Another step and another.

Closer and closer.

His teeth are white, bared in a snarl. The sword is raised over his shoulder, ready to strike.

I raise the gun and pull the trigger.

And again.

Flashes of red and the smell of cordite and those sounds, so loud in the darkness.

Ramsey bellows in pain.

I shout over my shoulder.

"Behind you, Leary. Coming fast. Watch out."

I turn back.

The gray light in Ramsey's eyes goes out, the sword falls from his hand with a clatter and he slumps to his knees.

He is down.

No time to check on him.

A snarling scream, like the roaring of a banshee from the hallway leading to the kitchen and the servants' quarters. I run towards Leary, to where he is standing in the throat of the hallway.

"No! Leary!"

It is no more than two dozen steps, but it feels like eternity. Like time has once again turned to treacle in this hellish place.

Another screaming snarl, high pitched and piercing, like nothing I have ever heard before.

Coming closer at impossible speed.

It is impossible to see anything.

I reach into my coat pocket for my torch.

Leary shoots, the shotgun blast like thunder in this enclosed space. Blinding.

With trembling fingers, I flick the switch and wave the torch in my offhand into the hallway. Swaying left to right, but there is nothing to see.

Flickering, dancing light and emptiness.

And then that bile of a scream again and—Lord help us—it is above us. I drop to my knees and point the torch at the ceiling. There. Less than seven feet away, and scampering across the ceiling like a camel spider. Mouth open in a hellish grin, it leaps at Leary.

Fast. So fast.

The shape humanoid, and yet not: limbs twisted and contorted like no mammal ever should be.

I shoot over Leary's head. He fires the shotgun and then it is on him.

An arm like a blade swinging, jaws open at an impossible angle as it tries to rip off his face.

I surge to my feet. Leary is on the ground, fighting as the thing lowers its enormous, fanged jaws onto his face. I aim, hold my breath like he showed me, breathe out and fire.

Risky, I know, but those fangs are moments from tearing his face to shreds.

And, because in this new-found incarnation of mine, I am Zoe Hearty, Amazon and Warrior Queen, I hit the fucking thing. Square in the head.

Boom.

Blast.

Over.

Like in an old Batman cartoon.

I fall to my knees.

And sob.

Until the ground beneath me is damp with my tears.

#

Leary is hurt and moaning in pain.

I get to my feet and stumble towards him. He is on the ground and the creature that attacked us is lying on him. Except, of course, it is no longer a creature.

He cries out in pain as I push the thing, the woman as it now is, off of him.

I can't help crying out in horror.

Adele, Ramsey's partner.

That makes a certain sick and yet inevitable sense.

They came here together, looking for what? For us perhaps. Although it beats me how they could have known we were here. Maybe something different, something the cult had left behind. And I know this is deflection, I am focusing on what is not important, rather than the actual consequences of what just occurred. By some fluke we intersected, and now they are both dead, and we, Leary and I, are none the wiser. That is the reality. One I am not ready to face.

And then I hear Ramsey moan, and watch in horror as he tries to lever himself to his feet. I grab the shotgun from where it fell between Leary's legs and aim it at Ramsey who is leaning on his arms and flexing his legs like a damaged spider.

My first thought is to shoot the fucker, but I know that without him, we have nothing.

I step towards him. His head swivels at the sound of my approach. His eyes are pale and monstrous.

You know that feeling of revulsion you have when a cockroach skitters out from under the fridge? That sense of difference, of fundamental mutual unintelligibility, and that shock inside you at such a primal invasion; that is what I saw in those eyes, except a thousand times worse. A truly alien intelligence that was both malignant and threatening.

I raise the butt of the shotgun and swing it into his forehead. To shut down the light in those eyes.

Hard.

Very hard.

His head snaps back and blood wells from the wound. He slumps to

209

the ground, prone. I wait long enough to be sure he is out, then I check his pulse. Alive. For now.

Blood is spilling from a gash across Leary´s cheek and there is an ugly bite mark leading from his neck to his shoulder. I rip off my jacket and press it against the bleeding.

He smiles up at me weakly. "Hurts like a bitch."

I smile back and rub my hand along his cheek in a gentle caress. This fat ugly man, this gentle kind man, has been my rock through all this; I could not bear to continue without him.

"Can you move?"

"Course I bloody can. Not done for yet." His face is haggard and his eyes small and gleaming. He is in way more pain than he is letting on.

"Get me back to the farm. You can patch me up there."

"You need a doctor."

"Like a hole in the head. I have everything we need at the farm, Zoe." He grabs hold of my hand and holds it tight. "We can't risk getting outsiders involved."

"Ramsey is alive."

He smiles. "I gathered that, and then I heard what you did to him."

"Just a gentle whack. His noggin is as tough as yours."

"Fuck."

"I know."

"We need him."

"Get the car. Reverse as close as you can to the door."

I pause, hesitant. Not wanting to leave him here, wounded and in pain.

"Go, woman."

I still hesitate.

"Go! I'll be fine. But give me the shotgun in case that fucker wakes."

Chapter 30

Looking back, I don't know how we managed.

Ramsey was still out when I got back. He was a large lump to pull and carry, even with the rope from the back of the truck.

It seemed to take hours, and it was nearly the end of Leary, but we got him into the back of the SUV. Driving to the farm, I almost bit through my tongue with worry. Leary was out of it, mumbling to himself, and pale as a winter-worn statue.

I drove up to the back of the farmhouse and reversed up to the old shed after opening the double doors.

Pulling him out of the machine and onto the ground took every scrap of energy I had left, but I had no choice but to keep going.

Tie Ramsey up. Make sure the knots are tight. Never mind the knot in your stomach and your trembling hands.

Get to it.

Lock the doors. Drive the car to the farmhouse. Get Leary inside.

He had a medical kit. Of course, he did. A good one too—would have put many a Mash unit to shame. Disinfectant, gauze, and bandages wrapped tight. Painkillers and a large helping of good whiskey put Leary to bed.

I collapsed there right beside him, still dressed.

I dreamed of eyes in the night, eyes in the darkness, covetous eyes. They were outside looking in. They were envious of what we had in the house where we were.

Thieves in the night.

Planning to murder us in our beds.

Alien eyes in the darkness staring at you as you sleep. I bet you have dreamed of them too?

#

I am not proud of what I did next.

I am not proud, nor did I enjoy it. It made me sick to my stomach. Profoundly ill in a way very little else has in my life. It sullied me and took from me. It damaged me and made me a lesser being.

I am not sure I can say that about anything else I did. All those monstrous things you accuse me of. Violent things, yes, but how could I really feel bad about killing monsters. As often as not, it was either them or me.

Adele, or whatever she had become, would have killed us. So would the others. I was—as I was slowly beginning to realise—at war. A war for my sanity, for the lives of my family, and perhaps even for the lives of others.

To listen to Leary, we were fighting for the future of humanity.

Fine.

I was a soldier.

But the torture of Ramsey made me ill. It destroyed a part of me that has never since recovered. Judge me for this, if you wish. Do not dare judge me for the rest.

Decide that it was wrong, if you must. I understand, but I felt then I had no choice. I feel the same now.

I do know I would do it again.

I had no other option if I wanted to see Sarah and Sean again.

Let me tell it quickly and be done with it.

I woke with a start beside Leary, snoring like a bear.

Fast asleep, moaning quietly.

His wounds were deep, but I knew he would survive if they did not get infected. It would take more than that to put a man mountain like him down. We were lucky. I was. Looking down on him, I knew this with deep certainty and some of the agony of my torn and battered heart was soothed.

I rested the palm of his hand against his face for a long moment. No fever. I kept my hand there until he stirred and said something incoherent.

When he was fully under again, I went to check on our guest.

Sitting in a puddle of his own piss, pulling against his binds, struggling like an animal, face red with effort, one eye swollen shut, and blood caking his face.

In another life, I might have had sympathy, have gone easy on him, but he knew. He knew what had happened to Guy, I was convinced. He knew where Jimmy and the kids were.

And there was little that was left of him that was human.

When his eyes settled on me, I felt like I was being swarmed by red ants. Those pale eyes. That gray, unnatural ashy colour.

I got a knife. A rusty knife and I used it on him. On it. Until he told me what I needed to know.

It went like this.

#

They had, of course, heard me scramble back to the house that night: the night that Guy disappeared.

Ramsey told me because I threatened to cut off his balls with a rusty saw in the shed on the deserted farm which I shared with Leary.

"It was Banning's decision," Ramsey wheezed through the pain. "Had to be done. A sacrifice in the name of Ka. The quack knew too much, and could wrest you and the kids from us. We needed them. Back then we were still unsure about you, if we could turn you, but the young are precious and malleable. We needed your kids, and we needed the quack out of the way."

Ka, the thing both inside and without, the prime mover of the deceit and lies they worshiped and were working towards. The worm that is the rot that will be the end of us all. The souls of aliens.

I think I drove the blade deeper into Ramsey's wound at that point. I remember him gagging blood. Even Ka cannot protect completely against physical pain.

When he recovered, this was what Ramsey told me:

"After we heard you running back to the house, I punched your husband's shoulder. Hard, to get him to focus on our mission. Zoe is a loose cannon, I told him. The quack knows about us, and Ka/Banning cannot let that stand. Your wife has witnessed too much. It's too dangerous to risk her leaving you and the quack has to be gotten out of the way, for he enables her. Ka/Banning has willed it so.`

"Jimmy did stare after you. I think even then he might have reneged. I believe part of him tried. It showed in the flush of colour that filled his face, and the broken red capillaries in the whites of his eyes. A fierce struggle, but pointless. His Ka prevailed. Ka always does, for so it is ordained. Me, I think he wanted to save himself. His children. Sarah and Sean. Never you. You were not that much to him."

And it smiled then at me, and it knew that the wounds its words stabbed me with were as painful as any I could inflict on him.

"What did you do, you sick shit? What happened to Guy?"

Ramsey was in a bad way at this stage. I had been working on him and his inner demons for a day and a half, but he did regain enough clarity, or perhaps humanity, to tell me the story.

"Jimmy wanted to go after you. I knew that was not wise. You were not ready, not yet one of us. The chosen are chosen for a reason, and though Ka wanted you, you were never his receptacle. We almost came to blows, but Jimmy relented. He knew. He knew we could not trust you. He knew the value of the mission placed in our hands. You had seen too much, told too much, trusted too much.

And so, we drove to the therapist's house. It was not far, a fifteen-minute drive. The air was hot and the A/C in our van did not work, so I had the windows down. We could hear the sound of nightjars in the fields to the east when we parked halfway down the long entry way to his house. His two-story cottage was at the rear of a dark cul-de-sac, gatehouse to an old gentry house that had been burned in the first war. No neighbours, no busybodies to phone the cops, but still, we were careful. We walked in single file, lightless, the rest of the way. He was in his living room, pacing, a telephone in his right hand. Staring at it as though the numbers on the dial were runes. That made me nervous. If he called the police he would set in motion powers we were not yet ready to face. The Ka within me squirmed in fear and I understood its worry. We were still few and vulnerable. The work of the chosen was nowhere near complete. If this man brought the powers of the world down upon our heads, that work might be delayed. We could not take that chance."

I hurt Ramsey again, I could not help it. He sobbed as the thin blade of my knife sank deep into already mangled flesh. I twisted the blade and he cried out. I had become a monster. They had made me one, but no matter how bad I got, I would never be as monstrous as they would be. I spat in his face.

"Tell me what you did to him!"

He took great gasping breaths, tears rolling down his cheeks.

"Fear drove us on then. I could feel it pouring off Jimmy too, but the Ka was great within us. We jogged towards the red-painted door and rang the bell. I stood to one side out of view as Jimmy rang the bell, again and again, the shrill sound inside deafening. I took deep breaths and waited. Jimmy kept pressing the bell. The quack knew. Had to have known it was us, or somebody like us. What if he rang for help? What if he ran? Our plan was not exactly foolproof. And then the door opened.

"Jimmy, what the fuck do you want here?"

The little man had a look on his face that could scare lions, but he was a little man, and Jimmy didn't give a fuck. Until he saw the putter held over the fella's shoulder like a mace.

"Careful, Doc," said Jimmy. Hands out wide, backing off a little. "Just wanted a quick chat. About Zoe. You know, my wife. The woman I am married to. You are her therapist after all."

Silence then for a long moment and I felt a, for want of a better word, professional hesitation in the doc.

"Your wife is my patient, Mr. Hearty. But you are not. You are not welcome here. This is my home, Mr. Hearty. Now please be so kind as to fuck off out of here before I call the police and get you thrown behind bars."

"Behind bars." Jimmy mimicked his tone, a whiny drawl as he edged away from the door.

And then the Brit stepped forward and his goose was cooked."

"What did you do to him?"

Ramsey looked up at me, a gleam in his eyes as ugly as the thing within him. A sickly, gray-eyed gleam, foreign and hateful.

His face changed. His skin contracted, the air around him became chill and the beast was made visible as it emerged for a few moments. Him, and not him at the same time. There, and not there. Two things happening at once.

I had seen this before of course, but no matter how often it happens, you cannot prepare for the sudden disconnect. It is like a change in air pressure, like the strange noise you sometimes get in your eardrums, that hissing peeping sound, except this is louder and involves other senses. To look at it is to feel vertigo.

How can this and that, these two disparate things, be real all at once. It is the sound and the smell and even the taste of strange.

It is hard, hard to describe, but then how do you describe the impossible? This shit feels biblical, and yet you can reach out and touch it and smell the rot in your nose and taste the darkness on your tongue.

It looked out at me, this creature, from behind Ramsey's eyes.

It looked at me, and its eyes were pale with contempt. Its eyes were corrupt and aged. Its stink was damnation and oblivion. It was the end of us all.

Crazy murderous bitch, you say. And maybe you have a point.

Maybe, but wait till you see it. Tell me then that I was wrong.

And see it, you will.

Now pay attention and you might still learn how to save yourselves.

#

They killed Guy, of course.

Dumped his body.

Ramsey was carrying a baseball bat. Old and made of ash. When Guy stepped forward, Ramsey, still unseen, swung overhead and smashed him with it on the crown of his head. Guy sunk to his knees with a groan. They stood looking at one another for a long moment, stunned by the enormity of their act.

The Society's warriors had drawn first blood in the long struggle ahead, at least according to their lights. I imagine even for them, in this incarnation, that must have been a moment of decision. A quickening of purpose.

Jimmy snapped out of it, reacted first. He grabbed Guy under the arms and barked at Ramsey to shift his hole.

They manhandled Guy to the boot of their car, and in renowned mafia style, stuffed him inside.

I imagine Guy then, his small frame stuffed into that dark space, blood oozing from his scalp. Moaning. Neither conscious nor unconscious. I wish still I could reach out to him, save him. Get him out of that terrible place. He might have saved me. He might have had the strength to keep damnation from my head. I will never know.

They drove him deep into the mountains, into the place beyond the Comeraghs, where the three lakes meet. Somewhere in a forest of spruce, they took a turn up a logging road. Ramsey got out and pulled aside the unlocked barrier. Jimmy drove slowly uphill into the trees, the lights of the car flickering and feeble in the dark, the road narrow and unpaved.

They stopped at a bend where the narrow road widened and pulled open the boot. As Ramsey tells it, Guy was conscious and leaped out at them, fighting, arms flailing, spitting, and screaming.

He never stood a chance. Ramsey had ditched his baseball bat for, of all things, a Samurai sword. Jimmy had the bat. They beat Guy, stabbed him. I remember Ramsey, or the demon within, looking up at me with something akin to wonder. Guy still would not fall.

Bleeding from half a dozen cuts, his skull and face a mask of blood, and on his knees. He refused to give up. Jimmy swung at the back of his head and knocked him face down onto the ground.

Ramsey hacked at his neck. One, twice, again and again.

And then Guy´s head was separate from his neck. Though I did not know it then, all the hope I had left in this world drained away with his life`s blood.

Draining into the muck, a little rivulet, dark as the night in that empty place.

They buried him in a levee a few hundred meters from the road, deep in the trees and far from people and hope.

To the best of my knowledge, he has still not been found.

#

On the third day, Leary woke. Must have sensed something. I doubt he could have heard anything from where I was. He was there when I looked up from my bloody work, with a face that could best be described as inscrutable.

We never did speak of it after, but I know he disapproved. Not in a moral or judgmental way. And I understood. He would have been more elegant.

More precise and more effective.

It was done.

Ramsey slumped forward, moaning.

I had everything I needed.

We had a way forward.

#

We are getting ready to leave for the ranch Ramsey told us about—when it happens.

There is a loud piercing scream from the shed.

When I was seven, I stayed a week on my Granddad's farm. One day, the men cornered a pig. It knew it was about to be slaughtered and it screamed and fought. A loud pitiful high-pitched squeal of protest.

This is that and so much more.

A being in extremis.

In shock, I drop the duffel bag I am carrying to the truck. It lands with a loud thud. We are a well-prepared mini army. We will have to be. Leary comes storming out of the main door of the cottage. His bandages are still in situ, but his energy is back.

He has recovered more quickly than I could have believed, but then Leary is a bull of a man.

He has a gun in both hands in front of him and he nods to the shed.

The plan has been to leave Ramsey here until we get back, if we get back. On no account can we let Ramsey escape. Our only hope is surprise.

To surprise Banning and the rest of the alien cultists at the ranch and free the kids.

We run to the shed together.

My heart is thumping and I can feel fear-sweat building.

We are so close to leaving, so close to finally getting to the kids. There is no way Ramsey can be a threat any longer. Not after what I put him through in the last days.

Surely not.

And yet for some reason, I am worried.

Leary pulls open the barn door and stops as if he has walked into a forcefield. He takes a step back, something I could never have imagined happening. I pull up beside him and gag.

Ramsey is no longer lying on the ground. He is floating near the roof of the shed, his body raised about ten feet into the air, spreadeagled as if being crucified. Demon possessed, as in a horror movie. He screams again, his mouth wide open and his jaw shatters as his body writhes and buckles. He looks down at me, mouth now a gaping hole, right into my eyes, and his eyes are human and pleading.

I vomit then.

All over my shoes.

For I sense what is coming.

He screams again, even louder, ear-shattering, in agony. He begins to gag as if choking. A long thin sliver of what looks like molten silver peeks out from his throat. For a long moment, there is silence except for the muffled attempts of Ramsey trying to breathe. Then the silver thing tears out of him like a reverse bullet towards the ceiling of the shed, It smashes through it as though it is composed of wet paper.

Ramsey crashes to the ground, face first; his neck bends and twists on impact.

Askew in a truly unnatural fashion.

For what is left now is the true Ramsey.

The human shell, the remains. His eyes open, human now, only human.

Leary is red-faced looking up at the shattered ceiling, shaking his head.

"Figures," he says after an indeterminate time.

"What's that?"

"There is that Bruce Springsteen song. 'We Take Care of Our Own.' This was that."

"Huh!"

"The parasite or whatever it is that they are. Biological weapons. Alien downloads. It has just returned home to its masters. To its colleagues. To whatever and wherever the fuck they come from."

I laugh. A hysterical high-pitched laugh that sounds obscene in the sullen silence of this bloody place.

"What the hell, Zoe?"

Shaking my head, I look up at him. "All those philosophers. All those gurus. Pondering what comes after death. What is the weight of a soul? Where does it come from?"

"So?"

"Guess we have proof of a sort that a soul can exist."

Leary stares hard at me with worried eyes.

I laugh again. A laugh of strained relief, for what else can one do on the face of this horror, and I wink.

"The alien soul has risen," I say straight-faced.

"Cut the bullshit, Zoe."

"We could make it official. Call it ascension day."

He shakes his head and sighs. "Crazy bloody woman." But there is a smile in his voice.

Which is good, for my smile masks a scream almost as primal as that of the pig in my memory.

As we turn and leave that Godforsaken place for good, I feel the reproach of Ramsey's emptied eyes upon my back.

At night now, in this cell, and in torment of my dreams, I still feel his eyes upon me, blue and dull in the darkness, calling me out for the violence I inflicted upon him.

I tortured him for my own needs. He was a shit, but nobody needs to die like that.

Chapter 31

Our destination is east and then south. It is a good day's drive away. We stay off the main roads. Leary drives over the mountains into the dim light and drifting clouds at the top of the world. It is like we are in a cocoon of mist and fog, only dimly aware of the towering peaks west and north and the sheep in the green fields and the forests of spruce and ash that we pass.

"So, it was never Ramsey?" I pause, gathering my thought. "I mean, I know what I did. What I had to do. But it's easier if it wasn't Ramsey. Not really human." I can hear my desperation.

Leary flicks his head at me and sighs.

"You have to let it go, Zoe."

"It was that thing inside him. That is what I was hurting. It wasn't him. Not truly."

I am staring across from the passenger seat, intent on his face. He grimaces.

"I said forget it."

"What do those things want?"

"I told you already. We are at war. It might not be decided today or tomorrow, but those fucking things," He points at the sky and we both know what he means, "they want us gone. Sidelined. Out of the fucking way."

"That's crazy, Leary. There are too many of us."

"There were also a lot of dinosaurs once."

"Crazy shit," I murmur, but without conviction. "Crazy."

But it isn't. Not really. Not anymore. Ramsey, or the thing that was a parasite in Ramsey, was driven almost mad in the end. It spoke in tongues. It wailed and screamed and eventually told us where the cult had gone. A dilapidated farm on the grounds of an abandoned estate that was once an army barracks near Middletown. Apparently Banning had bought it on the cheap. And whatever they were up to there would be something like the endgame. I had sensed that through the madness.

If Leary and I are soldiers, I think, then so are they, these alien parasites. Soldiers and explorers. And they are here to do us harm in order to profit themselves. And then it strikes me. They have come to conquer, yes, but also to dominate.

There is no shortage of analogues in human history. The East India Company. The Dutch. All those freebooters and schemers roaming vast seas with but one goal in mind. Wealth and power. And look at the destruction they wrought on the indigenous inhabitants they came across. The toll in lives lost and destroyed or enslaved, the societies they ruined, the generations they forced into poverty as servants, disenfranchised workers, dope addicts, prostitutes, and worse.

"Leary?"

"What?"

"They aren't just here to destroy us. I mean, to wipe us out."

"They aren't?"

"Think about it. What are we to them?"

"I don't know. Ants. Pests."

"It is more than that. That is what these War of the Worlds things always do. Humanity is to be wiped out. But that makes no sense. However many they are, they cannot be enough to populate a world as large as ours."

"So wipe us out. Clean slate. Time to make shitty, new, little aliens in a brave, new, shitty world. The world is their oyster."

"I think we are more than that to them."

"What?"

"A resource. For now, at least. Think donkeys and cows. Horses and pigs. We can be used."

Leary laughs sourly. "Really? They want to domesticate us. To turn us into farm animals. Porky pig snorting on the farm."

I laugh too at the image. "Not literally, dumb-ass. But, yeah, in a nutshell. To harness us. To make us do their dirty fucking work."

"You really are serious."

"Think of Adele. She was with Ramsey, but not as a human."

He thinks for a moment then whistles. "Shit. You may be onto something there, love."

"She was his bodyguard. Designed, I figure, to protect him. Twisted and warped into whatever. If they can do that once, they can do it again."

"I don't know, Zoe."

"Why?"

"There are a hell of a lot of humans. And we are notoriously Bolshie. This is a technologically advanced race of dickheads. They can´t need us all. Not by a long shot."

"No," I say quietly. "No, they probably can't."

We are silent, listening to the sound of the engine growling and the tires spinning on wet tarmac as we speed to the gathering gloom, into the night and what awaits us there.

#

We arrive after dark.

Leary pulls up outside the broken-down walls of the old estate. On the drive, I had looked up its provenance. An old country home, torched by locals after the war. Angry and still under the cruelty and hard hardheartedness of the landlords during the Great Hunger. Rebuilt on a smaller scale as a ranch-style house by a returned Yank in the fifties; fallen to general neglect since. His family had returned to the States when he was murdered in his sleep, his killer never caught. The army bought the grounds and turned it into a barracks, later deserted after cutbacks in the eighties, but not before more deaths. A jeep full of enlisted men on a bright summer´s day drove off a wide road and crashed into a ravine in the early eighties. All 6 on board died.

A haunted house, with equally haunted grounds, that the Society must have snapped up for a song.

Leary turns off the engine, and the silence is deafening. A silence born of my whole life up to this point. Like the way people say your whole life flashes before your eyes when you are dying. This was like that. A moment of silence that felt stretched and entangled. Call it a quantum moment, a moment out of time, when my life was neither a wave nor a particle, neither here nor there, neither real nor unreal.

A long moment, out of time, when all the choices I had ever made were weighed and evaluated. And I must have been found wanting; for they had all led here. To me sitting with a man who was not my husband in a car in the darkness with my children still lost to me and in imminent danger.

We simply had no clue what to expect.

That long moment passed with a pop —like air expanding—and life returned, in all its sad glory.

#

Or perhaps, observed from one perspective, it never did.

I know I will struggle from here on in. Struggle to fully remember the dark events that were inflicted on the world and all of those who lived in it that night.

So much of this long story is clear to me, like glass etched by a diamond, sharp and brittle and clear as day.

Nothing of that night is: it is a dense London pea soup, a fog of memories and disjointed moments. Please forgive me and trust me on this. I have been nothing but honest up to now and I will still endeavor to reach the end of this story, but I refuse to embellish what I cannot hope to remember.

The gaps are there. Read between them, if you must. All I can do is record what I remember and place it in whatever context seems the most likely.

I do remember the noise after the silence. Leary sparing me a long look. He reaches out to cup me on the side of my head, and I lean into him and we kiss.

Just that once. A brief moment only, but also an eternity.

The spark that keeps me going still.

"Let's get this over with? Get your kids back."

He smiles and I smile back. His eyes are liquid in the moonlight. I know that he is filled with the same trepidation that weighs on me.

A feeling of reaching an end, of things coming to some abject conclusion. For we discussed this earlier. We have no plan. We have no way of knowing what awaits us. We have come too far to delay.

It is all or nothing. In this forlorn barracks, one way or another, are the answers and, if my children are not there, then we will have failed.

So, we both open our doors. I have a pistol, Leary his trusted shotgun. We are parked outside the barracks at about nine in the evening. The rounded wooden gates are pulled back and fully open, there are no guards posted and nobody to stop us from entering.

Strange, I remember thinking, for we had talked through all the possible scenarios we could think of on the way here; they all had involved us entering the grounds of this place using force of some sort.

Leary glances at me and I shrug. Side by side we walk forward like gunfighters into the corral.

#

It is deserted, or seems to be.

To the west the large ranch-like building, a massive bungalow with a wooden patio in the front and looming over it the ruins of the old house leering and broken in the light of the moon. All very Gothic.

The barracks themselves are spread out on the grounds to the east. A parade ground in the shape of a quadrangle surrounded on three sides, and visible in the distance is an assortment of various smaller buildings.

Admin and offices and presumably living quarters to their rear.

A huge place, even for an organization like the Society.

Where the hell is everybody?

#

And that is when the night starts to splinter in my memory.

We walk together to the barracks buildings. I remember thinking how run-down they look. Shingles missing from the roofs, rubbish piled up to one side of the quadrangle, and a smell that is the smell of rot and worse.

Death. Decay. Age.

The closer we get to the building the more spooked I become, the more worried. I cannot stand the idea of the kids not being here and that idea, that concept, is a vice squeezing my forehead.

We almost stumble on the first corpse. A young woman lying naked on the parade ground, her hair long and dirty, her body ravaged with pustules and what look like imploded wounds. Her face is a stiff mask of agony, her hands darkened claws reaching out to us.

"Get back, Zoe," Leary hisses. I was about to reach out to the woman, ready to offer help, but he waves me back, his face urgent and agitated.

"Get back! Get back!"

And we do.

Like I said, my brain was foggy that night. Disjointed. I know I was unable to join the dots, but Leary did. And quickly too.

He is holding me back, arms wrapped around me and whispering in my ear.

"Remember what we talked about? Disease and death? Remember?"

It takes time, but I do. I remember. Biological warfare. The death of humanity or some such. The aliens have a purpose, and their purpose is our destruction.

Later we are standing looking in the doorway of one of the barracks buildings. Death lives within, is grinning at us from row upon row of beds. The stink of rotting bodies drives us out, gagging, into the night air.

Sometime later, a glow of white alien light appears overhead and seems to land by the ruins of the old house. Leary leads now and I follow, for I know I am no longer capable of thought and action.

I am lost, as though stoned on opioids, flipping from moment to moment like a flat stone skimming water. I remember a small group of sect members wandering across the quadrangle, walking towards the dim light.

Alive, scarred by the pestilence, damaged. No longer human.

Leary tries to talk to them, to ask about the children. To appeal to our common nature. They stare at us uncomprehendingly. They have trouble with all but the most simple ideas, their eyes are dim and their faces scarred with broken pustules. They try to answer, but they do not speak English, or any language I know of. It is an alien sound, almost animalistic, like barking. There is a profound emptiness in their voices, a lack of will and self-awareness.

As we walk from them in despair, I think that this is the master plan.

They intend to wipe out the majority of us with this plague and know that the survivors will be mere putty in their hands in the new world order they hope to create.

Humanity reduced to dim obedience or worse.

#

And we do what we must.

We follow the light to the ruins. We kill what threatens us and torch some buildings.

Our goal. The alien light in the distance, for where else is there for us to go?

Except, when we get to the ranch house, Leary tells me, as if on some sudden impulse, to wait. He hops onto the patio, and pushes open the unlocked door. When he returns, his face is set in stone and hard as concrete.

As if he had seen something that had caused his heart to freeze over.

"What is it?" I ask. "What just happened?" The fog in my mind is a cloud, obscuring thought.

My voice comes from far away as though I am speaking through a hollow bucket.

He shakes his head, reaches into his pocket, and holds up a slip of paper.

"It does not matter now. Later, Zoe. We'll discuss it later." In a quiet voice, unconvinced. "It is not important. Not now. We have come too far." He glances back at the house with troubled eyes. "It doesn't matter. It cannot. Not now." He waves the paper at me. "This, though, might be something." He almost falls back, onto the old rocking chair on the porch, and sits there slumped backward. Looking old for the first time. Devoid of energy. Hollowed out. Defeated.

Something in the house has shaken him to his core.

I make for the door, but he holds up a warning hand.

"No, Zoe."

I stop at the tone. Half an order, half a desperate plea. He stumbles to his feet and places himself in front of the door. "It is too dangerous. Trust me."

He smiles wanly.

I make to push past him. After all who the hell does he think he is? But that is a reaction to the other men in my life, my father, Jimmy.

Not Leary.

Him I need to trust, so I stop and put my hand on the crook of his elbow and smile at him.

"What's that on the paper?"

He shakes his head. "I think it is something. An address. Details of some delivery. A truck. Let me check."

And then my memory fades again.

I know Leary stayed behind. I know I was called. Forced to move almost against my will. Towards the light.

Into the cold.

I don't remember much. The fragments of memory are a kaleidoscope that never seem to connect. I walked to the deserted ruin of the stately old house in the moonlight that was subject to the ashy gray of alien light.

Banning was there, standing in front of some ruins and to the right of what could have been a space capsule. Small and thin and shaped like a cigar. But Banning was not, of course, Banning. He was Ka. A man and an alien both. A creature of immense age and cruelty. Tall and thin and pale. An alien vampire. An alien god. And he told me everything. His people are called the Nal-Lith. The people of the purple star. Driven from their ancestral homes by internecine conflict, spurred on by religious reasons. They were promised a paradise by their holy prophets, and earth is that paradise, and their new home, and we would be forced aside. Leary had been right, or mostly, for they were researching death and control. Death for the large majority, and control for the rest. We would become their beasts of burden, their bodyguards and soldiers, and even their food; for what were we to them? Short-lived like flies and ultimately destructive to the world we had been born into. Our intelligence a brute, overrated aspect. Little better than the apes from which we had evolved but infinitely more dangerous. They would control us and restore the world to its pristine beauty, for the Nal-Lith lived long and did not breed in great numbers, and their technology was as much biological as mechanical.

Spacefaring elves, of a sort, and like most elves, they were dicks.

They would exterminate us—as we would an infestation of rats—and use the survivors as chattel, beasts of burden, to build a new and better world.

A world of diversity and riches where humans would once again be subordinate and weak.

A world made in their image, not ours. The weird thing is, I kind of got the feeling that Banning was enjoying himself, that his exposition was fun, that he was getting his jollies off at my expense.

And would a sane creature really enjoy the mental anguish of an inferior being?

I didn't think so then. I don't now. The Nal-Lith know we are, if not quite their equals, then close. They know we are sentient; they just don't care. And that makes them much more human, I imagine, that they are willing to admit. I figure there is a word for genocide in their language too.

Chapter 32

"We have them, Zoe!"

We are in the car again though I don't remember how we got here. Banning's awful influence on my messed-up brain is gradually dissipating but still present like some alien fog.

"This is it." He slaps at the paper in his left hand. "This is it. Finally. The key. Fucking amateur shits. Leaving this behind. Having it in writing in the first place. They must think we are morons."

He hands it to me and I scan. Jimmy's handwriting. The scribbled notes a bit cryptic but the address is clear and so is the gist.

Details of a rented van.

Plans in code. Nicknames, dates.

"They are moving their shit to the quays in Middletown?"

"Seems so." He leans over to me and places a fat finger on two names. "I looked them up. A cruise ship leaving the day after tomorrow. Stopping off all over the Med. Spain. Italy. Egypt. And here, a container ship headed for the States."

And I have a sudden image in my head of Banning leaning over me, his finger on my forehead, for we had not communicated with words but by touch.

I could see it.

The deaths in the barracks, those diseased bodies, were nothing but the trial run.

The plan was to release a pathogen, but something new, like an airborne cross between a virus and a parasite. The virus kills and the parasite inhabits and controls whatever happens to survive, robbing it of self-will. Aimed only at humans, a targeted and lethal biological weapon. Turning us into shambling zombies like those we had seen in the barracks.

And we realise, with a sudden jolt, that we are the only ones who know enough to stop it.

"They have a mini-van. It's not just Jimmy and the kids. There may be others." I pause, my heart speeding with a mixture of fear and excitement.

And I parse another set of images. Jimmy and the kids boarding the cruise ship. The pathogen is in a little plastic vial that Jimmy breaks when they are at sea, and slowly the passengers develop mild coughs and snuffly noses, symptoms they spread at every stop until four or five weeks in. The incubation is as slow as it is deadly; a fever develops and then black pustules on the neck and stomach. My kids would be ground zero.

And that would be all she wrote for them and humanity.

Eighty to ninety percent mortality and the survivors lost to the parasite that has infected and spread through their brain like fungus.

I look up and Leary is looking at me, his face contorted with conflicting emotions.

He wraps his arms around me and sighs.

"You up for this, Zoe?" His face serious as he kisses me. "You up for this still?"

That image again. The children lost in the forest and chased by ghouls and demons with the faces of Jimmy, of Ramsey, and the gray monstrosity that is Banning.

I nod into his chest as tears squeeze hot and burning from my eyes.

Last chance, I think.

Last fucking chance to save them.

"Coming guys," I mouth silently. Coming to save you now.

#

We get to Middleton in, of course, darkness. Looking back, I do not remember much daylight in those days. We seemed to live in the shadows and the gray light that was the alien infection. It was all one undifferentiated gloaming, as constant as it was unnerving.

The streets are deserted. A developing mist is rolling in slow waves from the ocean. Our GPS takes us to the East of town where we take a two-lane bypass past the industrial area to the harbour beyond. Middleton downtown—two miles north of where we park—is a pretty town ringed by pleasant tree-lined streets with a yachting harbour and a fleet of small commercial fishing boats. East Middleton, though, is a rundown commercial container port in serious decline. Graffiti-smeared warehouses that seem abandoned and forlorn and a few bars that are dimly lit and inward-looking. Pale streetlights that are so faint they are effectively useless.

The bars are the kinds of places where you can sulk into a drink and ignore those around you, unless they are selling or buying what you need to get through the night. The kind of place where violence is just a heartbeat away.

The address that Jimmy left behind is above one of these awful speakeasies with no obvious entrance except through the dark hole that is the front door of the bar.

Leary has his Uzi in the jacket of his coat and the shotgun is in the bag he is carrying, but we decide against being too rash.

We have no idea who is in there. We know that Jimmy may not be alone, but we have no idea how many other minions, monsters, or otherwise infected compadres he has. To rush in now would be reckless. We decide to check out the harbour first and walk down the long Jetty past evening darkened buildings, many desolate and boarded up. The container ship is still loading at the far end at a short row of gantry cranes. The occasional sounds of machines quietly straining and men barking commands echoes over the lapping waves that hit the old stone quay.

"They can't have boarded yet, I reckon," Leary whispers, in a voice that is almost a prayer. "Not yet. Not with all that commotion. We still have time."

The quays follow the shoreline in a semicircle that is narrower at the front like a horseshoe with an open mouth. The cruise ship is berthed on the northern quay directly opposite, and from here appears to be a gleaming hotel soaring above the water. We walk to it, Leary striding fast and breathing heavily. Close up, it is clear the cruise ship is nothing but a tired old lady and cannot have berths for more than a couple of hundred passengers. Some sort of cheap-ass version of the scandalous luxury embodied by the Queen Marys of the cruise world.

"Still enough passengers and crew to wipe out half the world if they are all infected and spreading their crap in half a dozen countries," Leary says when I mention this. And he is not wrong.

In my mind's eye, I imagine the passengers, a little tired and dispirited by the less than stellar once-in-a-lifetime experience of disembarking in the bleak surrounding of Middletown industrial harbor. And if the aliens have their way, the once-in-a-lifetime experience would also be a last-in-a-lifetime experience. A horrific slow death or transformation into some mutant new form of controlled humanity.

"Wait here a moment," Leary drops the bag at my feet and marches to the gangway leading to the ship. He waits at the bottom of the gangway and calls to one of the two sailors at the top who waves him up. They huddle close for a moment or two and Leary reaches into his wallet.

Money or his old police ID, the one he never did hand back when he retired. Or both?

There is a brief delay, one of the crew leaves and returns with a clipboard and what looks like an electronic scanner. They pore over it for a moment and there is a series of brief flashes as Jimmy takes photos with his cell phone.

He strides back to me with a bounce in his step and a lopsided grin on his homely face.

"Got them. Got the fuckers."

"What is it?"

"Boarding for new passengers begins after eight tomorrow, and they set sail at noon. We cut it close, Zoe." He puts his arms around me and squeezes gently. "But we got here in time. Look." He holds his phone out to me with a smile. "See there. Jimmy's name on the manifest."

Two rooms. Suites, I note sourly, and the best aboard the fucking ship—for whatever that is worth on this particular vessel. Only the best for our Jimmy. Even as a host for his alien master, even as a puppet and a traitor to the human race, he still expects to be treated as King Jimmy. Leary sees my face darken at the thought and He leans in and holds my chin.

"Let it go, Zoe. Forget that shit. You are so close. So close."

And Leary is right. Of course, he is. Two double rooms. That must mean that Jimmy and the kids are planning to leave together.

"Sarah and Sean, they must be listed too. Their names. Can I see it again?" I can feel the hope return, and that quiet desperation. That impatience.

We have come so far and are so close, yet they remain so distant.

Leary glances away and closes his phone and puts it into his pocket and turns from me. "Jimmy hasn't supplied the ship with names of the other passengers. Least that's what I was told."

Something there. In the shape of his shoulder, in the timbre of his voice.

Something that worries me.

Why is he so rattled all of a sudden?

"I'll see if I can find out anything at the container ship, yeah?"

"You do that," I say, and I stare after him as he strides purposefully down the quay to the container ship.

I look after him and notice how his shoulders are slumped forward, as if in defeat, and I cannot help but wonder what has gotten into him.

Chapter 33

"I paid with good cash. To the first mate. Had to dig deep too, smarmy fucker. They gave me a guided tour. No new random berths, so no human-sized rats have snuck on board. Still, the captain did confirm that he had been informed about a new crew member they were to pick up in Middletown before setting off. Hasn't seen him yet."

"And when do they sail?"

"Early in the morning."

"That´s it. That has to be. The timing."

"You said it. Two ships sail from here in different directions and in two months, the world as we know it, is finished. Jesus. What in God´s name are these morons thinking?"

Jimmy and the other cult members. Those intent on genocide. More than that. Something for which no word exists. Anthropocide, perhaps? The deliberate destruction and murder of the human race.

"They are no longer thinking, Leary. You know that."

He shakes his head and slaps the dashboard of the car.

"I can't buy that. No matter how brainwashed or how deep those parasites have their hooks into them, something human must remain. Something that would make them pause and stop. I mean, Jesus. The children. All the children." A lone tear makes its way down his cheek.

I am ashamed to say I did not know back then how to react and just turned away.

#

It is almost time.

We wait in the parked car on the opposite side of the street, hidden but with a view of the front door of the bar, watching the comings and goings of the place. None who leave are Jimmy and all who leave are too ragged to be in any way dangerous. One old man with a biblical beard pisses against the wall just yards away from the car, cursing loudly at whatever gods had offended him. Other drunks come staggering out, loud and bilious or quiet and barely capable, staggering to the winds.

Midnight passes. The bar closes. The last stragglers are thrown out. And still, we wait.

Leary's idea. Catch them cold in the early morning, just before sunrise, when they are at their lowest ebb, if these alien fucks even have a low ebb.

As good a plan as any, I suppose.

Just after five, with the dawn a boastful hint in the east, we slip out of the car, closing the car doors quietly behind us. I shiver in the damp salty air. A bitter wind has picked up and the waves are bashing against the seawall at the head of the quays.

Somewhere a gull croaks and the sound is both fierce and lonely.

Like us, I remember thinking.

Fierce and lonely as us.

I am wrapped in my parka with a dark beanie on my head. I hold an unfamiliar gun in my hand and both trepidation and hope war in my heart. I will do what needs to be done to get to the children and get them away from Jimmy's clutches. Deep down I know, though, that they may be changed, that they may be already in thrall to the aliens. The thought fills me with terror, of course, but I know I will save them. I will get them away from here and I will save them, heal them, make sure that whatever is within them is expunged, and that they remain safe for the rest of their lives.

Zoe Hearty, Warrior Queen, and destroyer of all alien worlds and the human shits that intend to stand in my way.

And yet, the violence is, for want of a better word, still alien to me.

Leary gives me one last look as we make our way to the door. I see him then for almost the last time, and in many ways for the first time; a strong man, a powerful man, tortured in his soul perhaps, but driven by his notions of what is honourable and right. He is, in his own gobshite way, a hero. I blow a kiss at him and he gestures for us to move on, and fast.

I can almost hear his voice in my head. "Would ye ever get a move on, Zoe, and stop standing there like some silly bleeding moving statue blowing kisses at me?"

I smile then.

He smiles back.

And that was the last time I would ever see him smile. If I could have one moment back of all those terrible days, one moment that I could freeze in aspic and carry with me as my own memory chain, it would be that one.

#

When it happens, it happens quick and hard. Leary jimmies the heavy wooden door open. It creaks, way too loud. Leary slips into the semi-darkness ahead of me. I follow behind, leaving the door ajar. We do not need to hear that sound again, thank you very much.

A hallway leads into the narrow main part of the bar, the wooden counter to the left, mirrors behind it, wooden high stools in front of the counter, and a half dozen or so round small tables scattered throughout the floor area; wooden chairs with narrow backs placed haphazardly around them. A small army of beer glasses are assembled on the counter, and the place stinks of stale beer. I stifle a cough at the rank smell mixed with equally stale cigarette smoke and something worse—the stink of despair and desperation. A smell I had known only too well when I lived with Jimmy.

Despair and self-pity and the stink at the end of the bottle.

We weave carefully around the tables which are littered with the last empty soldiers of the evening. Leary points ahead. An open door, and in the darkness what I take to be the stairs to the floor above. Footsteps sound, coming down the stairs. Fast and hard and alarmed.

Leary kneels in partial cover behind one of the wooden tables. I am behind and to his left and kneel with my shoulder leaning against the counter.

The heavy footfalls stop suddenly, somebody still out of view, at the bottom of the stairs.

And then there is a sound that begins with a heavy sigh and becomes someone (something?) sucking in the air.

"Watch out!" I yell.

For I know that what is coming is not human, or is no longer human.

Down the last few steps, around the corner, and into the room a blur like a shock wave of air.

I know it is a body, it must be corporeal but it does not seem like that in the gloom. It flies through the air, for all the world like a bat, screeching a high-pitched sound that drives nails into my ears and causes me to stagger back onto my arse. I fire a shot that goes high and wide and then it is on Leary, who doesn't even get a shot off. He is blown backwards and knocks into a table spilling it over. Glass bottles go flying and smash onto the ground.

The flying bat thing—or whatever the fuck this is—lurches forward like some Dracula knock off and stabs Leary in the chest with a long kitchen knife. Screeching that shrill screech; this one sounding like a victory cry it raises itself off of Leary so I can see its face.

Think Nosferatu by Klaus Kinski on a bad hair day. Pale skin, fangs, creepy reddened eyes, and a long eighties mullet down to its shoulder. Behind the (make up? Transformation? Infestation?) I remember this guy. A Ramsey sycophant who was at the party. Randy something? I was still with Adele when he came sauntering over and told us some awful blue joke that Neanderthals with learning issues might have found funny.

And here he is leering at me, reddened eyes alive with delight and pride. He opens his mouth, and I see his long thin tongue protrude, start to vibrate as that sound builds again. A wave of sound that is piercing and numbing at once.

I raise my gun.

Try to.

It is hard.

So hard. That numbing sound boring into my brain.

So loud. Those eyes. Drawing me in. Pulling me towards him. God, they do have this vampire shit down.

Think, Zoe.

The kids. Break this fucker's hold. For the kids.

I struggle but to no avail.

My hand will not lift the gun in this fucking thing's direction. I stand there like some hapless sap in a B-movie waiting to be plucked, some Rando who was only introduced into the plot to be knocked off. Jaysus, Zoe. It's the kids' lives that are at stake. Do something.

No good.

Zoe Hearty, Warrior Queen, my ass.

It rises to its feet. Cocky now, and it can afford to be for its voice sounds deeper in my head.

Ta tum. Ta tum.

Like my heartbeat.

And then a command as if from God himself.

"Drop it!"

And I do. The pistol falls from my hand with a loud clatter. It, the alien that was once human, moves towards me, the screech now a clicking sound, a predator knowing it has won and celebrating.

Klik, klak. Klik, klak.

Its mouth opens, jaw unnaturally wide, teeth like pincers and long tongue pointing towards me, a tongue I see now that is not one thing but many; a filigree of wire-like threads.

That is it, I think.

The interface. They will latch on to me as the thing sucks blood or whatever the hell it does, and they will infect and transform me, deface and destroy me.

That will turn me into one of them.

That same smug sickness that I sensed from Banning is emanating like poison from this one. From the parasite within. A sociopathic vibe, and a barely hidden condescension. A conquistador staring at its first native villager and licking its lips at the potential to destroy the world it has stumbled upon and remake it in its own image. Whatever I am to it, I am not human. I am potential. Something to be gotten rid of, to be side-lined or used and abused before being cast aside like an old nag or a broken sex doll. It would be trite to say evil, not with the evidence of human history, but lacking in morality and empathy, nonetheless.

It moves towards me. The tongue protrudes even further, undulating like the waving feelers of a sea anemone. These tips, though, are metallic looking and I can already feel the sting as they latch onto my flesh and the course invasion as they grow within me. A dozen waving lines of alien biotics coursing through my blood and body until they reach my brain.

They failed once, the night at the party.

I do not think they will fail again.

But I am frozen. In thrall to the voice and the piercing red eyes.

Nearer. Ever nearer he moves. The feelers enlarge, spread out towards me, and are mere inches from my skin when the face of that fucking thing explodes.

Boom! That sound. The sudden unexpected violence.

Like the freeze-frame in an adult manga. The bullet enters the side of the head and explodes in a spray of blood and bone and the thing crumples to the floor at my feet.

"Got you, you fucker," Leary calls out weakly, coughing blood. I rush over to him, kneel beside him and tear off my beanie. I hold it against the blood pumping rhythmically from him as from a burst pipe. In moments the beanie is soaked and my hands are damp and sticky with his blood.

"Leary," I say in a low voice. "We need to get you out of here. Now! Let me get you to your feet."

He grimaces in pain as he shakes his head.

"No, Zoe. Never mind that." He coughs, spluttering blood. "Leave me, for feck's sake. But finish it. Finish it now."

I hesitate.

He coughs again. More blood.

"Go. Go!"

Waving his right hand weakly. And he is, of course, right. I need to find the children and stop Jimmy.

Jimmy the monster.

Funny, in the past, Jimmy was a monster only in my mind. The ogre in my house. The monster, not under, but in my bed. Now he is everyone's definition of a real monster. Obsessed, possessed, and homicidal.

And yet that old fear (not respect, never that) and sense of self-preservation make me hesitate. I know that I am better than him: truer, more honest, more loving. Imperfect in many, many ways but I gave him what I could, and he took from me and then he took again and still he took. And when the taking was not enough, he hurt me and gave me away. Me. To make himself bigger, badder, better.

Am I angry? Well of course I am. The affairs. The lies. The lack of intimacy and honesty. The fucking society of the Gray Eclipse.

It is time to set the record straight.

And still, I hesitate.

It is still Jimmy, and there are still memories of better times.

But fuck it. The past is the past and it will not return.

Time to move forward, Zoe, into the future. Time to do that. And to put the past in the craphole where it belongs.

#

I leave Leary gasping on the ground.

One of the hardest things I have ever done; leaving him gasping, slick with his coppery warm and still pumping blood.

Hard.

Hard not to turn around and just take him to the car and go. Begone. Leave all this shit behind. Even then I think I knew that nothing good would come of ascending those stairs.

I knew that death awaited. But, see, I had the kids to care for, and now suddenly the whole of humanity—its past and its present and certainly its future. Humans are imperfect, God knows. We murder and we destroy. We ravage and rape. People and the planet, both.

And yet we are all we have. And we can be better. Better versions of ourselves are within reach, just around the corner, so close. I truly believe that. So close we can reach out and almost touch it.

All the hidden potential.

I have seen this in my children. In the better versions of who we could have been. Sarah's gentle kindness masks a strength I never had. Once when she was five, she saw me toss a wrapper on the ground and reprimanded me. Scolded me even. She attacked an older boy in the schoolyard who was using a stone to murder ants. She will never, ever allow injustice to prosper. Quiet. Gentle, timid even, and hard as nails. What a great combination. And Sean is his Dad's son. Scrap that. He is the kid that could be the man that Jimmy—his parents and whatever else be thanked—could never hope to be. The best of both of us, but more Jimmy than me and yet kind and considerate. Driven yes, but so far as I can tell, never driving over others. I see him playing football. He is a leader but never a follower, gifted too with enough imagination to understand the charismatic power he possesses, and yet not let it into his head. Sarah is more intelligent, but he possesses a nimble cleverness that allows him to have friends that he does not have to fuck over.

Difficult, of course, to predict, for they are young if this is who they will eventually be.

But these traits have been evident from the beginning, and up to now, Jimmy and I have managed not to fuck them up too much.

Up to now.

That is a sad and terrible irony.

Up to now.

Up to then.

Who knows what has happened since I last saw them?

And that is enough to propel me up the stairs.

#

The smell is a barrier like a wall.

I do not mean that in any metaphorical sense.

It is a wall meant not to stop but to actively frighten us off. Us being humans.

We—again I mean humans—would have used fire, I guess, back in the day. Against the yellow-eyed wolves circling in the darkness.

When I was still in college, I did the backpacking thing in India. I remember getting off an overnight bus somewhere between Goa and Mumbai, desperate for a pee with all the other suckers who just could not sleep. It was clearly a regular stop, so there were food stalls at the side of the road, the smell of curry, cumin, and coriander wafting from simple metal pots on gas burners. Lentils and white bean doti, warm samosas on plates. The warm and comforting music of Hindi and the lilt of Indian English. Behind a low wooden building that had seen better days when Mountbatten was still Viceroy was the jakes. I made my way towards it and the closer I got, the more the stink was a hand pushing back against me, acrid and sour in the back of my throat.

I made it no more than halfway, couldn't go any further, then took a detour into the fields.

The smell on the way up the stairs is like that, but worse. It is alien. It is cold and foul and greasy and it makes me want to puke and flee at the same time.

A warning signal to other living creatures.

Come forward if you wish, but danger lies ahead.

I tear a strip off my blouse and wrap it bandanna-like around my face. It does not do much to help. The stink is a living thing pushing me back, a force field trying to weaken my will. I can barely see from the tears stinging my eyes, as though I had been sprayed with pepper spray. The fear in my stomach, the knot of terror that this cold wave pushes through me, threatens to loosen my bowels. The only thing that keeps me going is the picture I conjure in my head of Sarah and Sean waiting for me at the top of the stairs.

Smiles on their faces now at the knowledge of how close I am to them.

So I push forward towards them and at the top of the stairs. As I reach a long hallway with doors to rooms on either side, the pressure—for that is what the smell is—fades. Not to nothing.

It is still a bad stink left behind in an un-aired room, but very much faded into the background. The hallway is long, and the walls painted the vivid green you used to get in hospital wards. A naked bulb hangs on wires from the ceiling and cast dim shadows in the corners.

I walk to the end of the hall. The doors—there are four of them—to the adjoining rooms are open and the small bare rooms appear empty. One final door at the far end of the hallway.

The last door. One last push. One last moment. An ending.

I push the door open.

Jimmy is at the far end of the room, or the being that used to be Jimmy is. Near an old fireplace, leaning against it. He smiles when he sees me, as if I am an expected and welcome guest—which given the welcome afforded to us below makes no sense. But then we fell down the rabbit hole a long time ago.

Against the wall to my right is a bed and behind it, leaning forward is another one of these twisted creatures—this one looks almost like a badger—its teeth bared. From the door, I can see that behind it is a suitcase. The thing seems to be protecting it; its body angled towards me as if to ward me off.

I nod at Jimmy and then the suitcase.

"So that is it, Jimmy, huh? The ultimate betrayal. The end of everything."

Jimmy's smile broadens but there is a glint that might be worry in his eyes.

"It is the way of things, Zoe. The strong eating the weak and all that. In the long run, it is no big deal. Life itself goes on. Healthier even, without the human race battering the crap out it." He smiles a Jimmy smile, but the smile is somehow edgy, and why wouldn't it be. This is not the Jimmy of old, and I am a danger to his best-laid plans.

The badger edges forward, suitcase in one hand, trying to get beyond the end of the bed so it has an unhindered route to attack me."

"I have had enough of this, Jimmy. Enough of your shite and that of those alien pricks you have hooked up with. I just want the kids back."

I raise my right hand, gun fully extended, a one-handed hail Mary shot, and squeeze the trigger.

I hit the badger right between his eyes. It flops backwards, knocking over the briefcase, and sinks to the ground.

"Hah!" I gasp, partly in delight, mostly in shock. I did that. From this distance. Somehow that is unexpected and, even if I have just killed something, sorta cool. Don't get me wrong. I did not enjoy the killing per se. I am not a monster. It is just one of those things. You know, you had to be there: in the circumstances with Leary bleeding out below, the end of the world at hand, and still no sign of the children, I thought fuck it. Let's get this over with. And for once I did not hesitate.

Jimmy steps towards me, hands out palms facing me.

"Zoe. Zoe, love."

I shake my head. I cannot believe that he really thinks that this will still work.

That voice calling my name. Over and over like he used to when he wanted to make up with me, but still did not want to apologize or face up to the shit he had caused.

I was always a sucker for his voice. Deep and from his chest area. Just something that vibrated within me, that made me feel both wanted and safe at the same time.

And that is what he is doing now.

"Zoe, my love. My heart."

Cooing almost. And with every mention of my name, he takes a step forward. Closer and closer.

And try as I might, I feel it happen again. I am small and getting smaller as he approaches. Big, strong Jimmy is calling my name, and I am mesmerized as so often before.

He is almost upon me.

Girl, I ask myself, have you learned nothing? In all that you have been through have you still not managed to breach this damned dependency? I think of Leary lying in a pool of his own blood, of my children who are still missing, and the way Jimmy reacted after the rape/mind fuck at the big house.

And that is enough to break his hoodoo.

Almost, but this shit is powerful. Years and years of training. Be a good girl. Do as you're told. Don't rock the boat.

You know the deal.

First my parents and then the Jimmy man himself.

No.

Not anymore.

And then there are the eyes, for he is close to me now. Almost within touching distance, and while that shit-kicking grin is still plastered all over his face I can't help but notice how his hands are bunched as if into claws.

All the better to tear you open with.

But it is the eyes that seal his fate.

Those eyes and that ring of alien lights around the irises. This is not Jimmy. Not the man I fathered children with and swore to love for all my life. Shit, the real Jimmy would not still have been the man I married and loved back then, for he too had changed. Marriage can do that. But

245

this thing walking towards me, calling out my name as though ready to reach out to hug and kiss me.

Now.

This is not even human.

He reaches out a hand to me.

I shoot him in the stomach.

The look on his face then, the sudden pain. The surprise and disbelief just before he drops to his knees in front of me as if proposing all over again.

"Where are they, Jim?"

He moans in pain.

"Where are they? Sarah and Sean? What have you done with them?"

He is holding his hands to his wound, pressing hard, looking down. I place the pistol against his forehead. He looks up at me and smiles; the smile is not his. It is that of the thing within. The voice is not his, barely human. Barely words.

"Gone, Zoe. Long gone. But you know this."

I press the trigger one more time and blow my husband's brains out and step over and past him to the bed, grab the handle of the briefcase and turn and hightail it away as fast as I can. I have no desire to witness another alien soul ascend.

One of those in a lifetime is enough, trust me.

#

Leary is still alive, but not by much. He is sitting up, still coughing blood, pale and fading. He looks almost translucent already, a cold grayness infusing his face.

He glances up as I appear down the stairs.

"All sorted, Zoe, love?"

I nod and rush to him, but he waves me away, and brushes my hands from his when I reach out.

"Listen, Zoe. Look at me, please. This is the endgame. I know you know that."

I nod.

"Then you know what has to happen with that." He nods at the briefcase in my right hand.

"No!" I shake my head in sudden realisation. I should not have to go through this too.

"Look at me, love. Look at me."

I look into his eyes. I see love there, I see concern. The polar opposite of the white spinning lights in Jimmy´s now closed forever eyes. I see more though. Leary is leaving life. Has made up his mind. This is his end.

I shake my head harder, swallow the tears. "No!"

"It is the only sure way."

He reaches into his trousers, pulls out his wallet, his badge, and the keys. "Take these. They may be of some use. Help you to remember me, if nothing else." He tries to laugh, but instead gasps in pain. "Now let me have it."

I hesitate for a long moment, the tears still flowing, and then hand him the briefcase. I help him to his feet and he bends over in pain. Like an old man.

I almost scream at the thought for this is as old as he will get.

"Stay safe, Zoe. In your dark days, remember what we have achieved here today. And, love…" He hesitates as if uncertain. "Go back to the ranch. You will find them there in the bungalow. Go now before the police come."

With that, briefcase in one hand, he turned his back and with a wave left me there, disappearing into the chill of that early morning to the sound of the dawn chorus and the sea gulls' screeching.

I cannot know for sure what happened, but I know him well enough to imagine how it went down. He climbed the sea wall at the end of the quays and walked along the cliff edge above the roiling sea, above the multitudes of gulls, puffins, and razorbills living in the caves and ledges of those cliffs. When his strength gave in, he threw himself and the briefcase into the chill water and held it tight as he sank into darkness, making sure that it was safe with him forever.

Except for the one vial I had taken and put into my pocket.

I knew, even then, I knew that this would not be the end. I would need proof.

I would need my freedom to keep fighting Ka and his aliens.

Leary was right about so much but not this; this was not the end, this was closer to the beginning.

#

I do not wish to speak of it.

I do not, but I suppose I must. Those last terrible hours of freedom, if you want to call it that.

I took the car and drove back to the ranch, Leary´s last words were a terrible foreboding gong in my head.

I remember nothing of that drive, was probably blessed to arrive in one piece. The compound was quiet but for the presence of crows and ravens feeding on human flesh—like the scene of some medieval battlefield.

A wasteland after the battle gods drink their fill of blood.

All gone.

Even those who had wandered like zombies around us. All dead. Murder or suicide? I never did find out, but clearly a mopping-up operation. The Society must have found out that we had foiled their plan and they were making sure that there would be no blow-back, no suspicion, so they would be free and clear to start anew in the war against humanity.

And it was a war, I suppose, and we had won a battle, Leary and I. We had stopped them for now, driven them back, for a while. I wandered through the compound. I entered every barracks building. In a sense, I think I needed to, to bear witness to what Ka and his evil forces were capable of.

It did not strike me to bury the fallen or somehow hide the bodies. This mutilation and destruction had to be witnessed, not only by me, but by all who came here.

I was bearing witness. I was also prevaricating.

I made my way to the ranch house bungalow; with every step it felt like something—a sharp rapier perhaps—was piercing my heart.

I opened the front door, shoved it open so it banged against the wall, and called out. Hoping still. Hoping until the last.

The shades were drawn, and despite the light outside, the interior of the house was a nest of shifting shadows, as though the house itself had internalized the violence that had so clearly happened here.

That I could smell in the air.

I checked downstairs. Kitchen and open plan dining room. Empty. The hallway leading to the bedrooms, doors on either side, all closed. One by one I pushed them open, holding my breath each time; that rapier stabbing me even harder. I could barely breathe when I reached the last door on the right.

They were lying on the bed, hands folded in front of them, faces stiff and cold and graying. I fell to my knees and tore at my hair.

My babies. Dead. Gone from me.

An explosion of grief that was nuclear roared through me. I heard a woman screaming. That woman was me.

And then I faded away.

When I awoke, it took long, blessed moments before I opened my eyes and saw them again. Long blessed moments in an alternate world where they were still alive. Even today at night, I will myself back into that place between sleeping and waking where they are still alive. In my head still breathing.

Sarah looks so quiet. Sean is unnaturally still. I sit on the side of the bed for a long, long time. I feel trapped and at the same time free. Out of space and time. Out of meaning and purpose.

They are gone.

I lie down on the bed, Sean on my right, Sarah on my left. It is hard to know how they died. They do not have the pustules that most of the dead had, so it may not have been this dreadful disease. Their faces are—apart from the spreading darkness and cold—unblemished. Almost as serene as statues. I talk to them, tell them about Leary and everything that has happened to me since the car crash, edited for their age, of course. I tell them nothing about what Jimmy was up to, but simply say that their father still loves them. I tell them stories about us, our family, our history, and my childhood. I talk to them about their grandparents and how our house is beautiful in summer. I talk to them of canoe trips and picnics and deer in the forest and a path we discovered along a burbling stream falling over stone that led to an old ruin of a castle deep in the heart of the forest. I remind Sean of how he had to climb to the top of the broken wall and how I scream-shouted at him to come down, to be careful, both scared and proud at once. I reminded Sarah of her desire to one day restore the castle, rebuild it to its former glory and live in it with exactly five dogs, three cats, and a parrot.

And then I ran out of words. And time.

The hardest thing I have ever had to do was leave that room. I grabbed a strange gadget of alien design on the bedside locker, and hunted through the compound for petrol. Doused the house in the stuff and set it alight.

I watched for a while as the flames took and my kids went on their valiant way to the stars.

In my handbag, I stuck the vial of the treacherous virus, the uzi, Leary's stuff including his badge—much as I wanted to keep it—and that strange machine from the ranch and some notes I had made in a diary. I found a shovel and like an old-time pirate, settled on a redoubtable ancient oak in a ditch in the field opposite the estate and counted steps from it. The combined number of Sarah and Sean's birthdays. I buried it there. Proof that I am not just a kook, that my story, a story that is incredible, is also true.

And then I sat in the car and waited.

I should have left. I know that now. I should have gone on the run, for the battle may be won but the war is not over. Honestly, I had no energy left, and a strange naive belief that somebody would believe what I had to say would take the burden from my shoulders.

Instead, they locked me up without a trial and gave me Guthry.

Foolish woman, I hear you say. You had your chance. You should have fought on.

Don't worry.

That naivety is long gone.

I know the burden is mine. I will shoulder it and I will pass it on to those who come after.

For the sake of us all and our future children.

Epilogue

It is a dull gray day in early October, with geese flying south and a newly discovered chill rampant in the wind.

A car makes a turn off a busy street in a city. The gates blocking the car's path are dark metal, almost light absorbent in the October gloom. Huge, monumental, and solid; they define the very confidence of the men who built this place. The stone walls which constrain the facility have developed soaring graystone pillars and wings that bend ornately towards the gate. Electrified wire rises on metal poles to twice the height of the already high walls. Nothing ornate there. Function topping design.

The guard waves the driver forward and the gates open automatically. Metal pylons in the road direct traffic in a sharp bend left and right and ensure nobody can drive a car at speed.

No suicide bombers I guess, the driver thinks wryly. Bit of a waste, though. Aren't the suiciders and other crazies all locked up in here?

He chuckles, but there is no humor in the sound. He knows it just betrays his nerves.

He pulls over at the gatehouse. The guard checks his ID and emailed appointment.

"Mr. Reid?"

Reid nods, for what else is there to say? The guard waves him forward. There are two more he can see on the roof of the guardhouse and another high on a metal platform overlooking the street.

But he presumes there must be a lot more he cannot see.

A lot of dangerous people are guests of the state in this building: serial killers, gang leaders, terrorists.

And Zoe Hearty.

The driveway to the main building is longer than he expected and the building itself is hidden behind an S-bend.

He pauses the car for a moment when it comes into view; a two-story gable-fronted building in a T-shaped plan, surrounded by modern buildings which have sprouted with no appreciable plan like mushrooms.

Cruciform windows with mullions give it an almost church-like feeling. He lets out a whistle.

Impressed despite himself. There it is again, that sense of certainty and solidity. The signature of the good old days which were so bad. He smiles to himself.

A sign with blue lettering directing him to parking. He slams the door shut and waits half a dozen seconds until the car locks itself. Force of habit.

As a lawyer who has defended many of the mad, bad, and downright ugly (some of whom are still residents of this very building, he is unhappy to acknowledge) his life has not always been drama-free.

But nobody has tried to kill, maim or threaten him in a few years — there is that. Or he could be slowing down.

Guards in the guise of orderlies man the main doors. He puts his briefcase and wallet through the bag scanner and walks through a full-body scanner.

"Guess that means I must be safe here." The guard glares back at him and does not return his smile.

The unwilling inhabitants of this particular building are not just wackos, they are dangerous bloody wackos with their hands soaked in blood. Safety is relative.

He follows the signs to Guthry′s office—Herr Direktor himself.

After he introduces himself, a P.A. waves at a row of plain chairs and asks him to wait. He glances at his watch, annoyed. He is scrupulously on time always and today is no different.

And so, he waits.

Whistling to himself.

The personal assistant glances at him and frowns, so he whistles louder.

Fifteen minutes. Bloody cheek. Despots in their own little kingdoms and all that.

The secretary clears his throat. "Director Guthry will see you now, Mr. Reid."

"Fucking right he will," Reid mutters.

"Sorry, sir?"

"Nothing." He drags up a smile. "Through here?"

He pushes open the double doors into an office fit for a Russian oligarch. Three times the size of his own office, a view through a bay window out over the lawns, trees in the distance and beyond those the flat steel gray of Marlin Lake.

The desk is the oversized monstrosity the room deserves and Guthry is safely ensconced behind it. A slim man in a cheap gray suit. Balding with long, thin fingers and slim wrists.

Tinpot dictator, Reid thinks.

"Guthry," the man says, hand outstretched. They shake.

Guthry moves around the desk and gestures to the sofa and armchair near the bay window.

Reid takes the sofa, Guthry the chair.

"So, Mr. Reid. You wished to see me." He rubs his hands together. "The unfortunate tale of Zoe Hearty is still your concern, I believe."

The smile is crooked and odd, lacking even a trace of warmth.

"It is my understanding that you initially approved the recording you sent us? May I ask why?"

Guthry squirms a little. "As an internal project, not meant to go beyond these walls. Therapy, if you will. A way to document her psychosis. I hoped... we hoped it might shine a light back upon her. Throw some shadows of doubt on her fantasy world. It has been known to work with others in the past." He pauses. Fidgets with the buttons of his jacket and recrosses his legs.

Guthry nods as if this confirms what he fully expects. "So why exactly are you here, Mr. Reid? We sent you the recording. What more can you possibly need?"

Reid leans forward. "I am... my company is still considering representing Ms. Hearty. We remain unconvinced she was given the defense she deserved. Call this meeting fact-finding, if you will. It is a long shot, but we are curious as to what we might do to help her."

A sarcastic laugh. "Curious, I see. As I advised you when we spoke, woman is a potential threat to anybody she crosses. She is a deluded mass murderer. You cannot seriously want her free."

"Mr. Guthry, our intentions are not your business. Not at the current moment. We, my firm and I, we are merely curious."

Guthry shakes his head and makes a face, as though dealing with a simpleton or child. Wishing he could make it all go away with short imperative orders.

Reid allows himself a small smile.

Guthry knows he fucked up by allowing the knowledge of the recording into the public domain. Somone got a hold of it, hacked the institute's server by all accounts, and released it on the Darkweb. There are groups all over the world now. Small groups, mostly run by bat-shit crazies; but hey, that is the brave new world of social media. The Friends of Zoe, People for Zoe, Free our Zoe, Death to Ka, Zoe and the Revolution, to name but a sampling. All determined in one way or another to carry on Zoe's fight against the dark forces of the aliens.

The narrative is out of Guthry's hands now. The genie has escaped the bottle and is making magic whether he likes it or not. Zoe hearty is not a household name, not by a long shot, but in the deeper reaches of the web, she is a name and a movement both.

Has some people worried even.

"Like I say, simple fact-checking. Cross-referenced with what we already know, of course."

"I really would like to state for the record that I consider this a huge waste of time and a terrible idea. Very terrible." He shakes his head. "The woman is a danger. But that being said, I have been told to indulge you; so go ahead. Ask your questions."

Reid pulls out his electronic pad and swipes to and fro. The action is to buy time for him to gather his thoughts more than anything. He knows the questions he intends to ask, has done his homework, and visualized them.

"Okay. Let's talk about Leary for a moment."

"What about him?"

"His image was all over the news back when Zoe was committed." Reid looks at his pad and swipes through the images. "The detached house he shared with his deceased wife, the two of them arm and arm in summer. That cute golden retriever of his. The files detailing his time on the force. He was indisputably real. A real person."

Guthry shakes head. "That is the nature of Ms. Hearty´s´s illness. I made this clear in our correspondence."

"Bear with me. Explain it so even a simpleton like me can understand." An encouraging smile, leaning forward.

"Leary was real yes, whatever that means in this context. Of course, he was. The police showed us his file and we sent officers to authenticate everything. He was a policeman. A bent policeman by all accounts, though he was never convicted. He did in fact save Zoe Hearty from being mugged, though she is sparing with the details of their relationship at that point. It appears she may have had a brief affair with him in the weeks after. A fixation on her saviour kind of thing."

"So, the badge?"

"Ah yes, the famous hoard of treasure. Becoming in its own low-brow way more famous than Sutton Hoo in certain circles, I believe." The red flares of anger around Guthry´s eyes and the thinness of his lips betray his real emotions. "Utter toss, of course. The woman is delusional."

In certain circles. This guy. Jeez. The Internet is buzzing but hey, that is only certain circles.

"And yet she has the badge of a man who disappeared two years ago, who she claims was her partner, and you claim was a figment of her imagination."

"She suffered a psychotic break. She drove her car into a tree, killed, perhaps murdered her children, after being abandoned by her wayward husband. So, she sought solace in an old flame, a positive memory, a savior, and, in a way, lover. Listen to the transcript again. There was no Leary. She is Leary. Was Leary perhaps. That is yet to be determined. Schizophrenia, trauma, a psychotic break."

Reid smiles. Guthry is exactly as he had imagined. A little tyrant in a smallish pond who is not used to being forced to explain himself—especially not to the lowly commoners who live in "certain circles." Well fuck you, buddy, I have given my life to smashing the careers and high horses of such as you, to freeing those you lock up with mean tricks and subterfuge; even if they often deserve to be locked up. But you, friend Guthry, you and your mates, do not get to decide who shall be condemned or not. That is the one purity there is in this benighted world —Justice must be blind.

"So how do you explain the badge?"

Guthry sneers and bares his teeth. "She stole it. When they were together. Isn't that explanation enough?"

Reid shrugs. "We have considered the possibility. But it seems a stretch. Like she knew she would have a psychotic turn ten years later and need a badge. You can't have her both as psychotic and a long-term planner, surely."

"She took it as a mnemonic. Her husband, Jimmy, had multiple affairs. This was Zoe's only fling—that we are aware of—her only escape from that domineering man. It hardly breaks the bounds of credibility that she kept a memento. And what could have been more personal?"

Reid pauses, glances at the screen. He knows the questions by heart. His only anxiety has been the order in which to play them.

"And what about the deaths at the ranch? Thirty members of the Society of the Gray Eclipse dead of unknown causes."

"Completely irrelevant. A suicide pact. Something Zoe Hearty heard, latched onto, and built into her fantasy world. Nothing in the slightest to do with her. Nothing. I mean, even the premise of her story is flawed. A superior alien race that waits until we number in the billions to eradicate us. A superior alien race that chooses to possess nobodies like Ramsey instead of world leaders. Putin? Trump? Why not have them unleash nuclear war? These must be the dumbest superior aliens in all of popular culture."

Guthry is fuming so much, Reid imagines he can see smoke blowing from his ears.

"Let's move on. Zoe's hoard is becoming quite a phenomenon since we dug it up. It seems to many of us that not everything can be so easily explained away." He pauses and could swear for a moment that Guthry flinches. Like there is a crack somewhere he is anticipating.

"Do we really have to go through this item by item, Mr. Reid? Fantasists like our Ms. Hearty are expert manipulators, you know. Surely we need to stand by science and logic in this endeavor?"

"As I was saying," I barely swallow the *Herr* Guthry. "Zoe also hoarded a capsule she claims is the virus that would destroy us all."

Guthry laughs and this time his laugh is genuine. He is on solid ground. "It has been tested, I assure you and proven harmless."

"Yes? So, there was no virus?"

His mouth makes a moo. "As I say, it has been tested and proven harmless."

"Has there been human testing?"

"Christ no, man. Are you crazy? There is nothing in the results to suggest anything harmful in that vial."

"Does Zoe not specifically claim that the virus was manufactured solely to target humans?"

Guthry's face gets even redder, if that is possible. He could light up the room if I closed the blinds. Reid smiles.

"A tame virus that only targets humans. Nonsense. What about mutation? Pure rubbish, I tell you."

"And yet it is possible."

"Then why the hell don't you try it on yourself?" Flecks of spit follow the statement.

Reid holds a hand out and waves it in a calming (or is it condescending?) gesture. Guthry looks fit to explode.

"His ID was there too, you know, in a wallet. Leary's I mean. And then there is the Uzi. Where, Mr. Guthry, does a homemaker with two young kids acquire an Uzi without any trace that the police or my investigators can find? Not even on the dark web. And if she did, where did she find the time to learn the skills to cover her tracks the way she did?"

Guthry is looking at his hands, saying nothing.

"And then there is the object."

Guthry makes a scoffing noise. "The alien iPhone? Sorry, Mr. Reid, but at this stage, I really must call this, with every offense intended, bullshit. It is a piece of metal and nothing else. It has never been shown to work, to do anything at all. It is a dummy, and nothing more; a product of a sick and twisted mind."

"And yet its design is unique, and testing shows traces of very strange metals. You have heard of Technetium, have you not?"

Guthry nods but says nothing.

Reid makes a show of consulting his pad, though this too he knows by heart. "I quote: Not found on earth in its natural form. Radioactive, so it decays and is no longer to be found in the wild, so to speak. A shiny lead-like metal. We can produce it on earth, but you need uranium and nuclear fission. A particle accelerator. So how does humble Zoe Hearty build and design such a thing with such rare metals?"

Guthry laughs, a genuine laugh. "She didn't. You already gave yourself the answer. The dark web. Technetium does exist because it is made on earth. And some of it just disappears from the official records. After the fall of the Soviet Union tons of the stuff vanished. Who knows where it ended up and what it is used for? So, Mr. Reid, Zoe could easily have ordered that strange gadget online—perhaps as a package deal with the Uzi—and built it into her fantasy world. All you need ask yourself then is how she had access to the dark web, but please remember sir, that this is a highly intelligent woman. You underestimate her at your peril. She is pulling the wool over your eyes, Sir. Over your eyes, I say. And you are blind, as are all those calling for her release. As to her capabilities. She is cleverer than you and many like you. And behind it all, fueling her psychosis, and driving her, is an utter ruthlessness. She talks about aliens. She should, for she invented them; and in many ways, compared to you and me, is in fact an alien herself."

Guthry makes a hissing sound and rises to his feet abruptly. "I am afraid that will have to do. I committed to giving you an interview. I have fulfilled my end of the bargain. But I do not need to put up any longer with this claptrap."

Reid gets to his feet. He has asked the most important questions and gotten what he wanted already. Guthry's vehemence is to be expected. He has a reputation to lose.

Reid holds out a hand. Guthry pointedly ignores it and strides to the door, opening it in a show of impatience.

Reid, whistles as he walks past the PA. The answering frown is very gratifying. He is almost out of the anteroom when Guthry calls him.

"Mr. Reid!"

"Mr. Guthry?"

"I urge you, sir, to tread lightly. Zoe Hearty is more than she seems."

Reid smiles. "I believe that is the first time we can agree on something today, sir."

He turns and walks through the depressing corridors of that terrible place. He drives home by the coast, the water a leaden gray interspersed with flickers of light where the cloud cover breaks. On impulse, he parks near Killinny Beach. Wrapped in his coat he walks the beach to the squawking of enormous seagulls flying overhead. A shape bouncing on the water about three hundred meters out turns out to be a seal.

Even that does not serve to raise his mood. He knows in the end what he will have to recommend; as much as Zoe's story is compelling, it is not a case they have a snowball's chance in hell of winning. With a heart as leaden as the sea, he calls the office.

When he hangs up, he feels like tossing the phone into the water. Instead, he walks to the promenade above the beach and finds a dark bar with dim lights and good whiskey.

And he drinks to forget what seems like a betrayal.

Another Epilogue

It was always a long shot. The news that Reid and the other lawyers have shut me down as a project is not surprising. I would have been stupid to have gone all-in on that.

Old Zoe might have broken apart at the seams when given the news. Would have stared at the red flashing light above the door and imagined a gloating Guthry behind it.

Would have cried and made a holy show of herself.

But not me. Not new Zoe.

Saviour of the World. That's what they call me, I believe. Out there in the darkness. The small but steadily growing army of true believers.

I am their general. General Zoe, alien killer.

Can't say I am happy at the thought. I would prefer to be left alone. My heart is a sore and empty kind of place and most days I do wake up from dreams of Sarah and Sean and cry quietly into my pillow.

But I can no longer afford the indulgence of self-pity. Ka is still out there; walking amongst us once again. The Society, or whatever it is calling itself now, busy fooling a new set of patsies into doing their bidding. Their fleet of conquering ships is hidden somewhere above, waiting for the right moment to pounce.

So, my army is a necessity.

But largely useless without me.

I never really did imagine that Reid and his company of do-gooder innocence lawyers would come through. He had nothing to go on legally, but I did manoeuvre him into releasing the knowledge of the recording.

I don't think he had a clue what he was actually doing—he released my manifesto, my call to arms into the world and so many have responded.

And how do I know all this, I hear you ask?

"Are you not locked up in solitary confinement with no access to news or any media except books?"

Steven is the answer.

Steven the orderly. Skinny young Steven with acne who has always been shy and clumsy around me. Face it folks, I could melt him with a sultry smile. And that was before he listened to the recording.

Now he sneaks messages to me on paper and holds my hand just a touch too long as his face reddens.

Before I was a hot piece of ass he was too shy to look at, but now I am all that and his hero.

So, it is arranged.

Tonight he will be on duty in my ward. He will open the door to my cell. A friend of his, a hacker, will switch off the camera feeds. There are three other gates, but no other guards at that time of night, and Steven assures me he has keycards to them all. That just leaves the two guards at reception. And one of them, James, is another acolyte— brought into the fold by Steven.

So, we neutralize the other guard, use the master keys in reception to open the main doors, and waiting for me outside will be a truck with three others. James and Steven and Bob and Fred and Peter.

Call them the apostles, if you will.

They have a lead on a nest of society cultists in the north.

We will go there first.

Listen to me, Ka, you sick fuck, you and your alien buddies and the sympathizers you recruit.

I am coming for you.

Tonight.

Don't sleep easy.

Zoe Hearty is on your trail.

About the Author

TE Norris was born and raised in South East Ireland in Tipperary and has a Degree in English and Politics and Masters in advertising and education. He has been a thatcher and has also worked as a demolition man, but is now a secondary school teacher in a town near Hamburg. He speaks several languages and has lived and worked in Ireland, England, Spain, the UAE, and Germany. He is married with three children.

He has written other books and poetry and even won a few minor prizes. A novel, *All Dark's Children*, is scheduled for publication in the UK in early 2023.

If you enjoyed this book, check out my other books at:

https://tenorrisauthor.com

or contact me directly with praise or critique or anything else at

tenorrisauthor@gmail.com

Sign-ups for my newsletter will receive a free copy of my fantasy novel, "Tallamun."

"...a highly atmospheric and engrossing epic fantasy tale of brave journeys, fabled utopias, and dead prophecies which will be sure to tantalize and excite readers...with world building and atmosphere, which really does transport readers into this new world." K.C. Finn. Five-Star Review for Reader's Favourite

Book Extract

*An excerpt from the fantastic new
novel by Te Norris*

All Dark's Children

*Due to be published by Black
Spring Press, London in 2022*

CHAPTER ONE

The Dark

So, this is the room.

It is small, mean, bathed in the glow of pale streetlights. Flimsy gauze curtains cast shadows over the single bed pushed up against the far wall.

A distant hum causes the air to vibrate.

Lights flash from a machine near the bed, and a scream sounds far away.

On the bed a man lies flat on his back, arms tucked tight against his side. His face is impossible to make out in the gloom but the overall impression is one of complete stillness.

The fingers of his right hand twitch once.

Voices sound outside. Footsteps march past.

The man's fingers twitch again, his face contracts, his lips move— and then he is still.

But the world seems to shake around him, for something momentous has just occurred.

Something that will change this world forever.

I am back.

Am I?

But where?

I cannot move.

Oh, God. The dark.

An assault.   I flounder in it, gasping for breath.

Drowning in darkness.

Help me!

Someone?

Help. Please.

Help me.

Damn it. Breathe! Calm down, right! You can do this. Breathe. Nice and gentle.

Why is it so dark? I open my eyes, or I think I do. It makes no difference. I cannot move, cannot feel my limbs. *Help! Help!* The universe at the end of times all energy dissipated. No movement. No light.

Shut it! You think, therefore you are. And if you want to leave this place, you need to calm down. This is not the end. Don't you see?

It's not. It can't be.

Shush. Listen. Okay?

Right! Right! I can hear. Yes. Voices, dim and far away. Little more than murmurs in soil. But real and not me, and not the dark. That is something. More than something. Everything.

If they are real, then so am I.

Calm. Shush. Breathe.

I try to speak, to call for help but I am unable to make a sound. Cannot feel my lips or tongue.   My body is weightless.

And as I let it, despair fills me until I feel I am being buried alive in something like treacle.

I have to get out of here.

In my head, I am screaming for help, waving my hands, jumping up and down.

I am paralyzed. Blind.

I am?

Who the hell am I, then?

What is happening to me?

Why do I remember nothing?

Lord, help and protect me!

***

Calm. Be calm. We can find a way out of this. Just be patient.

Patient, my royal Irish ass!

I am like a busted tv with a poor signal. But at least there is reception.

Those faint voices feed the weak signal: gifting me vague memories of another world. A world full of colour. The light in *her* eyes—the way she lifted me with her smile. Children. Two of them. A vague collage of their faces. No names, but family. Mine. I know this. A place of love. A communion of souls in orbit around one another.

Where has it gone?

Why am I here? Alone. Empty.

I try to move. Darting fingers of agony hold me and press me down.

I was whole once, and now am broken, a twig afloat on tumbling weirs

Where the hell am I? What is happening to me?

My name is Chris. I am not sure. I may be dead, and how that can be, I have no idea. Something happened. Something unexpected and sudden. It is all dark. Trying to remember hurts: flashes of purple pain as if some thug is working me over

Focus, brother. Grab hold of something. A thread that will guide you from here. But it is hard. I close my eyes, or are they already closed?

It is too dark to know, and a sudden noise reverberates in this empty place like an alarm, and its threat is clear, and fills me with pain.

And I wake and scream and—nothing. My voice is nothing

Darkness and silence.

CHAPTER TWO

What Moves

Time passes. Long periods of empty time in which I intuit more. I am in a room. It is small, its lines functional. A place of little comfort.

And at the far end of the room is a sound: something creeping toward me.

I blink or try to as sweat pours down my back, and my heart is percussion. *Ta-tum. Ta-tum.*

It stalks me in this dark place with an intent foul and deadly.

I picture snakes slithering in darkness and spiders scattering around them, hairy legs pumping. I cringe and try to move, and close my eyes, and struggle to remember.

I don't think my name is Chris, after all.

But the name Chris evokes a new memory: a keychain with a Saint Christopher's medal.

Against the darkness, memory is light.

I picture us then: Four of us in a car, me at the wheel, driving into gorse and heather covered hills. A day out, cirrus clouds in a summer-blue sky, the memory of an ice cream cold on my lips and tongue.

Focus. Remember the clink of that medal and the joy and laughter in the car all around you.

And whatever moves in darkness is gone.

Holy Mother of Mercy, save me from this horrific place.

Tears fall. But my face is dry.

I did something, I think, or something happened because of me, and that is the reason I am here. What happened to my family? What did I do? Why do I feel so guilty?

More memories return.

A concert, lit up with neon. The two of us singing together, arm in arm, a child on my shoulder, and the wholeness I knew then.

"A guiding light"

I remember the name of the song, but I can't even remember their names.

I shake my head but know it isn't moving. Nobody ever needed a guiding light like me, but I would settle for a glimpse of your smile, love. All I have now is a threadbare sense of that other life and its fading texture.

And time passes. Or not. An eternity, or not. And I scream and no sound comes out, and my heartbeat sounds but I cannot hear it above my terror.

Who has done this to me?

***

A miracle happened. I woke, opened my eyes, and could see: a slender will-o'-the-wisp, flitting before my eyes. Very faint and fragile, yet it disputes the darkness. If it is real, then so am I.

If it can move then so can I.

I smile. My lips actually move.

And my heart swells with hope that I can escape this dismal grave. I keep my eyes fixed on the moving trail of light. *Hold to it. Hold fast. Life exists and darkness cannot keep you. It will bend and give in. It must.*

I stretch, flex my fingers. Nothing. *Try, you useless shite.* Try again. Nothing.

The dancing light is no longer a mote but shaped like a human eye, a pale blue wintry sky.

Another being.

"Arise"

What the fuck? I try to speak. It comes out as a muffled gasp. Progress, of a sort, though my heart is in my mouth and being chased higher by my balls.

"Arise, you dim shite. It is time. Away with ye now."

***

I am an eagle gliding on updrafts. Below is home, my people, my town.

To them I am a distant speck; to me they are ants struggling and striving.

Cars on Main Street.

High steeples.

Bells ringing.

I follow the river, cutting through the center, down by the quay and the old mills which house modern apartments, past the old stone bridge, the park with screaming children and until we are above the cemetery where my grandparents and my parents quietly lie.

I see them.

Sarah, her name is Sarah.

My children stand beside her, arms around her shoulder. She is somehow sunken, shorn of energy, dressed in black, a small crowd in a rough half-circle behind her and an open grave beside which stands a teak-colored coffin.

Death and mourning. Our local priest, a tall scarecrow of a man, more sinister than soothing, says something and Sarah falls to her knees.

I reach out to her and fall. Into darkness. Into the grave which shrouds me, this dark and miserable room. And die again.

***

"Wake up!"

I was gone and now am back. I pause, afraid. To open my eyes. To see. To see nothing. Which would be worse?

"Arise."

I force my eyes open. The eye is still there a glowing sapphire gem staring down at me, and in an instant I fall under its blinding spell.

In a blink I am back in the cemetery.

Wind howls and ravens perched on bare trees, caw. A blue moon casts a dim light. I am alone, windblown and cold, shivering in the darkness. The witch haunting hours after midnight.

"Walk and bear witness."

I start forward. This is an old place, and where I am is one of the oldest sections; headstones lie fallen or hang crooked and illegible. Death here is but a vague memory, long ago faded into dust and crumbling bones.

In the distance beyond the small stone chapel is our family plot, shadowed by a semicircle of trees. My parents lie to the right of a tall oak, their plots strewn with fallen leaves. Their parents lie behind them and to the right is a fresh plot.

Terror in my soul, confusion in my brain. The grave is open, the coffin lies broken on the dark soil above. Empty.

"See how they rise."

Distracted, I trip over a fallen headstone, coming to land face-first in a puddle of dark mud smelling faintly of dog shit. Typical. I get to my knees and wipe the muck from my face.

Restless. They walk. The earth spits them out.

Around me, faint sounds like broken whispers.

Not zombies from some B-movie, but the dead, aware and unhappy and damned and in pain. Aware of their death and yearning for life. Souls straight out of a Viking emptiness. Hel not hell. Not hordes but multitudes. Not violent but despairing.

The dead move slowly shuffling like birds with broken wings, emptied eye sockets seeing nothing, skeletal fingers reaching forward. They speak but no words come from those damaged organs. Choking ugly noises torture the darkness. The newly interred are worse, their humanity vanished, but not yet entirely other: features still recognizable amid the rot and decay.

They stumble toward me.

I fall backward, shocked and disgusted on seeing see myself. Me, myself and I. Only dead. A blank and empty gaze, mouth twisted in a grimace, a long strip of flesh hanging from my face, one eye missing and everywhere flesh putrid and swollen and black. The empty eye is a host to maggots and swarming blue flies. Death upon me. scream but no sound comes out. I rise to my feet and turn to run—but my feet do not move. I hear them approach, the multitude of the dead, and I am frozen. Trapped in my body.

A hand touches my shoulder, long nails, bruised flesh.

"Return."

I open my eyes. Back on the bed in this pitch-black room. Alone.

A shake of my head. A faint movement but real. Real! I move, therefore I am.

I am not dead. This is not a coffin, nor a grave. I am alive. Not dead. Alive and breathing. I smile and I can feel my lips move. A fraction, no more, but they do move.

CHAPTER THREE

Going Home

"Why are you doing this to me?"

Words come from my lips as if free of a huge weight.

I can hear them. They exist outside of me.

"Listen carefully, pal. You are trapped here, locked in this box. Sinister forces have done this to you and many like you. Sarah and the kids think you are dead. They buried you, mourned and are moving on. And you will remain here if you don't do something about it. But within you is the power to free yourself. Let go of this room and this place. Leave! Find Sarah. Get your life back."

The eye, but now it is more substantial, more than just an eye, the outline of a face that looks familiar, one I once knew. A brother? An old friend? A familiar.

"Tell me what to do?"

"Get up. Walk. Now! Move your ass and ditch this place."

I flex my fingers. Good. I concentrate on my legs. They twitch. Not movement, not yet, but close—and I can feel my body again, its heft.

The vast emptiness is gone and even the darkness appears lighter.

I try again and this time find I can move the toes of my right leg. Back and forward. I turn the whole foot on its ankle and know the greatest joy I have known since waking here. I am free and in control of myself. Real tears, glorious and wet roll down my cheeks.

I cannot wipe them off, not yet, but that will come.

It is painful, of course, and takes time, but time is a luxury I have. Unused joints and muscles scream in protest, stabs of pain shooting through me—but after some time, I am sitting. Then, the pain subsiding somewhat, I am standing. I almost fall, but forward.

I reach out with my hands and the bed saves me. I smile in delight at the speed of my reaction. Standing, I take a first tentative step. I shuffle rather than walk forward but do not trip, and I make progress. My eyes have adjusted to the darkness and I move toward what I make out to be a window and pull at a curtain. Light floods the room and blinds me for a long minute.

Outside an innocuous street of darker gray concrete, empty of people. I am on the ground floor of a building and the windows are crisscrossed with metal. I turn to the door. Metal with something like a closed peephole in the middle, about a third of the way from the top. A prison?

"The people who put you here have grown complacent. The window bars are rotten, though this is not visible. If you can find the strength, you can break through them. When you leave, move quickly. They will come after you and theirs is not a merciful code."

A pause, and in a quieter tone, "I have taken you as far as I can for the moment. Now it's up to you, Chris. Be safe, old friend, be careful and clever. Be gone."

I turn to look but know already, there is nothing. The eye, the voice, my friend whose name I cannot remember—all are gone.

Voices sound through the walls, distant and unintelligible but real, not echoes in my brain chamber. Once, there is a gallop of rushing footsteps outside my door—and later, the sound of someone screaming in great extremity. My friend's sinister forces, I presume, whatever that means.

I have no clue what they want or wanted from me: I still remember little except my name, and I not even sure of that, and Sarah. My memories, such as they are, are chaotic and jumbled. I do, however, have some inkling of how they kept me tamed. Drugs, no doubt, that kept me catatonic, that made me unable to speak or think or move. And if drugs, then there is hope they will wear off and my memory return.

I scan the room with a sudden urgency. The sounds from the rooms outside my direct prison make me more than nervous; what if someone should think to check on me?

Surely they would call for help and that being delivered, overpower me and send me back into the darkness, with no guarantee of ever rising again.

The room is uninviting, drab and puke-green. There are some portable trolley-like cupboards, a cheap wooden nightstand and a heavy-looking metal-backed chair. It is this that provides me with hope. I walk to it, faster now and sure on my feet, my confidence returning.

The chair is on casters and I roll it to the window, lift and swing it against the widow. It bounces off, of course, nearly driving me back to the bed. I swing again. The glass smashes, voices are raised and an alarm goes off. I swing again, mustering all my courage and strength and this time, the window frame and the metal bars crash forward as I let go of the chair.

The path is free. I take quick stock to find I'm wearing a jumpsuit, blue in color, such as a convict might wear. I have grown a beard which is scruffy and strange; I never was a beard man. Should I run into people on the streets, I will come off as a maniac, an escaped lunatic—which I might well be, but that is a secondary issue now. I will have to take my chances.

I step through the window, brushing broken glass aside, and into cold daylight and freedom. I ease myself onto the tarmac below and start running, hard.

Sarah, wait for me. I am coming home.

***

I run till my heart is fit to explode, but pass nobody, see nobody.

I reach Old Potter's Park after about ten minutes, and stop. I have no idea how long I have been gone from my real life, lost to the sinister forces arrayed against me in that dark room.

Yet, all things considered, I am in fine shape. The run has been only mildly stressful and hearing my heartbeat thumping is uplifting. I feel alive again. My muscles strong.

Strangely so, all things considered.

The sky is wintry but the air is mild: not warm exactly but more like a thaw in early spring.

A copse of gray alder with deep undergrowth provides a place to rest and think. I study the quietness of the park and decide to wait until dark. I am at home, in the town where I know I have lived the majority of my life. And that itself is strange, for why would sinister forces, those arrayed against me, have ever taken root in this place so far from the madding crowd?

I struggle to remember. Our town is a small one of no great importance, backing onto a chain of mountains which are in themselves, though beautiful, relatively untouched by mining or other industry. There is no deep layer of power or depth of wealth here to attract the greed and corruption of larger towns and cities. What then has attracted this affliction, these forces of evil?

Anyway: the question is irrelevant.

I have a family. My wife's name is Sarah.

And I am going home.

Sometime before dusk, the sun peeps from behind a wooden blanket of clouds, and smiles. My heart sings with it, a dumb cliché I guess, but there is heat in its smile and my blood warms in its caress. My home is but a short walk, less than three miles away.

And still I wait. I do not wish to be seen in this state and cannot guess who or what might be scouring the town for me.

Sometime after midnight, or so I reckon, I set off, keeping to dark shadows and avoiding streetlights. I hear cars and people but see no one, as I take backstreets and keep to the darkest of shadows in the loneliest alleys.

I hear him before I see him, at end of the narrow medieval alley I just turned into.

An old artery, this one, connecting Main and O'Connell Streets.

It is just narrow enough for two to walk abreast, empty of everything but the large plastic dumper bins from the neighbouring strip of shops on Main Street.

He is wearing a hoody, standing in the darkness beneath the archway connecting the adjacent buildings. He turns toward me, though there is no way he should have heard me. In the semi-darkness, the glint of his eyes reveals thin, dark pinpricks.

Knots of fear twist my stomach.

"He comes."

A high voice, almost falsetto, aimed at me. A jarring, whiny sound. "The spawn of Satan, pulled back from the dead and the flames. It seethes in your foul soul, clear as anything."

He starts toward me and a glint of something metal in his right hand has me desperately looking around for any sort of defensive weapon of my own.

There on the top of that square bin, and suspiciously provident, a large heavy-looking metal bar, rusted and raggedly broken at one end. I pick it up and weigh its balance.

He steps into the faint light cast by a window above. The hoody shades his face but I can make out the thin pallor, the blotchy face and the concave jaw.

Drugs.

When it rains it pours.

He points the knife hand at me, waving it in a circle. "Satan lives. Within you, it slithers."

He smiles a narrow smile, showing rotten teeth in that broken face. "I will cut it out. For you are the evil that walks in darkness."

I hold up the palm of my left hand, hoping somehow to still talk my way out of this madness but he lurches forward, clumsy but fast, the knife slicing past my face. I twist left and bring the metal bar hard against the arm holding the knife. It snaps, the sound clear in the dark. He screams and falls to his knees.

I back away.

His hoody is no longer covering his face and his drug-ravaged visage is visible now. Bald head, light eyes, clouded with pain and whatever he is high on.

"You! You are Lucifer!"

He spits the words at me, almost foaming and makes as if to stand. I turn and run back the way I had come, fast, unsure if he will follow or not, the words still echoing in my ears.

Running into trouble like this may have been coincidental, but that does not seem likely. Sinister forces at work, perhaps, and if so, what is the extent of their reach?

My home is a tall two-story in a street of other Edwardians. Painted cream and white, it gleams happily in sunshine. But now in the pale white cast by ornate streetlights, it looks back at me, dark and brooding. It appears empty, and that fact hits me like a sucker punch.

Where is Sarah?

Where are my kids?

I have no keys and dare not try a direct entry, for there is bound to be some neighbour awake, restless and aware, who would raise the alarm. No matter. Easily solved. I walk to the end of the street and make for the narrow alley between the two parallel rows of houses facing away from each other. Our house lies halfway down the eastern row. I scale the old stone walls with some difficulty and land in our small, rectangular garden, aware of memories sliding back into my consciousness almost like muscle memories—of a shared life together, of light and laughter.

The wide patio window on the left leads into the living room, and the back door leads to a short hallway and the kitchen on the right. I use a stone to smash a pane of glass near the window latch. Then I wait, tense and breathing quietly. An owl hoots flying nearby, and somewhere on a different street a dog howls, but my actions have created no undue attention.

I reach in, pull the latch open, push on the window and let myself into the living room.

Strange, the smells of this place. I had been expecting something else, more familiar, but the air in here is dusty and dry, and starved of life. Vague light from the nearest streetlight seeps through the windows, easing the darkness somewhat, but visibility is poor and I dare not risk too much light. I make for the kitchen and—rummaging on a shelf—find a small green flashlight. The kitchen feels hollow, but there are tins in the cupboards and though everything seems clean, a faint smell comes from the built-in trash bins and disposer.

I search the house with a wounded heart. The dusty emptiness is everywhere the same. The house is deserted and lost, like an abandoned ship on high seas and something of its emptiness frightens me. This is not casual desertion; this was a panicked retreat. In the bathroom, I kneel and touch flecks of dried blood. Not much, certainly not enough to worry even a neurotic parent, but the blood has not been cleaned, has been left in situ. I find no family portraits, no pictures of me or of Sarah and the kids, no knick-knacks, no forgotten gadgets or toys.

No personal items at all, not even clothes.

A barren shell, as if cleaned out, or—this is a much too depressing thought—*always* empty.

Doubt is again a squirming worm in my brain. What if there was never anyone here?

What if my family and the faulty memories I have of them are but confused and broken processes in my brain, phantasms or imaginary and fleeting dreams?

Maybe I am crazy after all, and the jailers I flee from are not my abductors but my healers.

I am fleeing not from prison, but a hospital.

I gather my woolly thoughts. Something has happened here. In the master bedroom, the bed lies unmade and the mattress darkened with stains. More blood? On the night table, I spot a book and an envelope. The book is a heavily annotated bible. I thumb through it. The handwritten annotations are cramped, tidy and neat, yet frenetic. I recognize numbers, names, some symbols but it makes no sense. The envelope is plain office standard, stamped and marked with the logo and address of the local parish church.

The priest, the one I had seen at my funeral. His name is listed as addressee.

Father Mahon. I struggle to remember.

A tall, thin and unpleasant man with a cynical smile and yet, in many obnoxious ways, a true believer. Certainly not your friendly local man-of-the-cloth.

Inside is a key and a sheet of paper. The key is large, spotted with rust, like the key to a pirate's treasure chest. Something ancient and strange. I pull out the sheet of paper, a letter written on coarse plain paper, and ease it open.

On the paper are four words, typed and faded. A real typescript, not a computer handout. Four words but repeated again and again as if some crazy chant, covering every centimeter of an A4-sized page, front, and back.

A herold. A herold. A herold. A herold. A herold.

A herold. A herold. A herold. A herold. A herold.

Evils surface Evil surfaces Evils surface Evil surfaces Evils surface Evil surfaces Evils surface.

I sit back stunned on the small armchair to the right of the double bed. The words sweep through my brain, crazed voices chanting crazed words.

A din, as of crows and vultures squawking. I close my eyes, trying to drown out this godawful racket and hold my head as my brain struggles to surface above the noise that swallows me whole.

***

"Hello, Christian."

I start awake. And yet am still asleep. A dream within a dream. But it feels real. For a moment, panic sweeps me but then calm returns. Even in this dreaming state, I can still move.

Not comatose, not back in prison, then, not captured. This is something else again.

A cough. I sit up and turn to its source.

A man sitting perched on the little sofa near the walk-in wardrobe.

"Pleased to finally meet you, Christian, though I am sorry to say—as I'm sure you have already realized—not in the flesh. Not yet. That will be an altogether less pleasant experience." He coughs. A racking, gasping cough that makes me flinch—and he gobs onto the carpet, green phlegm streaked with blood. "My name is Mr. Harnelo. I have been tasked with hunting you down and making you suffer for being such a wilful one, for putting us all to so much trouble."

He smiles darkly. "Wish I could say I will go easy on you, but I am afraid that is something I rarely consider and never enact. I like what I do, and I am afraid I have little time left on this mortal coil to exercise my particular skills. However, I am obliged—reluctantly, by my employer—to make you an offer. Surrender yourself to us and we are prepared to be merciful. Refuse and I will torture you and your wife, I will rape and bugger her, and make you and your children watch.

Then I will cut her to pieces and start on the others." He smiles, almost wistfully. "I can imagine the taste of your blood already." He laughs, mouth open, eyes twinkling with joy and his teeth are canine fangs reaching below his lower lip.

"We really should get to know each other better, Christian. Close your eyes. Relax. Let me tell you my story."

Made in the USA
Columbia, SC
22 July 2022

63662442R00174